Every Boy's Got One

By Meg Cabot

MEG CABOT

Every Boy's Got One

AVON
TRADE

An Imprint of HarperCollinsPublishers

HarperCollins books may be purchased for education, business, or sales promotional use. For information please write: Special Markets Department, HarperCollins Publishers Inc., 10 East 53rd Street, New York, NY 10022.

FIRST EDITION

Designed by Elizabeth M. Glover
Illustrations copyright © 2005 by Jennifer Lewis

Library of Congress Cataloging-in-Publication Data

Cabot, Meg.
Every boy's got one / by Meg Cabot.—1st. ed.
    p. cm.
ISBN 0-06-008546-0 (acid-free paper)
1. Americans—Italy—Fiction. 2. Women cartoonists—Fiction. 3. Camera operators—Fiction. 4. Riviera (Italy)—Fiction. 5. Friendship—Fiction. 6. Weddings—Fiction.   I. Title.

PS3553.A278E94   2005
813'.6—dc22   2004010884

05 06 07 08 09 JTC/RRD 10 9 8 7 6 5 4 3 2 1

For Benjamin

Many thanks to Beth Adler,
Ingo Arndt, Jennifer Brown,
John Henry Dreyfuss,
Benjamin Egnatz, Carrie, Feron,
Michele Jaffe, Laura Langlie,
and Greg and Sophia Travis

ALITALIA

Boarding Pass

Passenger Name
Langdon, Cal

Frequent Flyer Number
E17H616

From:
NYC-JFK

Flight
1516

Class
K

Date
13Sept

Departs
626PM

To:
ROMA-Fiumacino
GROUP 4

Gate
30

Boarding Time
550PM

Seat
21D

*Every
Boy's
Got
One*

1

ALITALIA

Boarding Pass

Passenger Name
Harris, Jane

Frequent Flyer Number
- - -

From:
NYC-JFK

Flight
1516

Class
K

Date
13Sept

Departs
626PM

To:
ROMA-Fiumacino
GROUP 4

Gate
30

Boarding Time
550PM

Seat
21C

```
        ≡⊕≡

      John F. Kennedy
    International Airport
        —Duty Free—


Reg #06              Tran#8971
Cshr#0084            Str#2411


1 New Republic Mag    $2.99
1 AA Batteries        $1.59


Subtotal              $4.58
Total                 $4.58


Payment          Credit Card
C Langdon
**** **** *** ****
Exp 2/08
March 25              3:59PM


  Thank you for shopping
     JFK Duty Free
   Enjoy your flight!
```

Meg
Cabot
_4_

John F. Kennedy
International Airport
—Duty Free—

Reg #06   Tran#8972
Cshr#0084   Str#2411

1 Gift PK Toblerone $9.99
1 Dramamine $2.29
1 Earplugs $0.79
1 Advil $2.29
1 Us Weekly Mag $1.99
1 Bottled Water $1.29
1 Bottled Water $1.29
1 Bottled Water $1.29
1 Bottled Water $1.29
1 Bottled Water $1.29
1 Travel Diary $12.95

Subtotal $36.75
Total $36.75

Payment   Credit Card
W Harris
**** **** *** ****

Exp 3/08
March 25   4:02PM

Thank you for shopping
JFK Duty Free
Enjoy your flight!

Travel Diary of

Holly Caputo and Mark Levine

On Their Elopement

Composed by Jane Harris, Witness

aka Maid of Honor

aka Holly's best friend since first grade and

roommate since freshman year at

Parsons School of Design

Dear Holly and Mark,

Surprise!

I know neither one of you would bother to keep a record of your elopement, so I've decided to do it for you! This way, when you're approaching your twentieth anniversary and your oldest kid has just wrecked the Volvo and your youngest has just come home from her cushy Westchester private school with head lice and the dog's thrown up all over the living room rug and, Holly, you're asking yourself why you ever moved out of the righteous East Village pad we shared for so long, and, Mark, you're wishing you'd stayed in resident housing down at St. Vincents, you can open this diary and go, "Oh, so THAT's why we got married."

Because you two are the grooviest couple I know, and totally belong together, and I think eloping to Italy is a BRILLIANT idea, even if you did steal it from Kate Mackenzie in Human Resources.

The eloping part, I mean. Not the Italy part.

But she HAD to elope. I mean, with in-laws like hers? What CHOICE did she have?

But you two are doing it for the pure romance of the thing—not because you HAVE to, because both your families are perfectly respectable.

Well, I guess there is that <u>teensy</u> religion thing with your moms.

But whatever! They'll get over it.

Anyway, that's what makes your elopement so special.

And I plan to record every detail of that special-ness, starting now, before we even get on the plane. Before I even meet you guys at the gate. Which, by the way, where ARE you, anyway? I mean, we were supposed to get here three hours before our departure time. You know that, don't you? I mean, it says that right on the ticket. <u>For international travel, please arrive no later than three hours prior to departure time</u>.

So. Where are you guys?

I suppose I could email you on my new BLACKBERRY, but as you keep reminding me, Holly, it's for WORK PURPOSES ONLY, which is the only reason the IT guys let you have them (thanks for mine, by the way. I mean, it's nice of Tim and those guys to think of me, even though I don't exactly work there anymore).

God, I hope nothing happened to you. I mean, on the way. People drive like maniacs on the expressway.

Wait—you didn't change your <u>minds</u>, did you? About getting married? You <u>can't</u>. That would be awful! Just AWFUL! I mean, you two are so perfect for each other . . . not to mention, it would be totally unfair to cancel on me. My first trip to Europe, and my travel companions ditch me? As it is, I can't even believe I'm really doing it. Why did I wait so long? Who turns thirty without having been outside the continental United States at least once in her life? No Paris with French class in the 11th grade. No "Cabo" for Spring Break in college. What's wrong with me, anyway? Why am I such a non-transcontinental flying freak?

And okay, seriously, what is with the guy with the cell phone over there? I mean, he's cute and everything. But why is he yelling? We're going to Italy, dude. Italy! So chill.

Okay, ignore the guy on the cell phone. IGNORE THE GUY ON THE CELL PHONE. I can't believe I'm wasting the first pages of your travel diary on him. Who cares about him? I'M GOING TO EUROPE!

I mean, WE'RE going to Europe.

I think. If you two aren't lying in the twisted wreckage of your taxi to the airport on the Long Island Expressway.

Let's just assume you were running a little late this morning and that you aren't dead.

Thank God you two are making me do this. You and Mark, I mean, Holly. I'm finally crossing the Atlantic, and for what better REASON? God, it's so romantic—

(Oh, wait, that's the same guy who was in front of me at the duty free! The one who was rolling his eyes because I bought all those bottles of Aquafina. Obviously he hasn't read this month's <u>Shape</u>. They say air travel is very dehydrating, and that you should drink half your body weight in water during the course of your flight if you want to avoid jet lag.)

And okay, they have water on the plane and all, but is it <u>good</u> water? I mean, as good as Aquafina? Probably not. I saw this thing on Ask Asa on Channel 4 where they sent the water from a plane to a lab and it was filled with all these microbes! And okay, it was the water from the tap in the plane bathroom, and no one would really drink that, but still.

Not that MY mom and dad wouldn't kill me if I did what you're doing, Holly. Elope, I mean. And to ITALY, of all places.

But it's just so totally you, Holly. God, you're lucky. Mark is so . . . grounded. And Mark, I know I give you a hard time about being such a sci-fi geek and all, but seriously, if I could meet a guy as—

(Oh my God! Cell Phone Guy just practically threw his phone at one of those little carts with the old people in it! The one taking them to their gate! And just because the guy driving it made that backing-up-truck sound to warn him he was in the way. God, what's got <u>his</u> panties in such a bunch? Although he hardly looks like a panty-wearing type of guy. Jockeys, more likely. Or maybe boxers.

Oh, no. How can I give this diary to Holly and Mark if it's full of musings about some random guy's underwear????

NOW what am I going to give them? I can't give them candlesticks or something. This is HOLLY. It has to be something SPECIAL.

Okay, well, one mention of underwear. You guys don't mind, do you? I mean, it's just <u>underwear</u>.)

Where was I? Oh yeah. Mark. So cute, in spite of the <u>Star Trek Next Generation</u> marathons he makes you watch, Holl. So responsible, with the whole doctor-and-health-column thing. Which reminds me, I need to ask him about this mole on my elbow. God, Holly's so lucky, she can get her moles checked for free anytime she wants. Why can't I find a boyfriend with a useful skill like that? All Malcolm can do is beat me at Vice City. And what good is that? Can a high score on Vice City save you from a life-threatening carcinoma? No.

Okay, now I <u>totally</u> can't give this to Holly and Mark. <u>What is wrong with me</u>?

Cell Phone Guy just hung up on whoever it was he was talking to. I just heard him go, "That is inexcusable," but that was all I could get because they've got CNN turned up so loud in here. Now he's got out his Blackberry. He's typing into it furiously. I will never be able to type that fast into mine.

But maybe that's a good thing. Cell Phone Guy is a classic example of a Type A personality, as illustrated in last

Meg
Cabot
8

month's <u>Shape</u>. I can practically SEE his blood pressure going up. I hope he doesn't stroke out on the plane.

Although I wouldn't mind giving him CPR.

Oh my God, I can't believe I just wrote that.

But he <u>is</u> kind of cute. I mean, if you like the tall, rugged, sandy-haired, razor-stubbled-with-piercing-blue-eyes-who-knows-how-to-use-a-Blackberry type.

Okay. Now I <u>definitely</u> won't be able to give this to Holly and Mark as a wedding present.

Oh, wait, I can just rip out the pages with Cell Phone Guy comments. Or black them out with a Sharpie.

Or maybe I should just get Holly and Mark a nice silver frame from Tiffany's instead. But that seems like kind of a lame present to get for someone who has held your hair back while you were throwing up tequila shooters as many times as Holly has for me.

Although of course I've done it for her often enough, most recently Friday night when the entire art department took her out for a bachelorette party. For two people who are supposed to be eloping, Mark and Holly told an AWFUL lot of people beforehand.

!!!! On CNN it says a plane is being held at the San Francisco airport under suspicion that a passenger aboard it has a highly contagious virus that they're worried will spread worldwide!!!!

You know what this means:

I need more snacks for the plane.

Seriously, those people have been on board that plane for TWO HOURS with no food service. If I go two hours without eating, I get that weird thing where I can't see out of one eye. And Toblerone won't do it. I need something with protein. Like smoked almonds. And maybe some cheese popcorn. Which I bet they don't even have in Italy. I better go back to the duty free and stock up, just in case. . . .

✉

To: Tara Samuels <tara.samuels@thenyjournal.com>
Fr: Cal Langdon <cal.langdon@thenyjournal.com>
Re: Travel Services

Where is everybody? I've been calling for the past half hour, and nobody there is picking up. Does Travel get half days on Fridays through September, or something, while the rest of us slobs have to give them up on Labor Day?

I asked you guys to book this ticket a month ago, but I'm at the airport now and they claim I'm in coach, not business class.

In a *middle seat*. For a *seven-hour flight*.

Freaking Frodo wouldn't last for six hours in a seat that small. How is a six-foot-four, two-hundred-pound man supposed to do it?

Someone had better pull some strings or you're going to have one very unhappy journalist on your hands.

C. Langdon

✉

To: Dolly Vargas<dolly.vargas@thenyjournal.com>
Fr: Cal Langdon <cal.langdon@thenyjournal.com>
Re: Last night

Thanks for last night. However, I think moving in together might be a little precipitous. And I don't think your husband would really appreciate it.

Let's just keep things casual for now, and see how things go. Okay? I'm off to some podunk part of Italy no one's ever heard of because Levine has some idiot idea he's going to get married there, but I'll be in touch when I get back in a week.

C.

....

✉

To: Cal Langdon <cal.langdon@thenyjournal.com>
Fr: Tara Samuels <tara.samuels@thenyjournal.com>
Re: Travel Services

I'm SO sorry, Mr. Langdon, we were in a budget meeting, which is why no one picked up. I've been calling the airline ever since I got back, and they're booked solid. I could get you in business class on another flight . . . but not until tomorrow. Would that be all right?

Again, I'm so sorry about the misunderstanding. I can't imagine how you ended up in coach. We ALWAYS book you in business class, as you know. Except of course when the plane you're taking is so small, there isn't a business class. Which isn't the case here. I can't apologize enough, really. Could we upgrade you to a suite when you get to your hotel?

Tara

....

✉

To: Cal Langdon <cal.langdon@thenyjournal.com>
Fr: Dolly Vargas <dolly.vargas@thenyjournal.com>
Re: Last night

There you are! I've only left ten messages on your cell phone. How COULD you have snuck out like that this morning, without even leaving a note?

And Peter and I aren't *married*, sweetie. We have an understanding—the same one you and I have.

And of *course* I wasn't asking you to move in permanently. Just offering you the spare guest room until you find a place of your own. I know how brutal the New York real-estate market can be.

Not that you'll have any problems, the way sales are going for *Sweeping Sands*. In fact, the penthouse across from mine just went up for sale, a steal at two million. Interested? I could speak to the co-op board on your behalf. . . .

In any case, darling, call me when you get back from Mark's little elopement.

XXXOOO
Dolly

Travel Diary of
~~Holly Caputo and Mark Levine~~
Jane Harris

OK, I asked Cell Phone Guy to watch my stuff for a minute while I ran to buy snacks, and he was TOTALLY rude about it. He said, in this very snarky way, "I highly doubt anyone is going to steal your <u>water</u>, miss."

!!!!!

Which wasn't even what I was asking him to watch. My water, I mean. Clearly, I meant my BAG. I mean, the last thing I need is for the airport to blow up my stuff because I left it unattended.

Whatever. It's just like Malcolm says. Some people just suck, and there's nothing you can do about it. I should have known Cell Phone Guy was one of them. Especially the way he keeps banging at the keyboard of that Blackberry. He's still at it. How can someone so anal retentive look so good in a pair of jeans? I don't get it. I mean, evolutionarily speaking, his kind should have been wiped out a long time ago. Because who'd want to mate with someone with THAT kind of attitude?

OOOOOOH, I see Holly!!!! Holly and Mark are here, at last! YAY!

I wonder where Mark's friend Cal is. The best man, I mean. We were all supposed to meet at the gate. . . .

✉

To: Mark Levine <mark.levine@thenyjournal.com>
Fr: Cal Langdon <cal.langdon@thenyjournal.com>
Re: Where are you?

I'm at the gate. I don't see you. You didn't take my advice and cancel the thing at the last minute, did you?

Forget it, you're not the leave-em-at-the-altar type.

So. Nervous yet? I've got the flask, don't worry. We're going to need it, too, there's a real nut job on this flight. Apparently she thinks there's a possibility we might crash land in the Sahara.

Hurry up and get here, I want to kiss the bride—

Oh, there you are.

Cal

Travel Diary of

~~Holly Caputo and Mark Levine~~
Jane Harris

Oh my God.

Cell Phone Guy is Cal. <u>Cal Langdon</u>, Mark's best buddy since elementary school, the one who's been traveling all around the world for the <u>Journal</u>, writing about social unrest and economic instability for the past ten years. The one with the new book that's just out—the one he supposedly got this huge advance for.

I wish I were on that plane that's stuck in the San Francisco airport instead of on this one. I would rather have a deadly virus than have to spend a minute more in the company of Cal Langdon, aka Cell Phone Guy, aka Mark Levine's Best Friend.

Oh, but guess what? HE'S SITTING RIGHT NEXT TO ME. That's what he was so mad about before. He was calling Travel Services at the <u>Journal</u>, trying to get them to change his seat so he could sit in business class, or at least on the aisle, and not in the middle, like he is now.

Ha ha. Ha ha, Cal In the Middle. Hope you like bumping your elbow into mine every five seconds, Mr. I-Highly-Doubt-Anyone-Is-Going-To-Steal-Your-Water,-Miss. Because I am SO not giving up my aisle seat. No way.

And don't expect me to share my water with you, either. OR my Toblerone. Or my cheese popcorn. I don't care how long we're stuck on this runway, or what kind of virus might get into the ventilation system. You're getting nada from me, mister.

I'm not telling Holly how much I hate her husband's best man, though. I don't want to spoil this special time for her.

I am so not going to be able to give them this travel diary as a wedding gift. Oh well. It's probably just as well, since my handwriting is barely legible, thanks to the Armrest Nazi next to me. Excuse me, Mr. I'm-So-Big-I-Need-To-Take-Up-Your-Space-Too. Could you please move your stupid hairy arm with the stupid waterproof watch that tells the altitude and the exact time on all seven continents which I know you so need, being such a fancy world traveler who knows so much about foreign policy and things a poor little cartoonist like me couldn't even begin to understand?

I'll tell you one thing: if this is a setup, Holly is dead. I mean, I know she doesn't like Malcolm, but could she seriously, even for one second, entertain the idea that I might like Mister Nothing-Comes-Between-Me-And-My-Blackberry here? Please! He asked me what I do for a living (he was so just making conversation because Holly and Mark are seated right behind us, and he didn't want to look like the Uptight Anal Retentive Control Freak he really is in front of them), and when I said I was a cartoonist, he was like, "You're kidding."

Totally deadpan. You're kidding.

And get this: he's never heard of Wondercat.

Never. Heard. Of. Wonder. Cat.

He has to be lying. He <u>writes</u> for the paper in which Wondercat was born.

And ok, he's abroad all the time, and you can't get the <u>Journal</u> everywhere. But doesn't he watch <u>television</u>? He may have been gallivanting all around the world for the past decade, but excuse me, he's back now, promoting his stupid book. Hasn't he seen Wondercat's commercial for energy-saving products on New York One? Everyone watches New York One, if only to check the temperature.

My God. Who is this guy? And why does Mark even <u>like</u> him????

I think I'm going to have to have a word with Holly. Does she know what she's getting herself into, marrying a man who'd be best friends with a guy who doesn't watch TV????

✉

To: Mark Levine <mark.levine@thenyjournal.com>
Fr: Cal Langdon <cal.langdon@thenyjournal.com>
Re: I'm going to kill you

What in hell is a Wondercat?

Cal

✉

To: Cal Langdon <cal.langdon@thenyjournal.com>
Fr: Mark Levine <mark.levine@thenyjournal.com>
Re: I'm going to kill you

Excuse me. I don't believe you are allowed to use these things on planes.

Mark

PS You didn't *tell* her you didn't know who Wondercat is, did you?

✉

To: Mark Levine <mark.levine@thenyjournal.com>
Fr: Cal Langdon <cal.langdon@thenyjournal.com>
Re: I'm going to kill you

You can't use them while you're in the air, according to the FAA— although I doubt the veracity of this, as I've left mine on plenty of times and none of my flights have ever plummeted into the sea because of it.

You can, however, still legally use them when you're sitting use- lessly on the tarmac while the air control tower guys are having a limbo contest, as they are apparently doing right now because I can see no other conceivable reason why we're not being allowed to take off.

And yes, I did ask her what a Wondercat was. Is that why she is busy scribbling into the travel diary she bought at the duty free? Because I offended her so deeply with my lack of knowledge about her cat?

Cal

....

Meg
Cabot
18

✉

To: Cal Langdon <cal.langdon@thenyjournal.com>
Fr: Mark Levine <mark.levine@thenyjournal.com>
Re: I'm going to kill you

Yes. And stop emailing me, Holly keeps asking who I'm writing to. I told her it was the hospital, and now she's mad that the hospital is emailing me when I'm supposed to be eloping.

Mark

....

✉

To: Mark Levine <mark.levine@thenyjournal.com>
Fr: Cal Langdon <cal.langdon@thenyjournal.com>
Re: I'm going to kill you

How would the hospital even know that, anyway? The word elope means to run away with a lover with the intention of wedding in secret. How secret is your wedding going to be if the hospital knows about it?

C

✉

To: Cal Langdon <cal.langdon@thenyjournal.com>
Fr: Mark Levine <mark.levine@thenyjournal.com>
Re: I'm going to kill you

I had to tell the hospital I was getting married. *And* the paper. They weren't going to give the time off, or let me out of my column, otherwise. DON'T TELL Holly. She still thinks the only people who know what we're really doing are the four of us.

And of course the entire art department at the *New York Journal*. But she doesn't know that I know that.

Mark

PS Quit writing to me. I'm turning this thing off.

....

✉

To: Mark Levine <mark.levine@thenyjournal.com>
Fr: Cal Langdon <cal.langdon@thenyjournal.com>
Re: You Dog

Your secret's safe with me.

But seriously. Is this girl one of those cat people? For the love of God please tell me I'm not going to be stuck in a middle seat in coach next to one of those cat people. She doesn't carry around pictures of it in her wallet, does she? Her cat? Because I will suffer an aneurysm midair if that's the case—

AT THIS TIME THE CAPTAIN HAS REQUESTED THAT ALL ELECTRONIC DEVICES BE TURNED OFF AND STOWED AWAY UNTIL WE HAVE REACHED CRUISING ALTITUDE

What do you think of him?

> Oh my God, Holly. What is this, the ninth grade?
> You're passing me notes? On the PLANE????

Well, how else am I supposed to talk to you with the
stupid food cart in the way? And they won't let us
turn on our Blackberries. Come on, hurry up, while he's
asleep. What do you think of him?

> He's not really asleep. He's just faking it so he
> won't have to talk to me. I know because he's still
> playing armrest war with me. Every time I put my
> elbow on the armrest, he puts his there, too, to
> block mine.

You don't like him?

> Holly, he's never heard of Wondercat!!!!

Janie, he's been doing foreign correspondence for the
past ten years. They don't get family papers like the
ones that run Wondercat in places like Kabul.

> But you said he moved back to the US a couple of
> weeks ago—

And you think he should have spent those weeks
catching up on YOUR comic, as opposed to, I don't
know, FINDING A PLACE TO LIVE???

> Well. He also made fun of me for bringing so many
> bottles of water onboard.

You do have kind of a lot.

> Excuse me. Nine out of ten people found dead
> after getting lost in the desert actually have
> water left in their canteens, they were just so con-
> cerned about conserving it, they didn't drink
> enough of it to survive. It's true. I saw it on the
> Discovery Channel.

Okay, okay. But what do you think of him???? Do you
like him? He's cute, right? I told you he was cute.

> He seems very . . . smart.

The Blackberry thing. I knew it. I *told* Mark to tell him
to put that thing away. I know nothing freaks you out
more than guys who are smarter than you.

> I can't believe you just wrote that. First of all,
> it's not even true, and second of all, in no way is
> Cal smarter than me. I mean, yes, he has trav-
> eled all over the world covering news stories
> about grisly wars and Ebola outbreaks and has
> written a book and stuff, but that does not
> mean he is smarter than I am. I mean, can he
> draw a cat?
> Besides which, I happen to like smart men.

Right. Like Malcolm.

> Oh, that's low, even for you. I will have you know
> that Malcolm can do a 360-degree spin in midair
> and not lose his board.

You have got to stop dating snowboarders and musicians, Jane. You're 30 years old now. You've got to start thinking about the future, and date people who will actually stick around for a change, instead of going off to their next X-Game or gig.

> Maybe I don't WANT a boyfriend who sticks around. Have you ever thought about that?

Then why did you cry so much those first couple weeks after Malcolm moved out?

> I just felt bad for The Dude. You know they'd bonded.

Yeah, well, there's that, too. The Dude needs some stability in his life. He might not bite people as much if he had a positive male role model in his life. The same could be said of you. Plus, financially, you'd be much better off with a partner who actually has steady employment. As a freelancer, you are paying a premium for health insurance. If you married a guy who had his own insurance—through, say, the paper—that'd be a big chunk of change saved. Plus you'd have security. And a 401K.

> This is pretty funny coming from a woman who once spent an entire month's rent money on a pair of purple leather pants.

Hello. Can we talk about things that happened in this millennium, please?

Fine. You know what? It's very unfair of you to throw all that stuff about 401Ks and all of that into my face, when you know perfectly well that I HAD all that when I was dating DAVE, and you saw how THAT turned out.

OK, well, I'll admit walking in on your boyfriend in bed with your HR rep can be psychologically scarring. Especially considering it was Amy Jenkins. But you'll recall that I ALWAYS told you it was never a good idea to date a foreigner. You can never tell when they're lying.

Hello. Dave was BRITISH.

Yes, but that accent had us fooled. If he'd been from this country, we'd have known right away he was an HR rep–whoremonger. But really, Janie, just because things didn't work out with Dave is no reason to start dating unemployed losers half his age—

Need I remind you that Malcolm is not unemployed? You know he got that big Winter Cal Games contract. That's the only reason he left. I mean, he had to move up to Canada. For the snow.

And the fact that he was a chronic wake and baker had nothing to do with you ENCOURAGING him to move.

Well, at least he isn't an anal-retentive control freak like SOME people who happen to be sitting next to me, HOGGING THE ARMREST.

Jane, your bedroom still smells like the inside of a bong.

It is so typical of you to bring this up at a sensitive time like this. After all, YOU'RE the bride. I'm only the bridesmaid. Or witness. Or whatever.

Well, other than the "smart" thing, what do you think of Cal? Do you like him?

I get fan mail from Wondercat readers in SRI LANKA, Holly. SRI LANKANS have heard of Wondercat. But not Mark's friend Cal.

So? Have you ever read any of his articles on landmines?

At least I know what a land mine is!!!!!!!!!

Just try to get along with him, will you? Because otherwise it's going to be a really long trip.

No problem. Now stop writing to me, please, my food is here.

Benvenuti in
(Welcome to)

Alitalia Inflight Menu

Durante il volo da New York a Roma verra servita la cena e, prima dell' arrivo, la colazione. I piatta che gusterete sono stati preparati per voi. Buon appetito.

(During the flight from New York to Rome we will be serving dinner and then, prior to arrival, breakfast. The dishes on today's menu have been specially prepared for you. Enjoy your meal.)

✢ Cena ✢
(Dinner)

Farfalle al pomodoro pachino e foglie di basilico
Rolle di tacchinella e broccoletti accompagnata da caponata
de melanzane e patate
(Farfalle pasta shapes in a fresh pachino tomato and basil sauce
Turkey roll with broccoli stuffing served with
aubergine stew and potatoes)

Oppure
(Or)

Filetti de pescatrice con potage de zucchine e insalata Catalana
(Monk fish fillet with green zucchini potage and Catalan style salad)

Assortimento dei fromaggi, accompagnali da composte
di frutta e cruditees
Caffe "Espresso" e cioccolatini
(Cheese assortment accompanied by crudites and
fresh fruit compote
Italian "Espresso" coffee and chocolates)

Travel Diary of

~~Holly Caputo and Mark Levine~~

Jane Harris

Oh my God. The Italian food on the plane is better than the Italian takeout around the corner from my apartment. And I thought their insalata caprese was to die for.

   The movie is starting. It's the new Hugh Jackman! OH MY GOD, I HAVE DIED AND GONE TO HEAVEN! I AM GOING TO EUROPE WITH MY BEST FRIEND AND THEY ARE SHOWING A HUGH JACKMAN MOVIE ON THE PLANE.

   If only the Armrest Nazi would MOVE HIS ELBOW.

PDA of Cal Langdon

As usual, the food on this flight is barely edible. And what passes for entertainment in this country these days is truly depressing. The in-flight movie appears to be yet another romantic comedy about a harried young career woman who finds love in a completely unexpected place. My traveling companion is watching it with rapt attention, as she swills from her many, many bottles of water. She is clearly envisioning herself in the role of the harried young career woman.

I think I can say with a certain amount of confidence that she is NOT picturing me in the role of the handsome young leading man. In fact, her marked lack of enthusiasm for me borders almost on the comical. She is taking great pains never to allow her elbow to touch mine on our mutual armrest, as if she fears she might contract some sort of deadly virus from doing so.

And all this, because I happened to remark on her rather remarkable penchant for bottled water.

Oh, and the Crazy Cat thing. Or Wondercat. How was I to know *Wondercat* is a comic strip, and that she is its creator? I haven't read a comic since Mark and I were kids, and used to shell out 35 cents a week for the latest edition of *Spider-Man* at the Big Red Food Mart. I certainly have never made a habit of reading comic strips in the newspaper—not since I turned ten. The newspapers I choose to read don't *have* comic strips in them.

Although I don't suppose it would be politic to admit that, seeing as how the tome we all work for features two pages of comics daily—not to mention horoscopes and *Dear Abby*. In fact, now that I'll be living in one place for an extended period of time, I suppose I'll have to start subscribing. So I have that to look forward to. In addition to so many other joys I've missed while I've been living out of a bag, such as apartment hunting, buying various electronic devices like a toaster and stereo equipment, and waiting all day for the cable guy who promised to come between ten and two, and then didn't show.

Ah! Domesticity! How I haven't missed you!

But I suppose domesticity can have its benefits. Mark is happier than I've ever seen him. He seems almost to *welcome* the noose that awaits his neck at the end of this journey. Although I suppose when the noose looks like Holly . . .

And she does, I'll admit, seem to think about topics outside of her nails and yoga and Must See TV, unlike most of the American women I've encountered lately. I even had an intelligent conversation with her last week about Gore Vidal.

But I had intelligent conversations with Valerie in the early days, as well.

And as for this friend of Holly's . . . I don't know. I suppose allowances must be made because she's an artist.

But is cartooning really art? My mother would surely think so.

But Mom thinks the lint she picks from the dryer and hot-glues to clothespins is art. And sadly, she is supported in this belief by the art community of Tucson, where she's lately set up a studio.

Still, though she may be an artist, Ms. Harris does have very shiny hair. It's brown, like her eyes.

The tattoo of a cat head—Wondercat, I'm supposing—she wears just above her right ankle is somewhat off-putting, however. And her mouth never seems to stop moving. Now she's telling the flight attendant how much she enjoyed the male lead's last film, in which he played some kind of mutant.

This seat is so uncomfortable. I can just fit into it, if I don't inhale.

Oh, well. I've slept in worse places. At least there aren't any guerrillas hiding in nearby undergrowth, waiting for the opportunity to slit my throat. Or snakes.

God, I hate snakes.

So that's something, anyway.

Benvenuti in
(Welcome to)

Alitalia Inflight Menu

✣ Colazione ✣
(Breakfast)

Spremuta fresca di arancia

Omelette alle erbe fini con funghi, pomodori e bacon ala griglia

Assortimento di tieviti e pano tostate caldi

Caffe, te, latte

Freshly squeezed orange juice

*Herb omelette accompanied with mushrooms,
grilled cherry tomatoes, and bacon*

Assortment of pastries and croissants

Coffee, tea, milk

Travel Diary of
~~Holly Caputo and Mark Levine~~
Jane Harris

Cell Phone Guy was right. There is plenty of water onboard this flight. There's also a lot of wine. Being drunk by the very loud group of people behind us. Who keep yelling to the flight attendant in Italian so I don't know what they're saying. But it doesn't sound very nice.

I also don't think it's necessarily appropriate to drink wine with breakfast, which is what they just woke us all up to have. I would have preferred to sleep for the rest of the flight, since it seems like we just had dinner after all.

But they came around with the cart and asked us all if we wanted breakfast and that woke everybody up, and now we're all cranky. But especially me because I fell asleep with my mascara still on and I guess it got kind of gunked up underneath the sleeping mask they gave us, and when the flight attendant woke me up to ask me if I wanted breakfast and I took off my sleeping mask, I still couldn't see him because my eyelashes were all stuck together. And then he said, "Oh, no, I think not," about me wanting breakfast in a kind of horrified voice.

So then I had to hurry to the bathroom to try to pick the chunks of mascara from my eyes before Cal could see it. Which he didn't, thank God, because he was still asleep.

But that's not the worst part. The worst part is that Cal woke up while I was gone, and I guess went to the other bathroom, where I suppose he brushed his teeth with the little kit they gave us just like I did, because his breath was minty fresh when he replied to the question I asked him, which I only asked him to be polite and make conversation, something I'll be sure not to do again where he's concerned.

Anyway, I asked him if he was excited about the wedding, he said, "Not exactly."

Which is not especially something you want to hear from the best man of your best friend's husband-to-be, in my opinion.

I have to admit I was so shocked I just sat there and stared at the thing on the wall that counts down the kms until we get to <u>Roma</u> (425). I couldn't think what he meant by it.

It seemed to me that the only thing he could mean by it was that maybe he doesn't like Holly or something, which is ridiculous because of course who doesn't like Holly? She's very kind and pretty and is the art director for a huge urban news-paper, which is a thankless job that doesn't pay nearly as well as it should, considering the fact that she has to work with crazy cartoonists like me, not to mention all the other psychos at the <u>Journal</u>, like that Dolly Vargas from the Style section who is always on Holly's back for not making the reds in the Valentine's Day issue red enough.

Plus she completely adores Mark. So why wouldn't Cal like her?

So I asked him—maybe a little defensively, I'll admit, but hello, I've known Holly for years, and if it weren't for her, Wondercat would never have seen the light of day, but would still be just a silly sketch in my notepad, and I still wouldn't be able to pay my American Express bill every month—what he had against her, and he said, totally politely, "Oh, I haven't got anything against Holly. I think Holly's great and Mark's lucky to have her. It's just marriage I have a problem with."

So then I realized he's one of those monogamy-phobes.

So I told him about how lobsters mate for life, and if they can do it, why can't we, and he looked at me sort of funny and said, "Yes, but they're crustaceans."

To which I replied that I knew that, but that lots of mammals mate for life as well, such as wolves and hawks (at least that's what Rutger Hauer said in <u>LadyHawke</u>, so I assume it's true), and how I think it's romantic and the way things should be.

And then Cal said, "If it's so romantic, how come over fifty percent of marriages end in divorce? How come the leading cause of death for pregnant women in the US isn't complications from childbirth but murder by their spouses?"

What can you even <u>say</u> to something like that?

I swear, if this guy starts spewing those little factoids of his about divorce and murder rates while Holly's within hearing distance, I'll kill him. KILL HIM. She's got enough on her mind right now without hearing THAT kind of stuff . . . I mean, what with her mother and all.

Ack! We're landing! In a few minutes, I'll be on foreign soil, for the first time in my life! I'm sure the Armrest Nazi, being a seasoned world traveler, would think it's stupid, but . . . I'm so excited!

PASSPORT

*The Secretary of State
of the United States of America
hereby requests all whom it may concern
to permit the citizen/national of the
United States named herein to pass
without delay or hindrance
and in case of need to give all lawful
aid and protections.*

Jane Harris
_____

*Signature of bearer
Not valid until signed*

Entries / Entrée / Entradas

FIUMACINO
14 SE

Travel Diary of

~~Holly Caputo and Mark Levine~~

Jane Harris

I got it! My first stamp in my passport! It's kind of smudgy
and you can't really read the date. But it's THERE!

Though it TOOK long enough to get it. What is with the
LINES in this place? I mean, seriously, do you think they could
have opened more than one customs booth? There must have
been three hundred people in line ahead of us. This NEVER
would have happened in the US. I mean, Americans just would
not have put up with it.

Still, it gave me a chance to look around and realize right
away that my shoes are all wrong for this country. NO ONE
here wears Steve Madden slides. NO ONE. The Italian women
have slides, all right, but they have these wicked pointed toes
and tiny little heels. Plus they are all wearing long pants, not
jeans like Holly and I, and they have these cashmere scarves
thrown casually over one shoulder even though according to
the Weather Channel it's going to be 24 degrees Celsius every
day while we're here, which is in the 80s. I think.

So what's up with that?

Also, it was just SLIGHTLY disturbing when the Customs
guy was all, "And where in Italy are you staying," and I said, "Le
Marche," hoping I'd pronounced it right, and he made a face
and went, "Why would you go THERE?"

Frankly, I do not believe that by offering me his opinion on
my final destination that he was allowing me to pass without
delay or hindrance into his country, as my passport says he
has to.

Besides which, he's wrong. Holly always said her uncle's
house was in the most beautiful section of Italy there is. And
okay, according to my guidebook, Le Marche (also known as

the Le Marche in English) isn't that well known to foreigners. But her uncle seems to have liked it well enough to spend a million bucks on a sixteenth-century villa there.

Besides, what's not to like? Le Marche "forms the eastern seaboard of central Italy—with the Apennine Mountains, noted for their bare peaks and dramatic gorges, forming a natural boundary between it and Umbria and Tuscany. The areas nearer the coast are celebrated for their fertile rounded hills topped by ancient fortified towns."

Um, at least according to my guidebook.

And OK, maybe it's not super popular with anyone but Italians (except for my customs agent). But my guidebook also goes on and on about its unspoiled beauty. . . .

Whatever. Why is my bag always the last one to get through the fricking carousel? And why is Cal laughing so hard at it? My bag is not funny. OK, I painted a Wondercat head on it. But that's only because it's a black rolly bag, and there are only five billion other black rolly bags that look exactly like it. At least I can tell mine apart from all the others at a distance of a hundred yards.

Plus, my bag's not as big as HOLLY's. I mean, I didn't cram a wedding gown into MINE. Just because HE has this dinky little backpack, Mr. Jet-Set-Travel-Guy—

Oh, here's the taxi stand, at LAST. I can't WAIT to get to the hotel and take a nap. Even if it IS only ten in the morning here. I'm so TIRED. . . .

What is that incessant BEEPING coming out of my bag? Not just MY bag either . . . EVERYBODY is beeping!

To: Jane Harris <jane@wondercat.com>
Fr: Claire Harris <charris2004@freemail.com>
Re: You

I hope this thing works! You said you'd be able to get emails in Italy, so I hope you get this. Everything here is fine, don't worry. Well, Dad stuck his hand in the wood chipper again, but he was wearing his chain-mail gloves, so he just broke a blade, didn't lose a finger. He is so forgetful sometimes!

Anyway, I know I'm not supposed to say anything to Holly's mom about how she and Mark are eloping, and you don't need to worry, I haven't said a word, even though I saw her at book group last night and she was practically in tears when we were discussing the scene in which the couple in the book—another one by that nice man who wrote *A Walk to Remember* . . . he's just so talented. But why do all his characters have to die at the end?—got married.

When we asked what was wrong, poor Marie said all she's ever wanted is to see Holly settled. You know how Holly was always dying her hair purple and getting things pierced and dating the most inappropriate people all through those years you two were in school together. (Thank goodness you were never like that! You've always been so sensible. I thought your new friend Malcolm was so sweet when I met him last July. How is his investment banking job, anyway? I'm so happy you've finally found someone so responsible! And he looks so *young*! You'd hardly know he was your age. Must be good genes!)

I *really* wanted to say something to Marie like, "Well, you aren't going to have to worry much longer about Holly staying single," but of course I didn't.

Although I sort of wish I had said something now, since Marie went on to say, "I don't care who she marries, as long as he's a nice *Catholic* boy! I have nothing against this *Mark* of hers, but he's, you know. Not one of *us*."

Oh, dear. I don't think Marie is going to be very happy when she gets Holly and Mark's telegram telling her they've gotten married.

And Mark is such a *nice* boy, too. It's such a shame.

Well, I hope you arrived safely. Be careful of pickpockets in Rome. I hear they like to career past tourists on Vespas through those little narrow streets and snatch handbags and cameras right off by the shoulder strap! So be sure not to wear your shoulder strap slung across your body or you could be dragged to your death.

Love,
Mom

PS Love to The Dude!
PPS What is Mark's friend like? Is he nice? I'm sure he must be, if he's a friend of Mark's!

....

✉

To: Mark Levine <mark.levine@thenyjournal.com>
Fr: Ruth Levine <r.levine@levinedentalgroup.com >
Re: Hello!

Hi, sweetie! I know you're off to Europe today with your little friends, but I just wanted you to know that last night we had dinner with the Schramms—you remember, you learned to swim in Susie Schramm's backyard pool when you were four—and Lottie Schramm told me that Susie is a corporate lawyer in—get this—NEW YORK CITY! Yes! She works at a firm called Hertzog, Webber, and Doyle on Madison Avenue (so fancy!), and lives on the Upper East Side, not three blocks from your own place! Isn't that incredible? I'm surprised the two of you have never run into one another at H & H Bagels!

In any case, Lottie gave me Susie's email to pass along to you. It's sschramm@hwd.com. You really ought to drop her a line, Mark. Dottie showed me a picture. Susie's grown into a real beauty, and lost every bit of her baby fat (Dottie says because she does Pilates three times a week and hasn't touched a carb in three years).

Hope you're having fun! Don't forget to wear a sweater in the evenings. I understand it can get chilly there at night.

Love,
Mom

....

✉

To: Ruth Levine <r.levine@levinedentalgroup.com >
Fr: Mark Levine <mark.levine@thenyjournal.com>
Re: Hello!

Ma. Stop trying to fix me up with other women. I am in love with Holly. Got it? HOLLY.

Mark

....

✉

To: Holly Caputo <holly.caputo@thenyjournal.com>
Fr: Inge Schumacher <i.schumacher@freemail.co.it>
Re: Greetings!

I am understand you will have arrived today! This is perfect. I am making your uncle's house, Villa Beccacia, a home for you. All is ready except the towels which dry on line. I am understand three rooms beds to be made. You arrive by car tomorrow afternoon? You will call me at Villa Beccacia and I will greet you on the autobahn to show you way to villa.

I am hoping you do not mind, my great-grandson Peter visits me on school holiday during your stay. He is good boy, and drives each morning on his motorino to fetch the brotchen for you. Tschuss!

Inge Schumacher
Villa Beccacia
Castelfidardo, Marche

✉

To: Cal Langdon <cal.langdon@thenyjournal.com>
Fr: Tara Samuels <tara.samuels@thenyjournal.com>
Re: Travel Services

Success! I've booked you a seat to Rome on the 6 P.M. flight today. I'm SO sorry about the confusion, and to make up for it, we managed to upgrade you to first class. Enjoy your flight!

Tara

✉

To: Claire Harris <charris2004@freemail.com>
Fr: Jane Harris <jane@wondercat.com>
Re: You

Hi, Mom! I'm writing this to you from an Italian taxi cab! We're on the way from the airport to the hotel where we're staying for the night before going on to Holly's uncle's villa in the morning. Holly made the paper give us Blackberries for emergency use. I can see why they gave one to Holly, because she's the art director, so her job is actually important. But ME??? I'm a freelancer,

I don't even really work there anymore. But Holly talked them into it. Isn't that cool? Of course we have to give them back when we get home. But whatever.

It is so . . . different here. I mean, I'm only in the cab, but already, it looks way different from home. All of the billboards are in Italian! Well, I mean, I know you'd expect that, but I mean, REALLY in Italian. Like there are no recognizably English words AT ALL.

And all of the buildings have these roll-down metal shutters, painted in all these bright colors, to keep out the sun, because I guess it can get really hot, and no one has air-conditioning.

And there are window boxes EVERYWHERE, with CASCADES of red and pink and blue flowers frothing down them. It's so pretty!

And everywhere you look are these funny little half-cars, like Volkswagen bugs that got cut in half, called Smart Cars. In fact the biggest car I've seen here is the minivan we're in. I guess Italians aren't really having big families anymore. Either that, or they don't go anywhere with the kids.

I really don't think you have to worry about my bag getting snatched, Mom. The only people I see on Vespas here are fashionably dressed, skinny women, with long flowing hair, driving around in long, pointy shoes with tiny little heels!

I'm so tired, I can't type anymore. I can't WAIT to get to the hotel so I can crash. I need a shower in the WORST way.

Love to Dad. Tell him to keep wearing those gloves.

Janie

PS The Dude was fine when I left him. Julio, the super's son, is going to look in on him every day after school. I bought him some special tuna Pounce for a treat. For The Dude. Not Julio.

J

PPS Mark's friend is NOT a nice guy. He's totally awful! His name is Cal Langdon and he's some hotshot reporter who thinks he's all that. He doesn't believe in marriage and thinks Mark is making a huge mistake. I don't know how I'm going to survive a whole week in his company. HE'S NEVER HEARD OF WONDERCAT.

J

....

✉

To: Julio Chasez <julio@streetsmart.com>
Fr: Jane Harris <jane@wondercat.com>
Re: The Dude

Hi, Julio! It's me, Jane! I realize I've only been gone a day, but I just wanted to make sure everything is all right. You know, with The Dude. I know how he can get. Just make sure he gets two cans of fresh food a day (one before you leave for school, and one before you go to bed) PLUS dry food and fresh water, and he should be fine.

Be sure to wear the oven mitts if you have to touch him! And whatever you do, DON'T give him any catnip!

Thank you SO MUCH for taking care of him for me. You are the BEST!

Love,
Jane

✉

To: Jane Harris <jane@wondercat.com>
Fr: Holly Caputo <holly.caputo@thenyjournal.com>
Re: His Mother

Can you believe it? He got an email from his freaking mother about some girl from his hometown who lives in NY now. I'm going to lose it.

Holly

✉

To: Holly Caputo <holly.caputo@thenyjournal.com>
Fr: Jane Harris <jane@wondercat.com>
Re: His Mother

Um . . . why are you emailing me from inside the same car we are both sitting in? Also, I thought we were only supposed to use these things for work purposes.

J

✉

To: Jane Harris <jane@wondercat.com>
Fr: Holly Caputo <holly.caputo@thenyjournal.com>
Re: His Mother

I can't exactly talk to you about the email he got from his mother IN FRONT OF HIM, now can I? Except this way.

And how are they ever going to know what we use these dumb things for, anyway? How are you holding up?

Holly

✉

To: Holly Caputo <holly.caputo@thenyjournal.com>
Fr: Jane Harris <jane@wondercat.com>
Re: His Mother

Good. It's pretty here.

How do you know that his mom emailed him, anyway?

J

✉

To: Jane Harris <jane@wondercat.com>
Fr: Holly Caputo <holly.caputo@thenyjournal.com>
Re: His Mother

Duh. I read it over his shoulder just now. I saw you and Cal talking at the baggage carousel. What did he say?

Holly

✉

To: Holly Caputo <holly.caputo@thenyjournal.com>
Fr: Jane Harris <jane@wondercat.com>
Re: His Mother

Oh. Nothing.

J

✉

To: Jane Harris <jane@wondercat.com>
Fr: Holly Caputo <holly.caputo@thenyjournal.com>
Re: His Mother

Come on! SPILL!

Holly

✉

To: Holly Caputo <holly.caputo@thenyjournal.com>
Fr: Jane Harris <jane@wondercat.com>
Re: His Mother

Is this a setup? Are you and Mark playing Fix Up the Best Friends? Because I told you before, I'm TAKEN. Besides. He's not my type.

J

✉

To: Jane Harris <jane@wondercat.com>
Fr: Holly Caputo <holly.caputo@thenyjournal.com>
Re: His Mother

You have a *type*? What is it? The only thing the guys you've dated have in common is that they've all been unemployed. Or, if they HAD jobs, they were also screwing Amy Jenkins, like Dave.

Holly

✉

To: Holly Caputo <holly.caputo@thenyjournal.com>
Fr: Jane Harris <jane@wondercat.com>
Re: His Mother

Whatever happened to her, anyway?

J

✉

To: Jane Harris <jane@wondercat.com>
Fr: Holly Caputo <holly.caputo@thenyjournal.com>
Re: His Mother

Who? Amy Jenkins?

She married a rich lawyer, moved to Pound Ridge, and squeezed out two kids.

Holly

✉

To: Holly Caputo <holly.caputo@thenyjournal.com>
Fr: Jane Harris <jane@wondercat.com>
Re: His Mother

No! No, she didn't! Why did you tell me that? THAT'S NOT FAIR!!! She tried to ruin my life!!! Why should SHE have a happy ending?

J

✉

To: Jane Harris <jane@wondercat.com>
Fr: Holly Caputo <holly.caputo@thenyjournal.com>
Re: His Mother

You call living in Pound Ridge with a lawyer and two kids a happy ending? You so know she spends her days working out and helping the nanny make wheat-free snacks.

Don't worry. In a couple of years she'll pudge out and he'll trade her in for a younger model and she won't be able to get a job to support herself anywhere because she doesn't have any references, and one day you and Cal will pull into an outlet Benetton to pick up a pair of socks and she'll be working the cash register.

Holly

✉

To: Holly Caputo <holly.caputo@thenyjournal.com>
Fr: Jane Harris <jane@wondercat.com>
Re: His Mother

I don't want to talk about this anymore.

J

✉

To: Jane Harris <jane@wondercat.com>
Fr: Holly Caputo <holly.caputo@thenyjournal.com>
Re: His Mother

Why not?

Holly

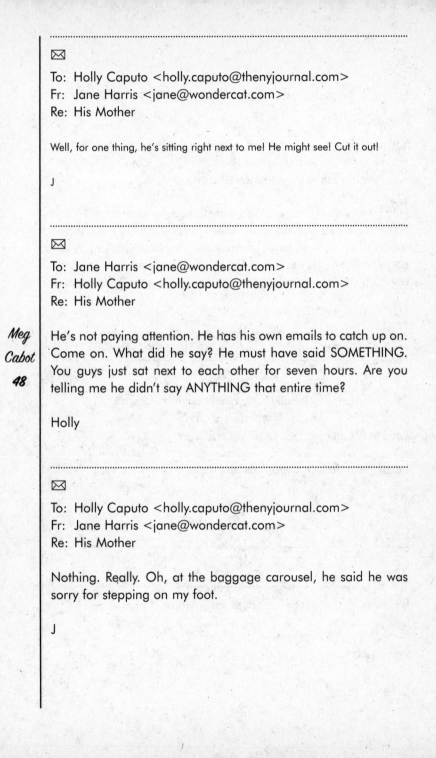

✉

To: Holly Caputo <holly.caputo@thenyjournal.com>
Fr: Jane Harris <jane@wondercat.com>
Re: His Mother

Well, for one thing, he's sitting right next to me! He might see! Cut it out!

J

✉

To: Jane Harris <jane@wondercat.com>
Fr: Holly Caputo <holly.caputo@thenyjournal.com>
Re: His Mother

He's not paying attention. He has his own emails to catch up on. Come on. What did he say? He must have said SOMETHING. You guys just sat next to each other for seven hours. Are you telling me he didn't say ANYTHING that entire time?

Holly

✉

To: Holly Caputo <holly.caputo@thenyjournal.com>
Fr: Jane Harris <jane@wondercat.com>
Re: His Mother

Nothing. Really. Oh, at the baggage carousel, he said he was sorry for stepping on my foot.

J

✉

To: Jane Harris <jane@wondercat.com>
Fr: Holly Caputo <holly.caputo@thenyjournal.com>
Re: His Mother

That's IT? Wow. That's weird. Did he talk about his marriage at all?

Holly

✉

To: Holly Caputo <holly.caputo@thenyjournal.com>
Fr: Jane Harris <jane@wondercat.com>
Re: His Mother

HIS WHAT????????????????????

J

✉

To: Jane Harris <jane@wondercat.com>
Fr: Holly Caputo <holly.caputo@thenyjournal.com>
Re: His Mother

God, use question marks much?

His MARRIAGE. He was married once, you know. He's divorced. I just wondered if he'd mentioned it.

Holly

✉

To: Holly Caputo <holly.caputo@thenyjournal.com>
Fr: Jane Harris <jane@wondercat.com>
Re: His Mother

He didn't say a word about this. But it explains an awful lot. Who was the NOT SO lucky girl?

J

✉

To: Jane Harris <jane@wondercat.com>
Fr: Holly Caputo <holly.caputo@thenyjournal.com>
Re: His Mother

Her name was Valerie Something. I don't know, really, it was ten years ago, back when he and Mark just graduated from college. They met in a bar. He was the newest cub reporter, and she was a model. They went out for about a month before he decided she was the best thing that ever happened to him and married her. They only lasted about a year. Apparently, as soon as the divorce was final, she married an investment banker, and Cal asked for an overseas post. According to Mark, she broke Cal's heart.

And what did you mean by that explains an awful lot?

Holly

To: Holly Caputo <holly.caputo@thenyjournal.com>
Fr: Jane Harris <jane@wondercat.com>
Re: His Mother

Nothing.

Oh, so you're saying he has a heart after all?

J

✉

To: Jane Harris <jane@wondercat.com>
Fr: Holly Caputo <holly.caputo@thenyjournal.com>
Re: His Mother

Come on. He's a nice guy. He's had a crappy time with women—I guess his mother left to "find herself" when he was still in high school, and lately, his little sister's followed suit. He was just put through the wringer by another model, and spent the past decade recovering in places where they don't have cell phone service. Or working toilets. Can you blame him for being a little rough around the edges?

Besides, he can't be THAT bad. Mark says Cal's always been a real ladies' man—that he's got a girl in every port, if you know what I mean. In fact, Mark was sure you two would hit it off right away. He said you're just Cal's type. Apparently, he's partial to brunettes.

He really must not like you.

Holly

✉

To: Holly Caputo <holly.caputo@thenyjournal.com>
Fr: Jane Harris <jane@wondercat.com>
Re: His Mother

Wow. That's really nice to know. Thanks so very much for that.

J

PS Oh, and thanks for trying to fix me up with him, but even if I COULD stand him, which I can't, he's a modelizer. You KNOW once a guy's had a model, he can never go back. So, nice try.

✉

To: Cal Langdon <cal.langdon@thenyjournal.com>
Fr: Mark Levine <mark.levine@thenyjournal.com>
Re: Benvenuto

The girls are emailing back and forth about us.

Mark

✉

To: Mark Levine <mark.levine@thenyjournal.com>
Fr: Cal Langdon <cal.langdon@thenyjournal.com>
Re: Benvenuto

That is blatantly obvious.

Cal

⊠

To: Cal Langdon <cal.langdon@thenyjournal.com>
Fr: Mark Levine <mark.levine@thenyjournal.com>
Re: Benvenuto

What do you think they're saying?

Mark

⊠

To: Mark Levine <mark.levine@thenyjournal.com>
Fr: Cal Langdon <cal.langdon@thenyjournal.com>
Re: Benvenuto

I honestly could not care less.

Cal

⊠

To: Cal Langdon <cal.langdon@thenyjournal.com>
Fr: Mark Levine <mark.levine@thenyjournal.com>
Re: Benvenuto

Don't you like her? Jane, I mean? Holly was sure you'd like her.

Mark

✉

To: Mark Levine <mark.levine@thenyjournal.com>
Fr: Cal Langdon <cal.langdon@thenyjournal.com>
Re: Benvenuto

She seems harmless enough.

Cal

✉

To: Cal Langdon <cal.langdon@thenyjournal.com>
Fr: Mark Levine <mark.levine@thenyjournal.com>
Re: Benvenuto

You don't like her.

Mark

✉

To: Mark Levine <mark.levine@thenyjournal.com>
Fr: Cal Langdon <cal.langdon@thenyjournal.com>
Re: Benvenuto

I didn't say that. All I said was that she seemed harmless. Much in the way an anaconda seems harmless, when it's wrapped around a tree branch ten feet above your head.

Cal

✉

To: Cal Langdon <cal.langdon@thenyjournal.com>
Fr: Mark Levine <mark.levine@thenyjournal.com>
Re: Benvenuto

She's not like that.

And she already has a boyfriend, anyway.

So get over yourself, fathead.

Mark

✉

To: Mark Levine <mark.levine@thenyjournal.com>
Fr: Cal Langdon <cal.langdon@thenyjournal.com>
Re: Benvenuto

Fathead. Harsh.

Cal

✉

To: Cal Langdon <cal.langdon@thenyjournal.com>
Fr: Mark Levine <mark.levine@thenyjournal.com>
Re: Benvenuto

Seriously. ARE you seeing anyone—anyone SPECIAL—these days?

Mark

✉

To: Mark Levine <mark.levine@thenyjournal.com>
Fr: Cal Langdon <cal.langdon@thenyjournal.com>
Re: Benvenuto

They're all special, my friend.

But special enough to shackle myself to her for the rest of eternity, the way you're doing?

No.

But your concern for my romantic well-being is, as always, greatly appreciated.

Cal

✉

To: Cal Langdon <cal.langdon@thenyjournal.com>
Fr: Mark Levine <mark.levine@thenyjournal.com>
Re: Benvenuto

Look, it's just that I know how tough things were for you after—

✉

To: Mark Levine <mark.levine@thenyjournal.com>
Fr: Cal Langdon <cal.langdon@thenyjournal.com>
Re: Benvenuto

Oh, look. The hotel. Stop e-ing me, please.

Cal

RICEVUTA TAXI-ROMA
Percoso:
Da . . . Fiumacino A . . . Hotel Alexander
Firma [redacted]
Importo Corsa 80.00 Euro

Benvenuto al nostro albergo!
(Welcome to our Hotel!)

Gentile Ospite,
Nel porgerLe il nostro cordiale benevuto, abbiamo pensato fe FarLe cosa gradita offrendoLe, al suo arrivo, un assaggio di acqua dalle proprietaria salutari.

Dear Guest,
We wish to express our warmest welcome to our hotel. Given our genuine care for our Guests, we invite you to enjoy the healthy qualities of this bottled water.

Travel Diary of
~~Holly Caputo and Mark Levine~~
Jane Harris

We're HERE!!!!!!!! At the hotel, I mean.

It's the sweetest little place, tucked into a side street that isn't wide enough to let a car coming from the other way pass by. And packed with people! I thought it was a pedestrian walkway and that the taxi driver was going the wrong way. But it turned out it was the Via di Buffalo, which is the street our hotel is on.

Still, it was kind of scary when those Italian school kids kept knocking on the car windows. I wonder what the driver yelled at them to make them run away like that. This is what comes of not having enough social programs for young people. Those kids should have had something better to do on a Saturday than stand around the Via di Buffalo, knocking on tourists' car door windows.

Not that I want to tell another country how it ought to be bringing up its children, or anything. But still.

All I wanted to do was get to my room and take a nap, but Cal had to start arguing with the taxi driver when he saw the receipt. He said over his dead body was he paying 80 euros for a ride from the airport and that the taxi driver might think he could bilk the tourists that way, but that he, Cal, had been to Rome before, and he knew the fare from the airport wasn't a cent over 40 euros. In English. Which it turned out the driver perfectly understood. And after a lot of grousing, he finally agreed that 40 euros would do.

So it's good Mark invited Cal along with us. I guess.

Anyway, my room is so adorable, a tiny little blue-and-white thing with gold curtains that, when I opened them, turned out to be for a window that looks out over the most beautiful courtyard, with white doves flying around it, and bougainvillea spilling from window boxes all over the place, and a sky stretched over it that, I swear, looks bluer than the sky over Manhattan, somehow. It is EXACTLY like Helena Bonham Carter's room in the pensione in <u>Room with a View</u>. Only there's no view. Well, except for the courtyard and the sky.

And there are big bottles of water right here in my room, for later, and I turned on the TV, and everything was In Italian!

I mean, I knew it would be. It's just SO WEIRD!

I thought I would be way too tired to want to go out and sightsee, but now that I'm finally here, I'm really stoked! I want to get out there and see EVERYTHING. After all, we only have about 24 hours in Rome before we leave for Le Marche.

On second thought, I didn't sleep very well on the plane, thanks to The Armrest Nazi. I suppose I shouldn't call him that anymore on account of him having been so tragically jilted all those years ago by that model.

But seriously, what did he expect, marrying a model? Mod-elizers get exactly what they deserve.

Maybe I'll just rest my eyes for a minute or two....

Funny. I miss The Dude. I'm so used to his big gray body curled up to mine in bed, I don't know if I'll be able to get to slee—

To: Cal Langdon <cal.langdon@thenyjournal.com>
Fr: Arthur Pendergast <a.pendergast@rawlingspress.com>
Re: The Book

Where are you this week? Nigeria? Well, wherever it is, just thought I'd give you the good news: *Sweeping Sands* made the *Times* extended list. Number 18. If you'd agreed to tour, we'd have probably debuted even higher. But I know, I know. You've got this wedding to go to. Oh, it's also number 48 on the *USA Today* list. Which isn't bad for a hardback.

Check out this cover sketch for the UK edition and let me know what you think.

Have you given any thought lately to what #2 is going to be about? The second book on your contract, I mean. No hurry, just that it's due in a couple months, and you still haven't submitted a proposal. Have you given any thought to dirty diamonds? That's a pretty hot topic these days. And I hear Angola is nice this time of year.

Arthur Pendergast
Senior Editor
Rawlings Press
1418 Avenue of the Americas
New York, NY 10019
212-555-8764

✉

To: Cal Langdon <cal.langdon@thenyjournal.com>
Fr: Aaron Spender <a.spender@cnn.com>
Re: Things

What's this I hear about you throwing in the foreign-correspondence towel and taking a post stateside? What are you, going soft on me in your old age? It can't be because of this multimillion-dollar book deal I hear you landed a while back, because the Cal Langdon I knew never cared about money. I distinctly recall you saying, that night we were trapped in that bomb shelter in Baghdad, that you never wanted to own any material goods because they might "weigh" you down.

All I can say is, you can buy a heck of a lot of pot holders with the kind of green you're raking in, buddy.

Anyway, if you're serious about staying home for a while, why work for that rag? Believe me, I've been there, and it is not where you want to be. Come on over to where the REAL news is being made. Print media is dead. It's all about television these days. I can set you up with a really sweet deal, if you're interested. Let me know.

Barbara says hello.

Aaron Spender
Senior Correspondent
CNN—New York

....

✉

To: Cal Langdon <cal.langdon@thenyjournal.com>
Fr: Mary Langdon <m.langdon@freemail.com>
Re: Mom

So I heard from Dad you're back in the States for a while—well, except for some jaunt to Italy to be a witness to some guy named Mark's wedding (it's not Mark from next door, is it? Didn't he end up becoming a doctor or something else really boring? Typical).

I also heard you got a cool mil for some book you wrote, and that they want a second one. What are you going to do with all that scratch? Try to lure the ex back from Mr. Investment Guy?

Why don't you send some of it my way? I'll keep it safe for you. This whole weaving thing isn't really working out, anyway, and I was thinking of heading up north with this guy who's got a tie-dye biz going out of his van.

Anyway, keep in touch. And welcome back to the good old US of A. It sucks just as much now as it did when you left.

Mare

PS Have you heard the latest about Mom? She actually has a SHOW. An ART show. Of her stupid lint/clothespin people. I don't know how SHE can get a show and I can't. My weavings are way more artistic than her lint people.

....

⊠

To: Cal Langdon <cal.langdon@thenyjournal.com>
Fr: Graziella Fratiani <graziella@galleriefratiani.co.it>
Re: You

What is this I hear about you coming to Roma and not calling to me? I would not have known a thing about it if Dolly Vargas hadn't happened to mention it during our interview. You are a naughty, naughty boy. Where are you staying? Call me. You know the number. I will come by your hotel and give you a true Italian welcome.

Ciao, amore XXXX
Grazi

PDA of Cal Langdon

Art sent the UK cover design for *Sands* today. It's got a very romantic feel to it that I'm not sure is entirely appropriate, considering the book's subject matter. Well, I suppose if it tricks unsuspecting readers into buying it, expecting it to be a work of fiction about a mummy's curse instead of a nonfiction treatise on Saudi Arabia's tiring oil fields, all the better.

I can't believe Aaron Spender is still among the living. I'd have assumed Barbara Bellerieve bit his head off and ate it on their wedding night. I still marvel at my own lucky escape from her clutches. If it hadn't been for that Daisy Cutter . . .

And Mary. I guess that grand I sent her last month didn't last very long. What the hell does she do with it all? It's not like she ever has anything to show for it. She can't smoke it ALL away, can she? I wish Mom and Dad had taken some control over her earlier in her adolescence. She probably wouldn't still be living out of some guy's van at the age of twenty-five.

But I guess they weren't necessarily the best role models, as parents go, considering Dad's obsession with the track and Mom's conviction that she's the next Grandma Moses. It's surprising, actually, that Mary isn't a bigger flake than she is. . . .

Much like some people I could mention. It was amusing, coming from the airport, to hear Holly's friend squeal at the sight of every monument—and every passing billboard. It's been a long time since I've seen anyone get so excited about a sign for mouthwash. I thought she was going to have a coronary when we drove by the Colosseum. I'm not entirely sure which impressed her more . . . the fact that it's stood for over two thousand years, or the fact that Britney Spears was recently there, filming a television commercial (at least, that's what Holly's friend announced to all of us).

There is something refreshing about American enthusiasm for antiquity. I guess I forget, having been away so long, that there is still a place on this earth where there are no structures older than half a millennium. It must be impressive to see something that existed fifteen hundred years before the *Mayflower*. . . .

Of course, if we hadn't slaughtered all the Indians and destroyed their native lands, it would be different.

Good Lord. It just occurred to me. What if that wasn't what she was impressed by? What if it was the Britney Spears thing?

But no. No, that couldn't be. Not even an artist could be that shallow.

I'll have to remember to change money later, if I can find a place with a decent exchange rate. I blew my last euro on that cab ride—

That was the concierge. Grazi is here. That didn't take her long. I called her less than half an hour ago. Still, I thought she'd be coming over later tonight, not NOW.

I guess it would be ungentlemanly of me not to see her, though. . . .

To: Julio Chasez <julio@streetsmart.com>
Fr: Jane Harris <jane@wondercat.com>
Re: The Dude

Hi, Julio! Me, again! Just checking in, since I haven't heard from you. How's The Dude doing? Does he like that salmon paté I got him? I figured he'd appreciate a few treats, with me being gone. I hope you found the Pounce. I left it on the counter, with the oven mitts. Really, you should only need the Pounce if he tries to attack. Which he really shouldn't, I mean, he KNOWS you. You two are buds. Right?

Well, let me know how he's doing as soon as you get a chance. No biggie. You can just email, if you want. Or call. From my phone in the apartment. That way it won't cost you anything. Don't worry about the time difference, you can call at any time. I don't mind being woken up, if it's for The Dude.

J

Travel Diary of

~~Holly Caputo and Mark Levine~~

Jane Harris

Oh my God, this place is FABULOUS! When I woke up from my nap, it was two, and I called Holly to see if she was hungry, and she was, but Mark was still asleep, and Modelizer/Armrest Nazi didn't pick up his phone (much to my relief) when Holly tried him . . . you know, to be polite, and not exclude him.

So Holly and I met in the hall and the two of us just strolled right out onto tiny Via di Buffalo, which I suppose is named after the mozzarella, which is made from buffalo milk, at least in Italy, and we started walking, and in half an hour, not five blocks from our hotel, we'd seen the Trevi Fountain, the Pantheon, the Piazza Navone, and a bunch of other sights I can't even remember, as they all involved monolisks with bumpy writing on them.

But that's not all! We saw portrait artists, right on the street—good ones, not like the cheesy ones in New York—and people eating gelati, and groups of senior citizens following around tour guides holding a flag, and I threw money in the Fontana di Trevi—I don't know how much, because it was Italian—which apparently guarantees you'll be back there someday. Which I hope is true, because it's a kick-ass fountain, almost as cool as Ozzy's pool on <u>The Osbournes</u>.

And we were solicited by a humpbacked dwarf with no shirt on and a tattoo that said <u>Antonio</u> on his shoulder, and I gave him some money, and then I bought a bottle of Diet Coke that cost five euros, which is more than a six-pack back home, and I realized I gave the humpbacked dwarf enough money to buy FIVE Italian Diet Cokes.

I really need to get a grip on this money thing. Although I'm sure Antonio (if that's his name) needs the money more than I need Diet Coke.

And then Holly wanted her picture taken with a hot guy dressed as a gladiator in front of the Pantheon, so I started to take one, but then this very blowsy older woman dressed in a toga came over and demanded ANOTHER five euros, just for letting me take the picture with her hot gladiator boyfriend! The guy just stood there looking all sheepish while this went on, but Holly was all, "I want it, it'll be funny," so I forked over five more euros and took the picture.

Holly said later that right before I took the picture, the gladiator handed her his plastic sword, and when she asked him, "What should I do with this?" he went, in a long-suffering voice, "Keel me. Please."

Which in and of itself was totally worth five euros.

And everywhere we went, lots of Italian vendors came up to us, another one every five seconds, it seemed, going "Bag, California?" I guess because we look like we're from California, even though of course we're not, though we are sort of tan thanks to Holly and Mark's share in East Hampton.

Only how they knew we were American I can't tell, though we were talking a lot, I suppose. And I am apparently the only girl in all of Rome who wears Steve Madden slides.

But then Mark called on Holly's cell and said he was hungry and Cal wasn't answering the phone in his room, so we agreed to meet Mark for a snack.

Except that on the way back to the hotel, we passed a church where a wedding was going on—or about to go on, anyway. I saw the crowd and assumed it was another sight we should see, but then it turned out to be a lot of tourists like us waiting outside a church with some flower girls and maids of honor, and we realized it was a wedding!

So then Holly said she had to stay to see the bride for luck, since she was getting married too.

So we edged into the church and stood there and waited and it wasn't long until a sleek beige Mercedes sedan pulled up and the bride, looking incredibly chic in an ivory sheath with a tiny veil got out, beaming and speaking in Italian to the little flower girls who started jumping up and down.

I got some very good photos of the whole thing and wanted to ask her if she wanted me to send her copies (the bride I mean), but I didn't know the right words in Italian, and besides, by that point her father had come out of the church and lent her his arm, and that's when Holly and I realized we were standing right in the aisle, with the groom at the front of the church with the priest, trying to see past us to catch a glimpse of his wife-to-be in her gorgeous ivory sheath.

So we scampered out of the way and I looked at Holly and saw tears in her eyes!!!!

I thought she'd been stung by a bee or something so I was like, "Let's go find some ice!" but it turned out that wasn't it at all. Holly looked at me all tearfully and went, "I want <u>my</u> father to lead <u>me</u> down the aisle! Only he doesn't know I'm doing this. And I'm not even going to have an aisle. Because we're going to get married by some clerk in some <u>office</u>."

Then she burst into tears right there on some street I can't remember the name of.

Of course I had no choice but to hustle her as fast as I could to the café where we'd said we'd meet Mark for snacks. Only I knew it was my duty as witness/bridesmaid to get her cleaned up before her future husband saw what a psycho he was marrying. Not that he didn't already know, since Holly cries at the end of every episode of <u>Seventh Heaven</u> she sees,

even the reruns, and won't pick up the phone on Monday
nights as a consequence.

But still.

We got a seat right away at the café across from the
Pantheon—an outdoor table, even. In New York, you practically
have to chew off your own foot to get an outdoor table anywhere. Maybe the waiter saw how dire our need was, considering Holly's tears. Anyway, he sat us under the shade of his
restaurant's big fluttery awning, and I said, "Un verre de vin
blanc pour moi et pour mon amie," forgetting I wasn't in 11th-
grade French, but in Italy.

The waiter totally took it in stride though. "Frizzante?" he
asked me.

I had no idea what he was talking about, but remembering
I was in Italy and not France, I managed to say Si and not Oui.

My first foreign language exchange! I'd spoken English with
the Diet Coke guy and Mr. Gladiator's pimp. And OK, the exchange hadn't been in the actual language spoken in this
country. But it had still been foreign.

Then the bread basket came, with a little pot of silky
white butter, and we dug in, because even when she's crying,
Holly can still eat, which is one of the many reasons I love her.

And I told her how lucky she is her father ISN'T here, since,
like her mom, he doesn't exactly approve of Mark. Which is ridiculous, because Mark is totally perfect husband material, being
completely sweet and thoughtful and funny and self-deprecating
and totally the opposite of his horrible friend Cal the Modelizer in
every way. Plus Mark's even reasonably good-looking. Oh, and a
doctor. With a weekly health column in a New York paper that's
read by millions. What more could the Caputos ask?

A Catholic, apparently.

Sometimes I get so mad at Holly's parents for what
they're doing to her, I just want to spit.

But then, Mark's parents are just as bad, in their own way.

"L—like it even matters to us," Holly sobbed, as the waiter reappeared with two glasses of white wine on a tray. "I mean, I haven't been to church since I was eighteen! Church was <u>their</u> thing, not mine. And Mark hasn't set foot in temple since his bar mitzvah. We have no intention of raising our children any particular religion. We're going to bring up the kids a-religious. And then when they're old enough, they can decide which religion—if any—they want to belong to."

I nodded because I had heard this many times before. The wine in the glasses the waiter was putting down in front of us seemed to catch the sun and dance around before my eyes like fool's gold in the bottom of that stream Laura found on that one episode of <u>Little House on the Prairie</u>.

"Why can't they just respect that this is the man I love?" Holly asked, picking up her glass and taking a gulp. "And, yes, he's Jewish. Get over it."

I sipped my wine too—

And nearly spat it out! Because it wasn't wine at all! It was champagne!

Only better than champagne! Because the bubbles in champagne usually give me an instant headache.

But these bubbles were tiny and light—barely there at all.

"What <u>is</u> this?" I asked, in wonder, holding my glass up to the light and looking at all the lovely bubbles.

"Frizzante," Holly said. "Remember? He asked, and you said Si. It's like . . .fizzy wine. Don't you like it?"

"I <u>love</u> it."

I loved it so much, I had another glass of it. By the time Mark joined us, I was in a VERY good mood.

Fortunately, so was Holly. There was so much people-watching to do in our corner of the piazza that she soon forgot all about the wedding we'd seen, and her yearning for her dad to give her away at her own. Soon we were able to pick out the American tourists as quickly as the Italians obviously could. I don't mean to say anything negative about my countrymen and women, but hello, the Fab Five have their work cut out for them.

Holly was instantly cheered, as always, by the sight of Mark. He asked for a menu and got one—in English!—and ordered mussels and an antipasto platter, and we sat and ate chunky crumbles of parmesan and fresh tangy olives and buttery slivers of salami and garlicky mussels and had fun watching other suckers get fleeced by the handsome, morose gladiator and his pimp.

Then the shadows started getting longer and Mark checked his Blackberry and said we should be getting back to the hotel to change for dinner. So we got the bill—which Mark insisted on paying—and started back, Mark with arm around Holly's waist, and her head leaning on his shoulder, her unhappiness from a few hours earlier blissfully forgotten.

And I wished SO HARD that awful Modelizer Cal was with us, so he could see how cute Holly and Mark are together, and how great a couple they are, and what sweet parents they'll make, and what a crime it would be if they didn't get married. I mean, how could anyone look at Holly and Mark and think, for even one minute, that marriage is an antiquated institution that ought to be abolished? They are living proof that it works. Just because Modelizer's wife turned out to be a money-grubbing beeyotch doesn't mean—

Ooooh! I got an email! On my Blackberry! PLEASE let it be Julio!!!!

✉

To: Jane Harris <jane@wondercat.com>
Fr: Malcolm Weatherly <malcolmw@snowstyle.com>
Re: Ciao!

Hey, babe! How's it hangin? So ya there yet? Whaddaya think? Pretty rad, huh? Yeah, I-ty blew my mind when I was there last year for the European Open. Even the freaking *coffee* tastes better there.

But I don't get the whole "everything closing from noon to four and lunch and everybody serving nothing but pasta after ten" thing. Bummer if you wake up at one and want a freaking waffle.

But make sure you try one of those bidets. It'll change your life!

Stay away from those I-ty Latin Lover types. I know how those guys operate. They only want a green card, anyway. Not that you're not, you know, totally hot.

Aw, gotta go, I'm up next on the halfpipe. Luv ya.

Mal

PS Know what? I kinda miss The Dude. Give him a big kiss for me, willya? Oh, you can't, cause you're in I–ty. Sorry.

Travel Diary of

~~Holly Caputo and Mark Levine~~

Jane Harris

Isn't that sweet? I miss The Dude, too. If he were here right now, he'd be curled up around my feet.

And my toes would be losing all circulation because he weighs so much. But still.

I don't understand why Julio hasn't written, though. What if he forgot? To feed The Dude, I mean?

But how could he forget? I stuck a giant sign on his dad's door, to remind him. . . .

Where was I? Oh, yeah. Walking through the piazza behind Mark and Holly.

Well . . . while I was looking at them, and thinking how cute they are, and what a shame it was that Modelizer Cal wasn't there with us to see them and all, I got a pang.

A PANG.

I'll admit it. I mean, I am totally happy for Holly and in full support of this elopement scheme. Really, given the situation, I don't see how she and Mark have any choice BUT to elope.

But seeing them together like that, her head on his shoulder, his arm around her—I felt a pang.

Because where is MY Mark? Really? Where IS he?

Because I know he's not in Canada right now, hitting the halfpipe—or the full pipe. Or even both, as in Malcolm's case. I mean, I like Malcolm and all, and we have a blast together. But I can't really picture him strolling through the piazza with his arm around my waist. Skateboarding through it, certainly. But having a nice glass of bianco frizzante as the sun sets? Not so much.

I'm sure he's out there, somewhere. My Mark, I mean. He has to be, right?

But what if I never find him? Or what if I already met him, and I messed it up somehow? This would not be unusual, since I mess up everything. I mean, what if My Mark was DAVE who cheated on me with Amy Jenkins (that whore)?

Oh, God, no. Fate would never be so unkind.

Or what if My Mark was Curt Shipley, who took me to the prom in 11th grade, and we made out in his Chevette afterwards, and then that summer, I found out he'd been making out, in that same Chevette, with Mike Morris after the fireworks on the Fourth of July?

Which means I must have turned Curt gay, because he certainly wasn't gay BEFORE we made out.

Oh, my God. What if Curt Shipley was the man of my dreams, and I TURNED HIM GAY?????

Killing self now.

✉

To: Mark Levine <mark.levine@thenyjournal.com>
Fr: Cal Langdon <cal.langdon@thenyjournal.com>
Re: Sorry

Sorry I missed it when you called earlier. I was dead to the world.
We still on for dinner tonight?

Cal

✉

To: Cal Langdon <cal.langdon@thenyjournal.com>
Fr: Mark Levine <mark.levine@thenyjournal.com>
Re: Sorry

Yes, I happened to hear how "dead to the world" you were as I
passed by your room on my way to meet the girls. I wasn't aware
that corpses were sexually active . . . at least, if I'm to assume
the heavily accented female voice calling your name with ever-
increasing volume as she climaxed was, indeed, coming from
Room 204.

Mark

✉

To: Mark Levine <mark.levine@thenyjournal.com>
Fr: Cal Langdon <cal.langdon@thenyjournal.com>
Re: Sorry

Oh. That was Graziella. She won't be joining us tonight.

Cal

✉

I am sorrier to hear that than words can adequately express. See you at eight.

Mark

PDA of Cal Langdon

It was a mistake to invite Grazi in. I should have insisted on going to her place. I'd forgotten how . . . *loud* she can be.

ANTIPASTI

Insalatina mista all'aceto balsamico
Carpaccio tiepido di manzo con parmigiano e rucola
Medaglioni d'astice con insalata di stagione

PASTA

Fusilli con pomodori e basilico
Garganelli con pesto, patate e fagiolini
Tagliolini con zafferano, gamberoni e zucchine

SECONDI PIATTI

Medaglioni di vitello in crosta di basilico con purea
de melanzane e parmigiano
Filetto di manzo alle erbe aromatiche
Tagliata di manzo con timballo de patate e cardamomo
Filetto di rombo al forno con limone e capperi

INSALATE DI STAGIONE

SELEZIONE DI FORMAGGI ITALIANI

DOLCI

Bavarese al cioccolato bianco con crema cocoa
alla liquirizia e latte di madorle
Mousse al cioccolato fondente con sedano candito
Crema al limone
Budino al cocco con frutto della passione

PDA of Cal Langdon

Insisted on paying for dinner, as spent majority of it pontificating on *Sweeping Sands,* and felt I had to make amends. Also, it was the least I could do after Mark's revelation regarding Grazi. Eight hundred euro, but worth it—especially the wine.

Don't think I made a friend of Ms. Harris, however. Which is a shame, because she looks rather fetching in heels—a point that was driven home rather hard when she stumbled outside the restaurant, and I was forced to pry her heel from where it was wedged between two cobblestones.

The tattoo IS of Wondercat. It's the same cat's head that she's got on her luggage. I've never been one for tattoos, but hers is rather fetching.

I can't believe I wrote the word *fetching.* This country goes to my head like prosecco.

Travel Diary of
~~Holly Caputo and Mark Levine~~
Jane Harris

Oh, my God, that restaurant was so fancy that they even had tiny little chairs for ladies' purses! Seriously! Like the waiter held my chair for me, then he pulled out this matching stool for my bag! The bag I bought off an outdoor table on Canal Street in Chinatown, then bedazzled with Wondercat's face! In a seat of honor!

It was almost too much. There was silverware on the table I had never <u>seen</u> before.

Plus, in the ladies' room, there were actual folded hand towels for every visitor. Not paper towels. But a huge stack of tiny hand towels, so when you dried your hands, you reached for one, then threw it into a laundry basket underneath the sink.

I have no idea what I ate for dinner. It was delicious, though. The waiter said a bunch of stuff, and Holly, who speaks a little Italian, and Modelizer Cal, who I guess speaks a little more than that, just nodded and went, "Si, si." And then plates began to appear, of squash blossoms stuffed with goat cheese, and perfect little circles of foie gras, and curls of endive dripping in butter and cheese. . . .

That meal had to have been three thousand calories, at least.

But I didn't care. Because it was all so delicious. THIS IS SO FUN!!!!!!!

Well, except for Cal. It's no WONDER he's never heard of Wondercat. I doubt he's ever read anything for fun in his entire life. Holly made the mistake—BIG one—of asking him what the book he wrote is about.

Of course a modelizer like him can't be writing something

cool like a spy thriller or dick lit, like Nick Hornsby or anything. Oh, no. HE has to have written a book about—get this—how Saudi Arabia's oil fields are on the decline, and soon won't be able to meet the world's demands. This, of course, is going to crush Saudi Arabia's economy, and have serious repercussions throughout the rest of the globe, as well.

Yeah. Who cares? Guess what, Cal? In Saudi Arabia, women aren't allowed to vote or drive cars. Why should I care if that nation's economy goes down the tubes? Maybe if they'd let women have some say in their country's governance, they wouldn't be in this sorry position in the first place.

Sadly, he SAW me yawning. Cal, I mean.

And instead of just politely accepting my apology— "Sorry, jet lag"—he was all, "This could have a profound im- pact on you, too, Jane. What do you think those water bottles you're so fond of are made from? Petroleum."

Geez! I love Mark to death, but why is he even friends with this guy? Oh, sure, maybe the ex left him a bitter shell of a man. But does he have to take it out on me?

Also, he may think he's slick, but when I was leaving my room to meet Holly and Mark for cocktails down in the lobby, I got a major eyeful of what he spent the afternoon doing, as she slunk out of his room and down the stairs. I don't care what Holly says about me being his type, it's a total lie. Cal Langdon's "type" is STILL clearly five-foot-eleven blonde mod- els, NOT five-foot-four brunette cartoonists into whose jeans TWO of said models could easily fit.

As if that's not bad enough, when we were waiting for a taxi to take us home, I looked over and saw Mark take off his jacket and wrap it around Holly, who was shivering a little in her sleeveless pink dress. Then he put his arm around her, and the two of them nuzzled each other.

NUZZLED. They were NUZZLING.

And I looked over to see if Cal had noticed, and he totally had, he was looking right at them.

And I will admit that it was impossible to tell what was going on behind those steely baby blues of his.

But I imagined—my second BIG MISTAKE—that he was feeling the way I was . . . that Mark and Holly are the cutest couple EVER and totally belong together and it's a CRIME what their families are doing to them, being so unreasonable about the differing faiths thing.

So I went, in a soft voice so Mark and Holly wouldn't over-hear, "Do you STILL think those two shouldn't get married?"

And the Modelizer went, "I give it a year. Two, tops."

!!!!!!!!!!!!!!!!!!!!!!!!!!!!!!!!!!!!!!

I couldn't believe it! I mean, where could he POSSIBLY be getting that?

So I went, "Are you crazy? They're totally in love. Look at them."

Cal: "You know love is just a chemical reaction in the brain caused by surges of phenylethylamine, don't you?"

Me: (confused) "You're saying Holly and Mark don't really love each other? That it's all in their heads?"

Cal: "I'm saying no one loves anyone. People are attracted to one another and pair up to breed due to our natural mating instinct. But that attraction doesn't last. As with all drugs, the body develops a tolerance for the phenylethylamine, and eventually, the attraction you once felt for your partner fades. It's all perfectly natural. You can get the same amount of phenylethylamine, a stimulant the mind craves, by ingesting vast amounts of chocolate as you can by, quote, falling in love, endquote."

Me: "So . . . you don't believe in romantic love?"

Cal: "I believe I just said that."

Me: "Because of the vast amount of time you've spent study-
ing the subject?"

Cal: "From my own personal experience, yes. And from the relationships I've observed around me."

Me: "So Holly and Mark are going to break up because there's
no such thing as love?"

Cal: "Oh, no. Well, yes, eventually. But well before that happens, they're going to break up because their back-
grounds are too different."

I really don't think I can be blamed for saying, "At least
they're both human, unlike the skank I saw leaving your hotel
room earlier."

I had the satisfaction of seeing him, for the first time
since we've met, completely speechless.

Sadly the effect was ruined when one of my stiletto heels got
caught between the cobblestones outside the restaurant. It
gouged away all the silver lamé. I don't think it can be fixed, either.

I'll admit the cobblestones are charming, but have these
people never heard of asphalt? It was totally humiliating too,
the Modelizer had to help me pry it loose. My heel, I mean.

His hand fit all the way around my ankle. You know, his fingers met his thumb on the other side.

Thank God I remembered to shave my legs in the shower
before dinner.

God, I'm so jazzed from all that good food, I don't think I'll
ever fall asleep. Plus, I keep thinking about The Dude. He has
to be all right, doesn't he? I mean, Julio would have called if
there was anything wrong. I left my cell number by the phone,
so Julio could call from my phone, and not wrack up a bill on
his parents' line.

And I just checked it, and he hasn't called. So The Dude is
good. No news is good news, right? The Dude HAS to be good.

It's just that we've spent maybe only five nights, total, away from each other since he was a kitten. Who is going to get up during The Dude's 4-AM windowsill yowl at the moon and comfort him if I'm not there? That yowl used to drive me insane. But now I sort of miss it. I'd give anything to hear that yowl right now. In fact, I don't think I'll be able to go to sleep without it—

✉

To: Customer Service New York Journal Travel Privileges
    <TravelPrivcustser@thenyjournal.com >
Fr: Mark Levine <mark.levine@thenyjournal.com >
Re: Car Rental

I realize it's Sunday, and that your offices are closed. However, when I made the reservation for a rental car in Rome, I specified that I needed a four-door sedan with trunk room for four VERY LARGE bags. I asked for a Jaguar or Mercedes, NOT a Toyota. Now I have to cram one of the bags in the backseat with two passengers, and we're going to be driving through MOUN-TAINS. Do you really think it's safe to drive through a mountain range with a large, overstuffed suitcase between passengers in the backseat?

I didn't think so. I'll expect to hear from you on Monday.

Mark Levine, MD

✉

To: Julio Chasez <julio@streetsmart.com>
Fr: Jane Harris <jane@wondercat.com>
Re: The Dude

Hi, Julio! I have to admit, I'm getting kind of worried. Is every-thing OK? I mean, you haven't written back to me, and I just want to know if everything is going all right. I know you're busy with school and hockey and all, but if you could just send me a tiny message, letting me know The Dude's all right, I'd really ap-preciate it.

I think I'll try your pager.

J

✉

To: Jane Harris <jane@wondercat.com>
Fr: Holly Caputo <holly.caputo@thenyjournal.com>
Re: Where are you?

?????????????????????

✉

To: Holly Caputo <holly.caputo@thenyjournal.com>
Fr: Jane Harris <jane@wondercat.com>
Re: Where are you?

I'm still in the dining room, finishing breakfast. Where are YOU?

J

✉

To: Jane Harris <jane@wondercat.com>
Fr: Holly Caputo <holly.caputo@thenyjournal.com>
Re: Where are you?

Outside. Hurry up and finish and get out here. You've got to see this. Mark and Cal are trying to cram all of our bags into the trunk, only they won't fit. So they're doing physics. All serious, like it's a puzzle or something. Something actually IMPORTANT. Get out here, or you'll miss it.

Holly

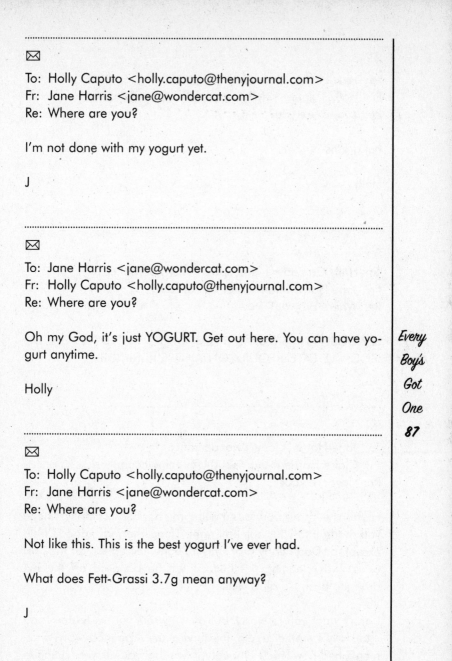

✉

To: Holly Caputo <holly.caputo@thenyjournal.com>
Fr: Jane Harris <jane@wondercat.com>
Re: Where are you?

I'm not done with my yogurt yet.

J

✉

To: Jane Harris <jane@wondercat.com>
Fr: Holly Caputo <holly.caputo@thenyjournal.com>
Re: Where are you?

Oh my God, it's just YOGURT. Get out here. You can have yogurt anytime.

Holly

✉

To: Holly Caputo <holly.caputo@thenyjournal.com>
Fr: Jane Harris <jane@wondercat.com>
Re: Where are you?

Not like this. This is the best yogurt I've ever had.

What does Fett-Grassi 3.7g mean anyway?

J

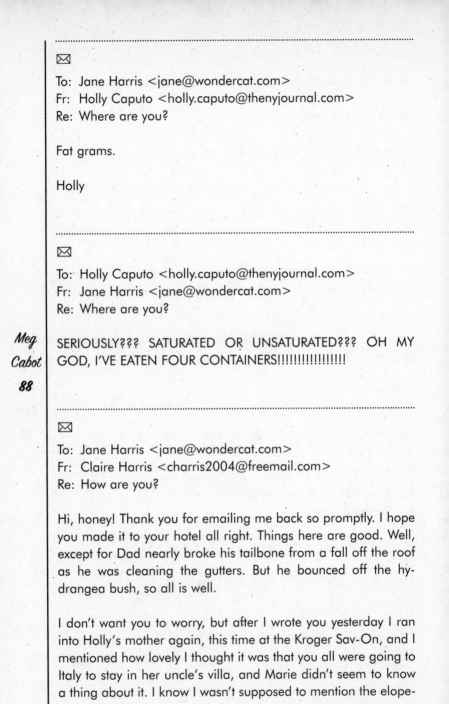

To: Jane Harris <jane@wondercat.com>
Fr: Holly Caputo <holly.caputo@thenyjournal.com>
Re: Where are you?

Fat grams.

Holly

To: Holly Caputo <holly.caputo@thenyjournal.com>
Fr: Jane Harris <jane@wondercat.com>
Re: Where are you?

SERIOUSLY??? SATURATED OR UNSATURATED??? OH MY GOD, I'VE EATEN FOUR CONTAINERS!!!!!!!!!!!!!!!!!!

To: Jane Harris <jane@wondercat.com>
Fr: Claire Harris <charris2004@freemail.com>
Re: How are you?

Hi, honey! Thank you for emailing me back so promptly. I hope you made it to your hotel all right. Things here are good. Well, except for Dad nearly broke his tailbone from a fall off the roof as he was cleaning the gutters. But he bounced off the hydrangea bush, so all is well.

I don't want you to worry, but after I wrote you yesterday I ran into Holly's mother again, this time at the Kroger Sav-On, and I mentioned how lovely I thought it was that you all were going to Italy to stay in her uncle's villa, and Marie didn't seem to know a thing about it. I know I wasn't supposed to mention the elopement, but Holly did tell her mother she was going to her uncle's, didn't she? I hope I haven't spoiled anything.

Love,
Mom

PS Cal Langdon, the reporter with the *New York Journal?* Why, I just saw him on *Charlie Rose* the other night! He was being interviewed about some big book he's just written. Apparently, it's selling very well. He's very handsome, Janie.

Still, imagine not thinking Mark should marry Holly. Those two were made for each other! And who's never heard of Wondercat? What has he been doing, living under a rock????
Well, I guess so, actually, since his book is about Saudi Arabia. . . .

Mom

....

✉

To: Claire Harris <charris2004@freemail.com>
Fr: Jane Harris <jane@wondercat.com>
Re: How are you?

Hi, Mom! Things here are fine. Well, except that Holly and I are waiting for the guys to go check out of the hotel so that we can rearrange the way they've packed the rental car. It's too small for all of us, plus our luggage, so Holly and I have to sit in the back with Holly's giant suitcase. Which we don't mind, especially, except that they packed our bag of Toblerone in the trunk. What good will it do anyone there?

We leave for Holly's uncle's villa today. It's about a four-hour drive from Rome to where the house is, on the Adriatic coast. I can't wait to see it! Everything here is just so different and fun. Even the yogurt is better.

But then I found out that's because I was eating full fat yogurt for the first time in my life. Oh well.

I wouldn't worry about Holly's mom. People in their family borrow their uncle's place all the time, since he's away so much.

Tell Dad there are people he can hire to clean the gutters.

Love,
Janie

PS You saw Cal Langdon on *Charlie Rose*? It figures. He is so full of himself. And as for his not thinking Holly and Mark are perfect for each other . . . Please! I don't even like to remember what Holly was like before she started dating Mark. I mean, remember the whole green hair phase?

And you'd have to have lived under a rock not to have seen Wondercat's recycling campaign at D'Agostino. There are circulars for it everywhere.

J

....

✉

To: Holly Caputo <holly.caputo@thenyjournal.com>
Fr: Jane Harris <jane@wondercat.com>
Re: What is up with this?

Why did you let Mark drive?

J

✉

To: Jane Harris <jane@wondercat.com>
Fr: Holly Caputo <holly.caputo@thenyjournal.com>
Re: What is up with this?

Hello? You were there. How was I supposed to stop him?

Holly

✉

To: Holly Caputo <holly.caputo@thenyjournal.com>
Fr: Jane Harris <jane@wondercat.com>
Re: What is up with this?

Yeah, but he sucks at it. I mean, really, really sucks at it.

J

✉

To: Jane Harris <jane@wondercat.com>
Fr: Holly Caputo <holly.caputo@thenyjournal.com>
Re: What is up with this?

Hello. It's Italy. Everyone sucks at driving. He blends.

Besides, I had to let him drive, after that whole thing with Cal re-arranging all the suitcases.

Holly

✉

To: Holly Caputo <holly.caputo@thenyjournal.com>
Fr: Jane Harris <jane@wondercat.com>
Re: What is up with this?

Yeah. What was UP with that, anyway? Why is Cal so . . . bossy?

J

✉

To: Jane Harris <jane@wondercat.com>
Fr: Holly Caputo <holly.caputo@thenyjournal.com>
Re: What is up with this?

Mark says it's because Cal has an enormous you know what.

Holly

✉

To: Holly Caputo <holly.caputo@thenyjournal.com>
Fr: Jane Harris <jane@wondercat.com>
Re: What is up with this?

Head?

J

✉

To: Jane Harris <jane@wondercat.com>
Fr: Holly Caputo <holly.caputo@thenyjournal.com>
Re: What is up with this?

No, you idiot. You KNOW what I mean.

Holly

✉

To: Holly Caputo <holly.caputo@thenyjournal.com>
Fr: Jane Harris <jane@wondercat.com>
Re: What is up with this?

Wait. WHAT??? SHUT UP!!!!!!!!!!!

J

✉

To: Jane Harris <jane@wondercat.com>
Fr: Holly Caputo <holly.caputo@thenyjournal.com>
Re: What is up with this?

Mark swears it's true. He says Cal has always been supremely self-confident because of the enormity of his you know what. Well, at least up until that model broke his heart and all.

Holly

✉

To: Holly Caputo <holly.caputo@thenyjournal.com>
Fr: Jane Harris <jane@wondercat.com>
Re: What is up with this?

You are making that up. About his you know what, I mean.

J

✉

To: Jane Harris <jane@wondercat.com>
Fr: Holly Caputo <holly.caputo@thenyjournal.com>
Re: What is up with this?

Um. Have YOU seen him sit with his legs crossed?

Holly

✉

To: Holly Caputo <holly.caputo@thenyjournal.com>
Fr: Jane Harris <jane@wondercat.com>
Re: What is up with this?

That doesn't mean—Oh, my God, you ARE serious.

J

✉

To: Jane Harris <jane@wondercat.com>
Fr: Holly Caputo <holly.caputo@thenyjournal.com>
Re: What is up with this?

Apparently, despite his ex-wife's desertion on what was to be their first wedding anniversary, he has every reason in the world to feel quite pleased with himself.

Does THAT make you think a little more fondly of him?

Holly

⸺⸺⸺⸺⸺⸺⸺⸺⸺⸺⸺⸺⸺⸺⸺⸺⸺⸺⸺

✉

To: Holly Caputo <holly.caputo@thenyjournal.com>
Fr: Jane Harris <jane@wondercat.com>
Re: What is up with this?

NO!!! Size doesn't matter, and you know it.

Well, not that much.

She really left him on their first anniversary?

J

⸺⸺⸺⸺⸺⸺⸺⸺⸺⸺⸺⸺⸺⸺⸺⸺⸺⸺⸺

✉

To: Jane Harris <jane@wondercat.com>
Fr: Holly Caputo <holly.caputo@thenyjournal.com>
Re: What is up with this?

He came home from work, preparing to change clothes and take her out for an evening of celebration, and found a note.

She'd had movers in while he was at the office. They took everything. Except the cat.

Holly

....

✉

To: Holly Caputo <holly.caputo@thenyjournal.com>
Fr: Jane Harris <jane@wondercat.com>
Re: What is up with this?

They had a CAT????

J

....

✉

To: Jane Harris <jane@wondercat.com>
Fr: Holly Caputo <holly.caputo@thenyjournal.com>
Re: What is up with this?

It was her cat. She left it with Cal because her new boyfriend was allergic. Cal took care of it for almost a year, hoping Valerie would change her mind and come back. But she didn't. So Cal got himself assigned to Iraq.

Holly

....

✉

To: Holly Caputo <holly.caputo@thenyjournal.com>
Fr: Jane Harris <jane@wondercat.com>
Re: What is up with this?

What happened to the CAT?????

J

✉

To: Jane Harris <jane@wondercat.com>
Fr: Holly Caputo <holly.caputo@thenyjournal.com>
Re: What is up with this?

Oh. The cat died right before he decided to leave. Of cancer. Mark says he isn't sure which left Cal more brokenhearted—his wife leaving him, or the cat dying.

Holly

✉

To: Holly Caputo <holly.caputo@thenyjournal.com>
Fr: Jane Harris <jane@wondercat.com>
Re: What is up with this?

You are such a liar. You made that whole thing up about the cat dying. What really happened to it?

J

✉

To: Jane Harris <jane@wondercat.com>
Fr: Holly Caputo <holly.caputo@thenyjournal.com>
Re: What is up with this?

He gave it to Tim Grabowski in IT.

Still. The cat COULD be dead now, for all I know. Poor, poor Cal.

Holly

✉

To: Holly Caputo <holly.caputo@thenyjournal.com>
Fr: Jane Harris <jane@wondercat.com>
Re: What is up with this?

You are so pathetic.

And I wouldn't feel too sorry for Cal Langdon if I were you. He's doing just fine for himself.

Promise you won't let Mark drive through the mountains. He will plunge us to our deaths.

J

✉

To: Jane Harris <jane@wondercat.com>
Fr: Holly Caputo <holly.caputo@thenyjournal.com>
Re: What is up with this?

Um. Yeah. Maybe I'll drive after lunch. Or we can get Cal "Large Appendage" Langdon to do it.

Holly

✉

To: Holly Caputo <holly.caputo@thenyjournal.com>
Fr: Jane Harris <jane@wondercat.com>
Re: What is up with this?

SHUT UP!!!!!!!!!!!!!!! You trust him to drive????

J

✉

To: Jane Harris <jane@wondercat.com>
Fr: Holly Caputo <holly.caputo@thenyjournal.com>
Re: What is up with this?

Yes, of course! Unlike some people, he's actually used to driving in a foreign country.

What is your problem with him, anyway? He was perfectly nice during dinner last night, didn't you think? And he's been nothing but charming all morning. So what gives?

Holly

✉

To: Holly Caputo <holly.caputo@thenyjournal.com>
Fr: Jane Harris <jane@wondercat.com>
Re: What is up with this?

Nothing. Stop e-ing me, they totally know we're talking about them.

Thank God they don't know WHAT we're talking about, though.

Ew.

J

To: Mark Levine <mark.levine@thenyjournal.com>
Fr: Ruth Levine <r.levine@levinedentalgroup.com >
Re: Hello!

Is that any way to speak to your mother, I would like to know? I KNOW you think you're in love with Holly.

And I will admit she is a very nice girl.

But I don't think she's the RIGHT girl for you, Mark. You two come from two different worlds. Don't get me wrong, I completely appreciate the Italian heritage. They brought so many important things to the world, such as pasta and that nice Mario Batali from the Food Channel.

But what kind of future do you and Holly have together? What religion would you raise your children? Are you going to have a Christmas tree? You know the DiMarcos down the street have an entire holy manger scene in their front yard every year, made from cut-out pieces of plywood. Is that what you want, Mark? The baby Jesus in your front yard? Are you trying to kill me?

I'm just saying, I'm sure Susie Schramm has grown into a very interesting, vibrant girl. Why don't you see her, just for lunch? What could one lunch hurt? You have a little lunch, catch up on old times . . . who knows where it could lead?

Call me, Markie. I'm worried about you. Really.

Mom

✉

To: Holly Caputo <holly.caputo@thenyjournal.com>
Fr: Darrin Caputo <darrin.caputo@caputographics.com>
Re: Hello, it is your mother

I am using your brother's email to write this to you. Your father says I should not, that you are an adult and I should let you lead your own life, like your brothers.

But all of your brothers found nice Italian girls—except for Frankie with that stripper. But even she is a good Christian, when she is not taking her clothes off for money.

Even Darrin, even HE found a nice Italian boy. Bobby came over for dinner last night and finished up ALL my chicken parmigiani. Such a good appetite.

I don't understand why you cannot do the same as your brothers. What is so wrong with finding a nice Italian boy to settle down with? Even a Polish boy would be all right, if he were Catholic. Why do you have to be with this Mark? He is a very nice boy, but he is not Catholic. What does he know about anything?

I am asking you to think about what you are doing with your life. People are starting to think things about you and this Mark. I saw Jane Harris's mother in the grocery store, and she was talking like you and Mark are getting married. If you are not careful, other people will begin to think the same, and eventually word will spread to Father Roberto, and then how will I be able to hold my head up at Mass on Sunday?

Think about your life, Holly. Do the right thing.

Mom

✉

To: Cal Langdon <cal.langdon@thenyjournal.com>
Fr: Graziella Fratiani <grazielle@galleriefratiani.co.it>
Re: Yesterday

It was so lovely to be seeing you yesterday afternoon. You are a twenty-first-century man, not like these Italian boys I constantly meet. You know, still living with Mama, and expect all women to cook and clean for them. It's nice to be with a man who washes his own socks.

Did I tell you, I'm between shows at the moment, so I can take a little time off from the gallery. Might I to be joining you at your little villa later in the week? I think I can—"rough it"? Let me know.

Grazi

✉

To: Jane Harris <jane@wondercat.com>
Fr: Julio Chasez <julio@streetsmart.com>
Re: The Dude

Hey, Ms. Harris. I got your messages. Just wanted to let you know your cat is fine. Really.

And no, I haven't had to use the oven mitts yet. And yeah, he ate all his salmon pate. And the Tender Vittles. And the Science Diet. And the Fancy Feast. And the Sheba. And he tried to gnaw through a box of Girl Scout cookies you left on the counter, but I took it away before he could.

Also, he chewed a hole through your sofa. But I guess you knew that. And he took a pretty big chunk out of my thumb when I caught him eating a tube of your toothpaste and tried to take it away. But the doctor says I'll be fine. I guess cats have cleaner spit than humans or dogs or something.

Hope you're having a nice trip.

Julio

....

✉

To: Julio Chasez <julio@streetsmart.com>
Fr: Jane Harris <jane@wondercat.com>
Re: The Dude

Oh, my God, I'm so sorry about your thumb! PLEASE save your doctor's bills so I can reimburse you when I get back!

You are the BEST!!! I cannot thank you enough for taking such good care of him!

Yes, I know about the sofa. It's okay, really.

THANK YOU!!!! I'll see you in a week!

Love,
Jane

~~Holly Caputo and Mark Levine~~
Jane Harris

It's actually kind of hard to write this with the suitcase wedged onto the seat between me and Holly, but it's better than trying to make conversation, because everyone seems to be in a bad mood since we all checked our Blackberries after lunch. Well, except for me. Since Julio says The Dude is fine!

I'll have to make sure I reimburse Julio for his medical expenses, of course. But just knowing that Dude was in a good-enough mood to bite him must mean he's not missing me too much.

I don't know what's eating everybody else in this car. . . .

Well, I sort of do. It turns out Mark, who was supposed to be the one in charge of bringing CDs to listen to in the car, forgot. So the only thing we have to listen to is Italian radio (Hello. You do not know what disturbing is until you've heard Italian rap) or the Queen CD Cal happened to have in his backpack.

Yes. Queen.

I have now heard "Fat-Bottomed Girls" twelve times. Holly joked that it's going to be her and Mark's wedding theme song.

Thank God Mark pulled over when we got to the foot of the mountains and let Cal take over. You never saw such narrow, twisty roads in your life. I thought I was going to heave. Thank God I had Dramamine with me.

Plus, every time we made a turn, Holly's suitcase fell on me. Well, not really fell, since Holly was holding onto it, but it LEANED HEAVILY on me. By the time we pulled over for lunch, I was chafed from the stupid thing rubbing against my shoulder, and in a pretty bad mood myself . . . especially when I saw the restaurant Cal had pulled up in front of.

I mean, God forbid he should choose a place in an actual TOWN. Oh, no, not Mr. I've Backpacked Around the World With Nothing But a Razor and My Queen CD (and some condoms, I hope, if he makes a habit of porking supermodels at every stop with his ABNORMALLY LARGE APPENDAGE—if what Holly says is really true, which I doubt. She's probably only saying it to make me like him. Well, it's NOT going to work).

Anyway, Modelizer has to pick this ridiculous looking Ho-Jo type place with these plate-glass windows in the middle of nowhere, perched on a CLIFF, practically.

Only when we walked in—me trying to rub some life back into my shoulder—we saw that there were like a million people there, looking out the plate glass windows at this beautiful waterfall rushing right past the dining room.

And the waiter was totally nice even though we didn't have a reservation, and sat us at a really lovely table right by the waterfall window. And instead of giving us menus, he just told us (in Italian, of course) what they were serving, which Holly and Cal said Si to, even though I didn't understand a word.

And then the next thing I knew, a carafe of bianco frizzante appeared as if from nowhere!

And then the waiter brought a giant bowl of deliciously cheesy pasta, which he spooned out onto each of our plates, and which seemed to melt as soon as it reached my tongue.

And then he brought a HUGE fish, swimming in butter, for the table to share, and a giant bowl of crisp, fresh, vinegary salad, and all this bread, and the whole thing only cost—get this: twenty-eight euros.

That is five Roman Diet Cokes right there.

The real question is, of course:

Why aren't more women in Italy fat? That's what I want to know. Because the women in that restaurant looked totally normal weight.

Mark said it's because they aren't loading up on empty calories the way Americans do. You know, soda and fries and stuff like that.

And maybe so.

But a few more meals like that one, and I guarantee I won't be fitting into my one-piece. Which would suck, because Holly says the villa's got a kick-ass pool.

So then after lunch we walked around the parking lot a little to get our circulation back and take in the view, which was stunning. And I was standing there enjoying the sun on my face and listening to the rushing water when Cal—I mean, Large Appendage—came up to me, and was all, "About what you said last night . . ."

I assumed he meant what I'd said about Holly and Mark being so perfect for each other, and that he was going to apologize for saying otherwise—especially since they were over by the car bickering about how it was Holly's turn to drive and Mark was saying how he was more comfortable with stick than she was and it was a totally cute argument that was making me long for my own soul mate with whom to bicker.

Only instead, he went, "Graziella Fratiani happens to own one of the most popular art galleries in Rome, and is both an enterprising businesswoman and a good friend. She is hardly a—what did you call her? Oh, yes. A skank."

CAN YOU BELIEVE THAT???? I was totally shocked. I just stood there looking up at him (why does he have to be so tall, anyway? And why are tall men always so . . . hot?) totally unable to think of anything pithy or witty to say. As usual.

And in a way he DID have a right to be mad. I mean, I don't know Graziwhosits Fratiwhatever. Maybe she's not a skank at all. Maybe she's this totally kindhearted and generous woman who gives huge amounts of money to cancer research and volunteers at the local orphanage. . . .

Yeah, right. No one in her thirties has thighs that thin without the help of the medical community.

And no one who's had that much work done is hanging out with orphans.

Plus, no one who stops by guys' hotel rooms for an afternoon quickie isn't a skank.

And even though Holly had asked me to try to get along with Large Appendage, just for the trip, and is making him out to be this big tragic hero, on account of his ex leaving him for someone richer (I bet she regrets it now, if she saw that episode of <u>Charlie Rose</u> my mom was talking about), I looked up at him and before I could stop myself, was all, "Wow, really, one of the most popular art galleries in Rome?"

Cal: "Yes."

Me: "And she didn't, like, inherit it from her dad or get it in a divorce settlement from an ex-husband?"

Cal: (looking kind of chagrined) "Well. Yes. I mean, her grandfather started the business, but—"

Me: "I see. Well, it might interest you to know that there are women who've actually started their own businesses from scratch without any help from their fathers, and who've managed to land seven-figure development deals with the Cartoon Network due to their own hard work and perseverance."

Which is all true. I mean, I don't actually GET the seven figures unless the Cartoon Network picks up Wondercat as an animated series.

But he doesn't have to know that.

Besides, even without those seven figures, I'm doing fine: Just as well as Graziwhosits. Probably.

And even if I'm not, the money is MINE. I earned it from

MY hard work, not my grandpa's. And so what if I live in a studio apartment? He doesn't have to know that. What do I need a lot of space for anyway? It's just me and The Dude, after all.

He didn't even have the grace to look embarrassed, though. He was just all, "Regardless. You don't have the right to call her a skank."

So then I looked him dead in the eye—well, as close as I could, anyway, from my twelve-inch height disadvantage—and said, "Well, you don't have the right to say Mark and Holly shouldn't get married."

"Actually," he said. "I do."

AND THEN HE STALKED AWAY!!! Before I could get another word in! Before I could stalk away!

Which actually is probably a good thing because when I tried to stalk away in the other direction, my Steve Madden heel slipped in the gravel and I nearly fell down and I would have fallen if I hadn't grabbed hold of the fender of a Smart Car parked nearby.

He didn't see, though.

Anyway, this pretty much settles it:

Cal Langdon = Spawn of Satan.

But at least now I know where we stand. And I will be able to begin taking evasive action. Obviously, from this moment on, I can never

a) Leave Cal and Mark alone in a room together
b) Leave Cal and Holly alone in a room together
c) Leave Cal alone anywhere

I will have to watch him like a hawk. It would be SO like him to drop unsubtle little hints about phenylethylamine and the dissolution of his marriage here and there in order to shake Mark's conviction to go through with his.

And Holly, as I know only too well, is already wondering if she's doing the right thing. I CANNOT let that man destroy the one actual solid romantic relationship left in the universe . . . well, except for my mom and dad's, but ew, don't want to think about that right now.

The only thing is, he obviously thinks he knows what's best . . . not just for Mark, but for everybody. I mean, that bossy way he chose where we were going to have lunch, and then, once we were there, what we were going to have.

And yeah, it was delicious.

But still.

I have to find a way to let him know he is NOT in charge here—WITHOUT letting Holly suspect anything's wrong. Because Holly's worried enough about everything. If she finds out the best man doesn't even think this wedding is a good idea, it's all over.

I've got to prove to this guy that I am not at ALL impressed with the size of his member. His having a huge you know what does absolutely NOTHING to intimidate ME.

And you know, I don't think his thing can really be all that big because it's not like he walks all bow-legged or whatever. Curt Shipley's was HUGE and you could see the sun shine between his inner thighs when he was coming toward you. . . .

Oooooh, I have an idea. If his email is the same as everyone else's who works at the <u>Journal</u>. . . .

✉

To: Cal Langdon <cal.langdon@thenyjournal.com>
Fr: Jane Harris <jane@wondercat.com>
Re: Holly and Mark

It's me. What you said back there in the parking lot—about how you're going to do whatever it takes to make sure Mark doesn't make the biggest mistake of his life—that's pretty presumptuous of you, don't you think?

J

✉

To: Jane Harris <jane@wondercat.com>
Fr: Cal Langdon <cal.langdon@thenyjournal.com>
Re: Holly and Mark

Ms. Harris. What a surprise. You're emailing me.

From the backseat.

✉

To: Cal Langdon <cal.langdon@thenyjournal.com>
Fr: Jane Harris <jane@wondercat.com>
Re: Holly and Mark

Oh, please. Like you and Mark weren't doing the same in the cab yesterday.

I realize you and Mark are friends—good friends, since child-hood, just like Holly and I are.

But you haven't seen him in a long time. How do you even know what's good for him anymore? And you certainly don't know

Holly well enough to make any kind of judgment about her. How can you presume that you know what's best for either of them when the truth is, you hardly know them at all?

J

✉

To: Jane Harris <jane@wondercat.com>
Fr: Cal Langdon <cal.langdon@thenyjournal.com>
Re: Holly and Mark

You are certainly entitled to your opinion. Just as I am entitled to mine.

Cal

✉

To: Cal Langdon <cal.langdon@thenyjournal.com>
Fr: Jane Harris <jane@wondercat.com>
Re: Holly and Mark

You're not entitled to your opinion at ALL. Because it's WRONG. You have absolutely no factual basis for it. You can't know Mark is making "the biggest mistake of his life" by marrying Holly because you hardly know Holly. You're basing your opinion on your own personal biases against love and marriage. And that has nothing to do with Mark OR Holly. That was just your own stupidity.

J

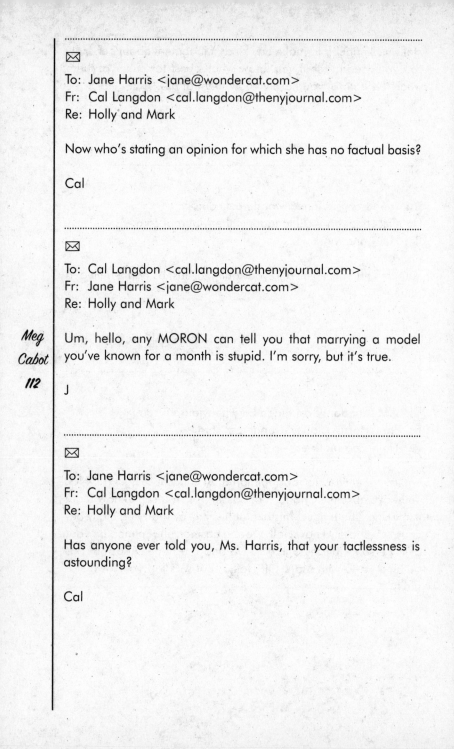

To: Jane Harris <jane@wondercat.com>
Fr: Cal Langdon <cal.langdon@thenyjournal.com>
Re: Holly and Mark

Now who's stating an opinion for which she has no factual basis?

Cal

To: Cal Langdon <cal.langdon@thenyjournal.com>
Fr: Jane Harris <jane@wondercat.com>
Re: Holly and Mark

Um, hello, any MORON can tell you that marrying a model you've known for a month is stupid. I'm sorry, but it's true.

J

To: Jane Harris <jane@wondercat.com>
Fr: Cal Langdon <cal.langdon@thenyjournal.com>
Re: Holly and Mark

Has anyone ever told you, Ms. Harris, that your tactlessness is astounding?

Cal

✉

To: Cal Langdon <cal.langdon@thenyjournal.com>
Fr: Jane Harris <jane@wondercat.com>
Re: Holly and Mark

ME??? I'm not the tactless one, Mr. There's No Such Thing as Romantic Love. Holly and Mark are in their thirties, not their twenties, and they've lived together for over two years. They are NOT making the same mistake you did. They are consenting adults—neither working in the modeling industry—who are in love. End of story.

J

....

✉

To: Jane Harris <jane@wondercat.com>
Fr: Cal Langdon <cal.langdon@thenyjournal.com>
Re: Holly and Mark

Perhaps we should discuss this face-to-face. My persuasive powers are at a disadvantage on handheld portable devices.

Cal

....

✉

To: Cal Langdon <cal.langdon@thenyjournal.com>
Fr: Jane Harris <jane@wondercat.com>
Re: Holly and Mark

No way! I don't want Holly getting wind of the fact that you aren't one hundred percent behind this wedding thing. She's freaking out enough about her family not being behind the idea. If she finds out the best man's against it too, she'll die.

J

✉

To: Jane Harris <jane@wondercat.com>
Fr: Cal Langdon <cal.langdon@thenyjournal.com>
Re: Holly and Mark

I meant sometime when Holly and Mark were not with us.

Cal

✉

To: Cal Langdon <cal.langdon@thenyjournal.com>
Fr: Jane Harris <jane@wondercat.com>
Re: Holly and Mark

Well, I don't see when that's going to happen.

J

✉

To: Jane Harris <jane@wondercat.com>
Fr: Cal Langdon <cal.langdon@thenyjournal.com>
Re: Holly and Mark

You don't anticipate that, during the next seven days we will be spending together, there will be a time when we will be alone together?

Cal

✉

To: Cal Langdon <cal.langdon@thenyjournal.com>
Fr: Jane Harris <jane@wondercat.com>
Re: Holly and Mark

God, I hope not. I mean, no, I don't. Let's just keep this conversation on paper. Or email. Or whatever. I don't want Holly getting wind of it. I—

AAAAAAAAAAAAAAH!

Travel Diary of

~~Holly Caputo and Mark Levine~~

Jane Harris

Well, THAT was totally humiliating. Holly's cell phone went off right when I was about to rewrite that last message to Cal, and I accidentally pushed Send.

Then Holly asked me to answer her cell phone, since she was concentrating on driving, and her purse was in the back-seat anyway with me and Mark (Cal, of course, got the front seat, since he's so TALL) and the phone was ringing.

And so I answered it, and this weird old lady was all, "Hel-looo? Hellooo-ooo?" and I was all, "Holly Caputo's line," and the old lady was like, "Vat? Vat?" with this German accent, and I was like, "Holly, there's a German lady on the line."

And Holly went, "Oh, that's Frau Schumacher, my uncle's housekeeper. She's meeting us at the exit to take us to the house since I haven't been there since I was little and I don't remember the way, and she says it's too hard to explain. Tell her we're on our way."

So I went, "Oh. OK. Hello, Frau Schumacher?"

And Frau Schumacher was all, "Helloooo, Holly?"

"No, this is Holly's friend, Jane," I said. "Holly can't talk now because she's driving. But she said to tell you we're on our way."

"Vere are you?" Frau Schumacher wanted to know.

So, to be helpful, I looked out the car window, and saw one of those green-and-white signs that let you know the name of the next city that's coming up.

"We're just outside Carabinieri," I said.

Which made Cal start laughing VERY VERY hard. Even though to my knowledge, I hadn't said anything funny.

"Vat?" Frau Schumacher sounded confused. But it was hard to tell with all the LAUGHING in the car. "<u>Vere</u> are you?"

"We just passed Carabinieri," I said into the phone. Now Holly was laughing, too. I leaned forward and swatted her, while Mark asked, confusedly, "What's so funny?"

"Jane," Holly choked, between chortles. "Carabinieri isn't the name of a <u>town</u>. It means police. We drove by a <u>police</u> station just then."

Really, I don't see what's so funny about that. I mean, how am I supposed to know what carabinieri means? I've only just gotten down <u>si</u>—yes—and <u>grazie</u>—thank you. I'm still trying to keep <u>buon giorno</u>—good day—and <u>buona sera</u>—good night—straight . . . not to mention <u>Non ho votato per lui</u> (I didn't vote for him) in the event of any rampant anti-Americanism that might rear its ugly head.

"Vere are the carabinieri?" Frau Shumacher wanted to know, sounding panicky. "Zey are following you?"

"No, no," I said, into the phone. "Sorry. No, I made a mistake."

"Zey zink zey own the roads, the carabinieri!" Frau Schumacher shouted. "In Germany, the polizia, zey know zeir place!"

"No, no carabinieri," I said. "There isn't any carabinieri . . . I made a mistake . . ."

"Give me that." Suddenly, the Modelizer was leaning over, trying to snatch the phone from me.

"I've GOT it," I said, outraged, and yanking the phone out of his reach.

"You guys," Holly yelled, jerking the wheel.

"I told you you don't know how to drive a stick," Mark said, as Holly's suitcase landed on him.

Then, because of the knowing look Cal threw me—as if, just because Mark was criticizing Holly's driving, they weren't destined for each other—I tossed the phone at him.

"Here, you big baby," I said—probably sounding like a baby myself. But I don't care.

Cal picked up the phone and began talking to Holly's uncle's housekeeper in smooth, fluent German. While the two of them were yakking away, I poked Holly in the shoulder and asked, "Why does your uncle have a German housekeeper in Italy, anyway?"

"How should I know?" We were almost out of the mountains now, but Holly was still paying rapt attention to the road. "She's just lived in the cottage next door forever, so Uncle Matteo made her his housekeeper."

This was a very unsatisfactory explanation.

About as unsatisfying as that email conversation with Cal. Just who does he think he is, anyway, presuming to tell me MY friend isn't worthy of his? And what did he mean by wanting to talk about this face-to-face? Is he high? I am never letting myself be alone in the same room with him. He might try to work his Large Appendage magic on me! Just like Curt Shipley used to! Girls—and, I know now, boys too—were powerless when Curt Shipley had them in his sights. It could be the same with Cal Langdon! Men who are supremely confident in the size of their own you know what do seem to exude a certain something. . . .

Although, really, he's so pompous, I can't actually see myself falling for him, Large Appendage magic or not.

He is kind of hot, though, the way his hair sometimes falls over his eye . . .

If only he'd shut up about stupid Saudi Arabia once in a while.

AAAAAAAAAOOOOOOOOOOEEEEEEEEEEOOOOOOOOOO

Sorry. Suddenly we went over this peak, and my eyes were DAZZLED by what I was seeing below us:

Meg
Cabot
118

Deep green valleys, over which tiny little cities are perched (the ancient fortified cities from the guidebook) clustered together within stone walls on brightly sunlit hillsides. . . .

Crumbling castles presiding over a patchwork of farmyards below them . . .

Sun-baked houses with orange tiled rooftops, with chickens in the yard pecking beneath brightly colored laundry hanging from lines outside shuttered windows. . . .

Oh, my God. I think we're <u>here</u>! Le Marche!

And that Customs guy was wrong. It's BEAUTIFUL.

To: Graziella Fratiani <grazielle@galleriefratiani.co.it>
Fr: Cal Langdon <cal.langdon@thenyjournal.com>
Re: Yesterday

If you really meant it when you said you'd come, you'd be entirely welcome . . . by me, at least. I can use an ally. My ego has taken about enough bruising as it can during this trip. The maid of honor is, to coin a phrase, a bitch.

Looking forward to seeing you.

Cal

☒

To: Cal Langdon <cal.langdon@thenyjournal.com>
Fr: Ruth Levine <r.levine@levinedentalgroup.com>
Re: Hello!

Cal, it's me, Mark's mom! How are you? I understand you're with Mark right now on his little European jaunt. I hear it's very nice in Italy this time of year. I hope you're getting plenty of rest and relaxation— you certainly deserve it after all that hard work you put in on your book. I saw it the other day at the Barnes and Noble. It was in the number-six spot for the bestsellers. Congratulations! That is fantastic.

Of course, Mark's father and I always knew you were destined for great things. It was pretty obvious from the day we met you, when you and little Markie took apart our vacuum cleaner's motor on the kitchen floor to see how it worked. It still ran perfectly well after you put it back together, despite those leftover pieces.

Well, I'm sure you're wondering why I'm writing to you after all these years, so I'll get to the point:

I'm worried about Mark. I'm sure this Holly is a very nice girl.

But I'm not so sure she's right for our Mark. She's the ARTISTIC type, for one thing. I know she has a very good job with the paper Mark sometimes writes that little column for. But let's face it: she doesn't exactly earn the kind of money I know some of Mark's past girlfriends are making now—Susie Schramm, for instance. You remember Susie, don't you, Cal? She's a lawyer now, with a very high-powered firm. I think Susie's SO MUCH more of Mark's type than this Holly girl.

And I DON'T mean because Holly's not Jewish. You know I NEVER judge people by their religion. After all, your family was—what was it again? Protestant?—and it never bothered me a bit! We quite enjoyed your mother's Christmas Eve cocktail party every year.

It's just that Mark has always been such a romantic. I'm sure deep down he thinks things like religious background don't matter. But you were always much more practical, Cal—not to mention, you've been around the world, and seen much more than Mark has—so I know you understand.

Plus, having been through a divorce yourself, I'm sure you wish someone had taken you aside in a brotherly manner and warned you not to rush into anything with that Valerie person. She was no good for you, anyone could see that. I knew it the minute I met her. What was she thinking, wearing that off-the-shoulder thing at your wedding? I realize it was couture and that Oscar de la Renta designed it just for her. Still, it hardly fit in at the country club here, now, did it?

And what about the children? Mark and Holly's, I mean, if, God forbid, they should have them? How are they going to raise the children? I don't want my grandchildren having no sense of identity because they've been raised in TWO religions. That's worse than being raised with none!

Anyway, I'm just hoping that since you're with Mark right now, you could try to talk some sense into him. He's always respected

you, and I just know if you told him not to rush into anything—
to give Susie Schramm a call when he gets home—he'd listen.
She has completely outgrown that underbite, you know. It's a
miracle what orthodontia can do.

Thank you, Cal. And please give my love to your parents. Except
for an annual Christmas newsletter from your mom, I haven't
heard much from them since they split up. But Joan's hacienda
in Tucson looks lovely—at least, judging from her newsletter. And
I hope Hank is enjoying himself in Mexico City, and that that little misunderstanding at the track back in Dayton got cleared up.

Affectionately,
Ruth Levine

PDA of Cal Langdon

Well . . . this is definitely going to be an interesting trip.

The bride-to-be's uncle appears to employ a German half-wit as a housekeeper, who went on ad nauseum about how things are so different now in Le Marche than they were right after the war (no need to ask which one . . . around here, there was only one war) and that Americans are welcome now with open arms, in spite of what they did to Ancona. No mention, of course, about her own country of origin's having started that war.

The groom's mother has another girl in mind for her daughter-in-law.

And the maid of honor appears to hate my guts.

This should be a lot of fun.

Sarcasm aside, Le Marche is an extraordinarily beautiful area of the world, filled with Renaissance towns still virtually untouched by American influence . . . no McDonalds, no twenty-four-hour convenience marts, no superstores. No wonder so many Italians flock here every summer. The waterfront resorts are reportedly packed from July though August. And there are even supposed to be some beaches down by Portoforno and Osimo that rival the Cote d'Azur for natural beauty.

Still, stunning vistas and Renaissance churches aside, Le Marche is not exactly where I'd choose to get married. If I were to make the mistake of getting married again. Which, of course, I never will.

And I feel a sense of responsibility toward Mark to keep him from making the same mistake as well. Not because, despite what Jane Harris might think, that I believe Holly is another Valerie. And not even because his mother asked me to. But because the guy has never lived! He's been in school for what, twenty years? And then he went straight from that to practicing full time. . . . the guy's done NOTHING. Never backpacked in Nepal. Never trekked the Amazon. Never swallowed the worm at the bottom of a tequila bottle in Belize. Adventure, to Mark, is a *Star Trek* convention.

And he thinks he's ready to get *married*? He's ready for a therapist's couch, is what he's ready for.

Holly's a great girl—I have no doubts about that. But marriage? No. Not now. The guy needs to have a life first. Then, if he and Holly were meant to be, they can attach the old ball and chain.

Obviously, I'm going to have to be subtle about this. Ms. Harris will undoubtedly be watching for any signs of mutiny. Which isn't necessarily a bad thing. She looks kind of cute with her chin thrust out in righteous indignation.

I can't believe I just wrote that. First fetching. Now cute. I think I need out of this car. And a drink.

She does have the worst problems with her footwear of any woman I have ever met. First the stiletto between the cobblestones last night, and today, the heel twisting in the gravel. I don't know how she manages to remain upright.

And she has this unnerving habit of staring at my crotch. Yes, she's short, but certainly not so much that this is where her eye level might naturally rest.

Ah, we've reached the exit where Frau Schumacher is going to meet us. She says she drives a silver Mercedes. Her grasp of English seems to have been derived from watching too many subtitled episodes of *Murder She Wrote*.

This should be an exceedingly entertaining week.

Travel Diary of

~~Holly Caputo and Mark Levine~~

Jane Harris

Oh my God, we're HERE. Villa Beccacia!

And it's GORGEOUS.

I will admit, at first I had my doubts. That Frau Schumacher—I think she might actually be as old as some of those castles we zoomed by. And, um, she's just SLIGHTLY in love with Large Appendage. It's sickening! Just because he speaks German! We got out of the car to meet her on the shoulder of the exit, and she was all, "Vich vun is Cal?" and when he raised his hand, you could practically see her melt onto the asphalt.

And she's got to be a hundred if she's a day! Who knew Large Appendage's magic works on centenarians?

The next thing I knew, the two of them were totally chattering away in German, leaving the rest of us out of the conversation.

Fortunately she had her great-grandson with her, Peter, who's fourteen and speaks English . . . well, pretty well anyway. Don't ask me why Peter is living with great-granny in Italy and not attending school, either here or his native Germany. Possibly she's home-schooling him? He does look a bit like he'd get the you know what knocked out of him in an American high school. I mean, he's a little on the chubby side and very soft-spoken, with an <u>X-Men</u> T-shirt under his jean jacket.

In any case, I didn't think it would be polite to ask. About why he wasn't in school, I mean.

Anyway, Peter asked us non-German speakers how the drive was, and if we were hungry, and said he and "Grand-muzzer" had stocked the fridge at the villa, so we should be all right until the "shops" opened again tomorrow, they're all being closed today on account of it's Sunday.

Mark asked him about liquor—you can tell sitting shot-gun while Holly drove had worn away his last good nerve—and Peter said, looking confused, "Vell, I zink zere are many bottles in the house now."

Mark looked visibly relieved.

Then Frau Schumacher said for us all to get back in the car and follow her. So we did. And we were driving along, me not being able to help notice that there was a big wall of clouds climbing over the nearby, castle-crested hill, and realiz-ing I probably wasn't going to be able to squeeze in an evening swim, when all of a sudden Holly went, "Look! The Adriatic!"

And there it was, this beautiful slice of sapphire blue, right there! There was no one on the beach, because being the middle of September, it's off season, of course . . . even though it's still in the 80s, temperature-wise (or the twenties, if you're going Celsius, like the Italians).

But somebody had still put out all of these white-and-yellow-striped lounge chairs, just in case.

And we drove through this adorable little seaside town, Porto Recanati, filled with the sweetest shops—a gelateria, and an Italian Benetton—and something called the Crazy Bar and Sexy Tattoo Shop, which I'm not sure really qualifies as sweet—and then hung a left onto a road I'm not even sure, technically, really IS a road. I mean, it's DIRT, and all of this dust was flying as we went down it, so that we had to close the windows.

Still, it was tree-lined, and through the spaces between the trees, we caught glimpses of the Centro Ippico—a horse-riding center down the road from Villa Beccacia . . . although not far ENOUGH down the road, if you ask me, since even as I write this I can hear neighing.

And there's a slightly horsy odor in the air when the wind shifts.

But whatever. We followed Frau Schumacher to this electric wooden gate, and waited while she hit a button and it slid slowly open. . . .

And then we saw it. Villa Beccacia, Holly's uncle's house, which has been around for a really long time . . . hundreds of years, since it was built in the 1600s!

Of course, it's been remodeled since then.

But not so you'd notice from the outside. As we drove down the long driveway, past fruit trees around which bees were humming and butterflies were flitting, past a deep green pond, its surface covered with lily pads, past rolling, grassy hills, the stone house, with vines creeping up all over it, came into view.

And it was just the way I'd pictured it!

Well, okay, there weren't any turrets. But really, it's LIKE a castle. I mean, it's really old, and inside, there are these darkly beamed and vaulted ceilings. And there are tapestries hanging on the walls, and in the old-fashioned kitchen, there's a brick oven.

You can't USE it . . . they put in a modern stove to cook on. But the brick oven is still THERE.

The casement windows are sunk into these deep walls with sills you can sit on, and open out like shutters. There are no screens, because if there were, you wouldn't be able to open the windows.

And out back, the pool is just steps away from the covered stone patio—the terrazza, according to Peter—with the ancient built-in grill/fireplace. This is apparently where Zio Matteo spends most of his time when he's home, since there was wax all over the wrought-iron table from the many candles that had dripped onto it while he was enjoying what Frau Schumacher intimated was one of his many enormous meals (from the photos I've seen scattered around the house, Zio

Matteo definitely enjoys his food). There was lots of firewood in the pile for the future, and a few sad-looking fly-strips hanging from the rafters.

The pool is gorgeous, 50 by 20 feet at least, with blue-and-white-striped lounge chairs all around, and palm trees at each end, the fronds swaying gently in the breeze (which is picking up, thanks to the approaching rain clouds). I am going to be so glued to the side of that pool as soon as the weather clears up.

Oh, and the whole wedding thing is taken care of.

Holly broke the news to Frau Schumacher as we were following the old lady around the house, listening to her rattle on in broken English about how there were plenty of clean towels but she'd just finished washing them and they were still drying on the line over at her cottage farther down the driveway.

Meg
Cabot
128

"You vill need lots of tovels," Frau Schumacher was saying, "for the svimming and the beach."

"Well," Holly said, glancing sweetly at Mark. "We aren't really here for the watersports, Frau Schumacher. Mark and I plan on getting married this week, over in Castelfidardo."

Frau Schumacher reacted the way a NORMAL—read, not Cal Langdon—person would react upon finding out a young and attractive couple like Mark and Holly were getting married: She clapped her hands for glee and wanted to know all the details, like what Holly would be wearing and did her uncle know and when were her parents coming.

To which Holly replied, her face getting red, "Well, I didn't tell Zio Matteo or my parents. We're eloping, actually—"

Which threw Frau Schumacher into a tizzy of excitement—once Cal translated, since neither Peter nor she was familiar with the word _elope_. She exclaimed, in her broken English, that she knew the mayor of Castelfidardo very well, and that if any problems developed, she was to be consulted immediately.

Where was the wedding breakfast going to be? What? We hadn't planned for a wedding breakfast? Well, there had to be a wedding breakfast. She would supply it—

Then Frau Schumacher's gaze fell on Cal (it never actually strays away from him long, I've noticed) and she glanced from him to me quickly and asked, no longer smiling, "And you two? You are having vedding, too?"

Both Cal and I hastened to assure the housekeeper that we were not—Cal a little more hastily than I think was actually polite, to tell you the truth. I mean, he may not know it, but he'd be LUCKY to be married to a girl like me. At least I can support myself without Daddy's—or some investment banker's—money, unlike SOME women he might know.

And I am at a completely normal body weight, and don't have to stick my finger down my throat to maintain it.

Plus, I have two television sets. How many does Cal have? Oh, that'd be none. I asked. Yeah, Cal doesn't "believe" in TV.

Right. You know what I don't believe in? People who don't believe in TV.

And then there's The Dude. Any man would be lucky to get to share a domicile with The Dude.

But whatever. His loss.

Not like I WANT to marry him. Or anybody. I mean, I have a development deal. What do I need a husband for?

Anyway, Frau Schumacher insisted on making us some snacks while Peter helped us take our bags upstairs. Mark picked up Holly's bag plus his own and Cal had his stupid backpack (Queen. That's the only CD he travels with. QUEEN. Although come to think of it, I sort of like Queen. But I'll never let HIM know that) so the only bag left was mine and when Peter went to pick it up he stiffened suddenly and said, "Vundercat?" in this astonished voice, staring at me.

Then Holly, halfway up the stairs, called down, laughingly,

"Yeah, Peter, didn't you know? Janie's the creator of Wonder-cat."

And Peter—to my everlasting gratification—cried, "You are Jane Harris, the artist of Vundercat? <u>Vundercat</u> is my favorite comic of all time! I have all of the <u>Vundercat</u> collection! I have Veb site dewoted to all things <u>Vundercat</u>!"

"Oh, do you?" I couldn't help stealing a look at Cal as he was following Holly and Mark up the stairs. Was it my imagination, or was he smiling a little ruefully? Yes, you BETTER feel full of rue, Mr. I Never Heard of Wondercat. Wondercat is INTERNATIONALLY RECOGNIZED. Oh, yes. Even strange, apparently home-schooled German boys in Italy have heard of Wondercat! I may not know what <u>carabinieri</u> means, buddy, but at least I can draw something that has INTERNATIONAL appeal.

"Well, while I'm here," I said, mostly to get Cal's goat, "I'll be happy to draw you some original Wondercats, Peter, for your Web site or whatever."

A look of total joy suffused Peter's round-cheeked face, and he raced up the stairs with my bag, chattering a mile a minute about his favorite Wondercat cartoons. I made sure to keep him talking too, so that Cal Langdon heard every word.

Villa Beccacia has seven bedrooms. Holly told Cal and I to pick whichever ones we liked best. Six of the bedrooms are huge, with ancient canopied beds with curtains around the sides, just like Scrooge's bed in <u>A Christmas Carol</u>, and walls lined with dark panels and bookshelves, on which sit copies of everything from books on bird-watching to <u>Valley of the Dolls</u> in Italian.

The seventh bedroom is tucked away beneath a sloping roof, its single dormer window facing the pool. It's clearly a boy's room, with dark blue bedspreads on its twin beds, and matching dark blue tiles in the adjoining bathroom. All of the paintings on the walls are of ships. The oldest one has the words <u>A sua eccellenza il sig Cav Francesco Seratti</u> engraved beneath it. Whatever that means.

I knew at once this was the room for me.

Peter was horrified. He said, "No, you don't vant this room. You vant the pretty pink room."

But I said, "Cal can have that one." (I know he heard me, too, because I heard a snort from the hallway.)

So Peter grudgingly put my bag down and went downstairs to see what his grandmother wanted, since she was bellowing for him (she has quite a set of lungs for such a tiny old lady).

And now I'm lying on one of the twin beds writing this, while everyone else is doing who knows what. All her life, Holly's talked about Villa Beccacia, the money pit her eccentric uncle bought with his first million doing . . . well, whatever it is Holly's uncle does. And now I'm finally IN it! And it feels as much like home as if Zio Matteo were MY uncle!

Oooh, Frau Schumacher is calling us. Authentic Italian (if German-made) snacks must be ready. Yum!

✉

To: Jane Harris <jane@wondercat.com>
Fr: Malcolm Weatherly <malcolmw@snowstyle.com>
Re: Ciao

Hey! Where are you? I haven't heard from you. Hope things are going good.

Listen, do you remember if I left my green ESPN hat at your place? Because I can't find it anywhere. I know I could just go buy a new one, but that was my lucky one. If you remember, could you let me know? And when you get back, send it to me, if you still have it?

Cool.

Rock out.

M

✉

To: Listserv <Wundercat@wundercatlives.com>
Fr: Peter Schumacher <webmaster@wundercatlives.com>
Re: JANE HARRIS

Listen up, kids! You are not believing what is happening! JANE HARRIS, creator of our beloved Wundercat, is here in Italy! Yes! IN THE HOUSE THAT IS NEXT DOOR TO THE ONE OF MY GRANDMOTHER!!! She is helping her friend to get the elopement in Castelfidardo!

And I have conversed with her! She says she will be drawing me some original sketches of our most favorite cat for this site! YES!!!!!

And JANE HARRIS is looking to be HOT! She has the dark brown hair (long, like we like it, boys!) and big brown eyes, and the very cute figure (sorry, girls!). She is looking very much like the beautiful vampire warrior Selene (played by the ravishing Kate Beckinsdale) in the finest film ever made of all time, *Underworld*!

And she has slain this mortal's heart!

I will be reporting more of the news of JANE HARRIS as it is happening!

Until then,

WUNDERCAT LIVES FOREVER!!!!

P. Schumacher
Webmaster, www.wundercatlives.com

Travel Diary of

~~Holly Caputo and Mark Levine~~
Jane Harris

Okay, I know the Italians have contributed a lot to our society, what with da Vinci and Mike Piazza, not to mention cannoli.

But seriously, why couldn't Holly and Mark have eloped to some country where they actually have electricity?

All right, all right, I KNOW Italy has electricity. In theory. In most areas. It just doesn't, apparently, extend to her uncle's house. When the stove is on, anyway.

Because the minute Mark turned the stove on to start boiling water for the pasta Frau Schumacher left us, all of the lights went out.

And when we called Frau Schumacher to ask her if her power was out, too, she was all, "No," and then when we explained what we'd been doing when the light went off, she cackled, "Oh, you cannot turn the owen on vile the lights are on as vell!"

Seriously. She was laughing like a crazy person at the idea of the stupid Americans trying to use a stove AND have lights on at the same time.

So then we asked her where the fuse box was, so we could turn the power back on (and I guess just eat antipasto for dinner) and she went, "Oh, yes. Vell, you go down the road to the gate—"

And Holly was all, "The ELECTRONIC gate? To the driveway?"

And Frau Schumacher was like, "Yes," as in, "What other gate would I be talking about, dorkus?" and then went on to say, "Go through the gate to the Wirgin Mary statue under the big tree—"

Seriously. THROUGH the gate. MILES from the house.

Well, okay, but like two hundred yards. TO THE VIRGIN MARY
STATUE. Under the big tree.

"—zen open her back and you will find the fuses."

Yeah. That's how they turn the power back on when it goes
out in Italy. They go DOWN the road, THROUGH the gate, UP
TO the VIRGIN MARY statue, OPEN her back, and flick the
switch.

Oh yeah. In the dark. And the pouring rain.

Since Holly thought she hadn't understood Frau Schumacher correctly, she handed the phone to Cal and made him
ask again, in German.

Same answer.

So Cal said he'd go do it.

Which I have to say is the first sign of generosity—well,
except for paying for dinner last night—from him so far. Especially since Frau Schumacher said she could send Peter.

But Cal insisted. He ran outside, and Holly and Mark and I
sat in the dark making jokes about all the escaped Italian
convicts that might be lurking outside, just waiting for someone to turn their stove on so that their lights would go out
and they could rob them.

After a little while we heard the front door slam and Cal
came back, dripping wet and cursing like a sailor.

But the lights weren't on.

"What happened?" Mark wanted to know.

Only Cal wouldn't say. He stumbled around in the semi-
darkness, found the bottle of Jack Daniel's Holly's uncle had in
his liquor cabinet, poured himself a stiff one, and downed the
whole thing in one gulp. Then he sat down—getting Zio Matteo's white couch all wet—and buried his head in his hands.

"Oh," Mark said suddenly, like he knew what was wrong.
"Was it—?"

Cal just nodded, not looking up.

So Mark went, "Okay. Never mind. I'll go." And grabbed the crummy flashlight we'd found in Zio Matteo's pantry.

Of course I couldn't let him go after that. I mean, I totally had to see whatever it was that had so destroyed the Modelizer.

And all it turned out to be was a little snake! A tiny one, curled up at the bottom of the fuse box, which someone had cleverly bolted to the Virgin Mary's back. Mark said Cal has been terrified of snakes his whole life.

Which is kind of sweet, in a way. You know, that he actually has a weakness? I mean, I can almost forgive him for the phenylethylamine thing.

Almost.

Except that now I'm soaking wet and one of my Steve Maddens got stuck in the mud in the road and came off and I had to pry it out with my fingers while Mark laughed his head off at me and now we can't make any hot food unless we do it by candlelight (even though Cal, recovering from the snake sighting, is out on the terrazza or whatever it is, trying to stoke up a fire in the stone barbecue thingie, saying we could

grill up the fish Frau Schumacher left us. As if somehow if he accomplishes this it's going to make us forget the whole part about how he was scared of that tiny snake. Yeah, so not going to happen, Mr. Million Dollar Advance for My Big Boring Book But I'm Scared of Snakes).

And I miss The Dude—even waking me up at 4 A.M. for a moonlit serenade.

And I can't seem to stop thinking about how I missed this week's ER because I was too busy packing to come here, and how it really is a shame that Holly asked me and not her brother Darrin to be her maid of honor. I'm sure DARRIN wouldn't be sitting in his room trying to dry his hair with a damp towel (what is up with these tiny Italian towels? They are the size of those hot cloths they handed out on the airplane on our way here—not to me, of course, but in first class. I just happened to see them because the line to the bathroom was too long in coach, so I snuck in to use the facilities in the forward cabin) thinking about Dr. Kovac.

No, at a time like this, Darrin—and his boyfriend Bobby—would probably be brainstorming about what to get for Holly and Mark. You know, as a wedding present. Like Egyptian cotton sheets, or a hand-tinted Audubon print, or a George Foreman grill, or something really meaningful like that.

Not a stupid travel diary that, guess what, I can't even give to them now because I've mentioned the best man's alleged Large Appendage a few too many times—

Holly just tapped on the door to say that Cal got a fire started and that he and Mark are trying to grill the fish and that it's hilarious and I should come down and by the way, do I like Cal better now that I know he has a phobia of snakes?

Trust Holly, at a time like this, when the elopement she's been planning for a whole year is finally just days away, to be wondering if Cal might be The One for me.

I can so totally tell she's hoping that Cal and I will fall in love and get married and buy a house next to the one you so know she and Mark are going to buy someday in Westchester (aka the Hellmouth) and send our kids to the same school and get together for barbecues on Saturday nights and sit around drinking Amstel Lights while spraying our progeny with Off to keep them from getting West Nile.

Yeah. Don't think that's going to be happening, Holl. The

best man doesn't BELIEVE in love. But don't worry, I'm sure his toast will be VERY heartfelt. . . .

Oh, wait, no, it won't. Because he doesn't HAVE a heart.

So now I'm wet and cold and sitting in my room with a too-small towel around my head, trying to scrape the mud off my Steve Madden, wondering what's wrong with me. I should be having fun. This is my first trip abroad, after all. And I haven't had a proper vacation in months, possibly years. I just spend all my time cooped up in my tiny studio apartment drawing stupid cats.

And I know that despite what the Customs guy said, Le Marche is supposed to be this magical place, even though since we've gotten here it's been pouring rain and the drops make this weird hollow sound as they hit the red terra-cotta roof tiles above my window and I swear to God if Cal Langdon and I end up cooped up in this house together for a week because of rain, only one of us is going to emerge alive, and it will be me because I know his weakness now.

But oh my God! What's with the mud and the everything being closed on Sunday and the power going out when you turn on the oven and the whole not-speaking-English thing? Not to mention, what is up with all the fish? I mean, I like fish, I guess, sort of, in small doses, and of course I am concerned about my Omega 3 fatty acid intake. Who isn't?

But I can certainly rectify that by having H & H throw a little nova on my bagel three times a week. I do not need to eat fish morning, noon, and night, like these Italians apparently do.

Wait. Could this explain why they're all so fit?

Oh, God, what is wrong with me? I am in an exotic foreign country, staying in a lovely house (except for the no-TV thing. And the Virgin Mary paintings everywhere—Holly's uncle seems to collect them, the ones whose eyes watch you wherever you go, so creepily that I had to take the one in my room down and put it in the wardrobe; oh, and the fact that there are no bathtubs, only showers, in any of the bathrooms. Oh, and my best friend's husband's best man keeps using words like <u>vicissitudes</u> and apparently wants to find some time to be alone with me so we can "talk." But other than that, the place is lovely) with my best friend, who is getting married, MAR-RIED, to the man she has loved forever. I should be happy for her.

It's just that really, with this storm overhead, pouring down buckets, we are stuck in this house together, with nothing but the Virgin Mary statues and the fish Frau Schumacher left us, and all I can think about is how crappy the weather is and how mean Mark's best man is and how much work I am going to have when I get back and how probably Julio is going to be resentful of The Dude's biting him and consequently forget to tape all my shows and then I won't know what's happening on any of them and I'll have to ask Dolly Vargas who will tell me all pityingly that a single woman who cares as much about television as I do has no life and why don't I let her introduce me to someone.

Holly is calling me. She says dinner is ready.

I swear to God, if any of them finds the playing cards some previously rain-swamped guests left behind and suggests we play bridge or something equally chummy, I am definitely going out to the pool, rain or no rain, and drowning myself.

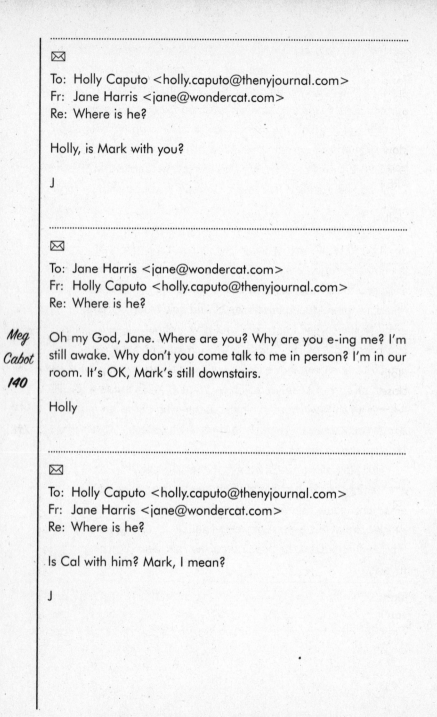

✉

To: Holly Caputo <holly.caputo@thenyjournal.com>
Fr: Jane Harris <jane@wondercat.com>
Re: Where is he?

Holly, is Mark with you?

J

✉

To: Jane Harris <jane@wondercat.com>
Fr: Holly Caputo <holly.caputo@thenyjournal.com>
Re: Where is he?

Oh my God, Jane. Where are you? Why are you e-ing me? I'm still awake. Why don't you come talk to me in person? I'm in our room. It's OK, Mark's still downstairs.

Holly

✉

To: Holly Caputo <holly.caputo@thenyjournal.com>
Fr: Jane Harris <jane@wondercat.com>
Re: Where is he?

Is Cal with him? Mark, I mean?

J

✉

To: Jane Harris <jane@wondercat.com>
Fr: Holly Caputo <holly.caputo@thenyjournal.com>
Re: Where is he?

How should I know? I told you, I'm in my room. I came up to bed because I'm exhausted. What is WRONG with you? Where ARE you? Why are you acting so weird all of a sudden?

Holly

✉

To: Holly Caputo <holly.caputo@thenyjournal.com>
Fr: Jane Harris <jane@wondercat.com>
Re: Where is he?

Nothing's wrong. I'm on my way to bed too. I'm in a downstairs closet. I just don't want to run into Cal. Go back to sleep. Sorry if I woke you up.

J

✉

To: Jane Harris <jane@wondercat.com>
Fr: Holly Caputo <holly.caputo@thenyjournal.com>
Re: Where is he?

Right. Like I'll be able to go back to sleep NOW. Janie, WHY are you in a downstairs closet? And WHY don't you want to run into Cal? Tell me now, or I'm coming down there and ripping that closet door open.

Holly

To: Holly Caputo <holly.caputo@thenyjournal.com>
Fr: Jane Harris <jane@wondercat.com>
Re: Where is he?

It's NOTHING, okay? After you went up to bed, and Mark went to see if he could find another bottle of scotch after we polished off the last one, Cal said he wanted to have a word with me alone before bed. That's all. Now I am hiding in the closet because I don't want to have a word with him. OK? Are you satisfied?

J

PS If you figure out where he is, let me know, and if he's far from the stairs, I'll make a run for my room. Then I can turn out all the lights and pretend to be asleep if he knocks.

✉

To: Jane Harris <jane@wondercat.com>
Fr: Holly Caputo <holly.caputo@thenyjournal.com>
Re: Where is he?

Janie, don't be such a freak! He LIKES you. He MUST. Why else would he want to see you alone? He probably wants to . . . you know.

And why not? You're both on vacation, you're both attractive, you're both single . . . why WOULDN'T you hook up?

Holly

✉

To: Holly Caputo <holly.caputo@thenyjournal.com>
Fr: Jane Harris <jane@wondercat.com>
Re: Where is he?

Um, why WOULD we? He is a modelizer, lest you forget.

And believe me, sex is NOT what he wants from me.

J

✉

To: Jane Harris <jane@wondercat.com>
Fr: Holly Caputo <holly.caputo@thenyjournal.com>
Re: Where is he?

Then what is it? What on earth do you think he wants to talk to you about?

Holly

✉

To: Holly Caputo <holly.caputo@thenyjournal.com>
Fr: Jane Harris <jane@wondercat.com>
Re: What on earth I think he wants to talk to me about

Oh, you might be surprised.

J

✉

To: Jane Harris <jane@wondercat.com>
Fr: Holly Caputo <holly.caputo@thenyjournal.com>
Re: What on earth I think he wants to talk to me about

Janie, you really have to get over this absurd prejudice you have about Cal. Mark and I were talking about it earlier, when you were doing the dishes, and Cal was cleaning the grill. You two actually have a lot in common. I mean, you both come from small towns. You both are extremely successful, and you both built up your careers from basically nothing. You're both attractive and creative. And you're both friends with us! You two would make an AWESOME couple. Just give him a chance. I know he's not up to your usual standards—seeing as how he has a job and is over twenty-five—but he might surprise you.

Holly

✉

To: Holly Caputo <holly.caputo@thenyjournal.com>
Fr: Jane Harris <jane@wondercat.com>
Re: What on earth I think he wants to talk to me about

Excuse me, but did you just use the word AWESOME?

J

✉

To: Jane Harris <jane@wondercat.com>
Fr: Holly Caputo <holly.caputo@thenyjournal.com>
Re: What on earth I think he wants to talk to me about

Stop being so silly. Come out of the closet. See what he wants!

Holly

✉

To: Holly Caputo <holly.caputo@thenyjournal.com>
Fr: Jane Harris <jane@wondercat.com>
Re: What he wants

Believe me, I know. And it is so not going to happen. Trust me on this, H. It's in your own best interest.

J

✉

To: Jane Harris <jane@wondercat.com>
Fr: Holly Caputo <holly.caputo@thenyjournal.com>
Re: What he wants

Well, I think you're being completely ridiculous. And I'm not having this conversation anymore. I'm going to get some sleep. We have a big day ahead of us tomorrow—you promised you'd go into Castelfidardo with us to petition for the marriage license and pick the day for the ceremony. I don't know about you, but I want to look good for the mayor's office. Good night.

Holly

To: Holly Caputo <holly.caputo@thenyjournal.com>
Fr: Jane Harris <jane@wondercat.com>
Re: What he wants

Fine, go to sleep. Traitor. I'm doing this for your own good, you know.

Well, no, I guess you don't.

And believe me, I intend to keep it that way!

Buona sera.

J

PDA of Cal Langdon

God bless Zio Matteo. The man may not care much about his home's electrical wiring, but at least he keeps a well-stocked liquor cabinet. Mark and I finished off the better part of a bottle of twelve-year-old scotch, and though it's a bit hard to type this, with my fingers feeling so numb, at least I got the picture of that snake out of my head at last.

The rain's finally stopped, too. The stars have come out, and there's a lovely warm breeze—slightly scented with horse manure—coming from the east. The pool and the wet stone surface around it are glistening in the moonlight, and somewhere in the distance—over the snoring of Mark, passed out facedown at the table beside me—I hear the braying of a donkey. It reminds me of those nights in Baghdad with Barbara Bellerieve, before she finally gave up on getting a ring out of me and hooked up with Aaron Spender—poor bastard.

Something which I realize has begun to happen with alarming regularity. Women I've slept with settling down with someone else, I mean.

I guess I shouldn't complain. God knows I'm not looking to register at Williams-Sonoma with any of them.

But it is a bit strange that all of my friends are pairing off. Mark, for instance. Well, not that I wouldn't have expected it of Mark, seeing as how he never exactly blazed any trails for rugged individuality in his lifetime. He does grill a mean turbot though.

But even people I'd pegged as lifelong bachelors—John Trent, for instance, over at the *Chronicle*—and Spender are taking the plunge.

Will it be long before I am the only single male my age left in the world? And if so . . . why? Don't these guys realize what they're getting themselves into?

I will admit, in Mark's case, the situation doesn't seem as dire as I once thought, despite what Ruth Levine might claim. Holly appears to be a cheerful, caring companion, who doesn't fall short in the looks department, either. She put together a wicked antipasto to go with the fish, an artfully arranged platter of marinated artichokes, mushroom, olives, fresh mozzarella, roasted red peppers, sundried tomatoes, and parmesan, all drizzled with olive oil and balsamic.

And when Mark mentioned something self-deprecating about his column, she chastised him, and proudly told me that his pieces are the Health section's most popular.

And when we sat down at the table her friend Jane had set—somewhat whimsically, with, I believe, every candle from the house on it, since we were dining al fresco on the logia, as the rain beat down just beyond the stone arches around us—Holly insisted on taking a picture, to mark our first meal at Villa Beccacia.

Then Ms. Harris—rather pointedly—insisted on taking a picture of Mark and Holly together—"To remember one of your last meals as an unmarried couple"—and the two of them wrapped their arms around each other. . . .

Well, I could see Jane's point about the two of them being perfect for each other. They are a lovely couple. Holly doesn't strike me—so far—as the type who'll, as soon as she gets a ring on her finger, quit her job and divide her days between Neiman-Marcus and her Pilates classes at the gym—

Must remember to stop judging all women by Valerie.

If Valerie had been at our evening meal, for instance, instead of Holly, she'd have consumed two of Zio Matteo's excellent bottles of montepolciano all on her own. And if Valerie had been here, she'd have made sure that the conversation, instead of flowing humorously from the troubles with the oven to the possible sex life of Frau Schumacher, would have revolved solely around her.

And afterward, of course, she'd have staggered to the toilet and heaved everything she'd just consumed into it.

Somehow, I can't picture Holly Caputo doing any of these things.

Still, that doesn't mean Mark is completely out of danger. A man can enter into a marriage thinking he's getting one thing, when the reality is, he's getting something very, very different. Mark's Holly may seem like a perfect helpmate at this point in their relationship, but who's to say once the blush is off the rose, so to speak, and they're declared man and wife—or *uomo* and *moglie,* as the case may be—she isn't going to turn into a stark raving bitch, demand that he make more money in order to buy her more expensive jewelry and spend all of her time obsessively weighing herself and recording every morsel that passes through her lips in a food journal?

I think Mark needs be made aware of this possibility.

And if he were conscious right now, I would make sure he knew.

As it is, however, I will have to wait until morning, and hope that we have another chance to talk privately before we make the trip to the marriage license office.

Speaking of hoping for a chance to talk, I mentioned to Ms. Harris that I was desirous of a private audience with her this evening, and she promptly disappeared into the house, never to return. I looked for her not long ago, and saw that she had retired to her room, the door of which was firmly closed. I have no doubt that, if there is a lock, she'd turned it.

For a woman who's capable of sending such blatantly hostile emails, she is remarkably reticent about face-to-face confrontations. It's always been my experience that women enjoy telling men what to do. Jane Harris, on the other hand, seems only willing to do this when it is her fingers, not her lips, doing the telling.

She strikes me as a very odd girl, overall.

But then, she is an artist . . . and a popular one, at least if the drooling half-wit boy from next door, who can't seem to take his eyes off her whenever they happen to be in the same room together, is to be believed.

How well I recognize his pain. I believe I had the same sort of all-consuming crush on my tenth-grade science teacher, Miss Huff.

Although Miss Huff did not exactly share Jane Harris's most impressive attributes . . . those slim ankles—the slenderness of the right one emphasized by that grinning cat's head—and that insouciant smile.

Insouciant. God. How in hell did I get a book contract, anyway?

Speaking of which . . . what in hell am I going to write about for my next book?

Oh, well. Much too tired—and too late—to think about it now. Will put this away and get to bed. It must be past midnight, and I'm still on New York time. Thoughts on the follow-up to *Sweeping Sands*—and further speculation about Ms. Harris—will have to wait until tomorrow.

· ·

PDA of Cal Langdon

One last thing before I go, though:

She still seems bizarrely fixated with the fly of my jeans. I am starting to wonder if Mark didn't resuscitate that ridiculous rumor from our days at Ohio State, about my having a super-sized wang, and share it with Holly, who in turn shared it with Ms. Harris. How else to explain why I keep catching her staring in that general vicinity?

If this is true, I will be forced, simply, to kill Mark. You would think that, at his age, he'd be over such childish pranks.

But he does work in the sciences, and those gifted in that arena do occasionally seem not to have quite as evolved a sense of humor as the rest of us.

Remember to ask him tomorrow.

✉

To: Listserv <Wundercat@wundercatlives.com>
Fr: Peter Schumacher <webmaster@wundercatlives.com>
Re: JANE HARRIS

Good morning all of you fans of Wundercat! I go now to take my motorino into town to get the brotchen for JANE HARRIS! She is not yet awake. I can see that she has not yet opened the curtains of her bedroom window.

But when she does, she will find that there is fresh brotchen to enjoy with her coffee! Courtesy of me, #1 Wundercat Fan Of All Time!

Wundercat Lives—4eva!
Peter

✉

To: Mark Levine <mark.levine@thenyjournal.com >
Fr: Customer Service New York Journal Travel Privileges
    <TravelPrivcustser@thenyjournal.com>
Re: Car Rental

Dear Sir,

Our great apologies for the misunderstanding concerning your vehicle. Our offices, as you discovered, are not open on Sundays. However, if you return the automobile you were assigned to the car rental agency in Ancona on Monday, we will happily allow you to exchange it for the four-door sedan you mentioned.

Sally Marx
New York Journal Travel Specialist

Travel Diary of

~~Holly Caputo and Mark Levine~~

Jane Harris

OK, everything I wrote in here last night about hating Italy and wishing I were home watching <u>ER</u>? Strike that.

I LOVE Italy. I LOVE it here.

Just now when I woke up, I pushed back the heavy curtains from my window, expecting to see more of the hard cold rain from yesterday. . . .

Gone. No more rain.

Instead, there was a cloudless blue sky. And a distant, green, castle-topped hillside straight out of a fairy tale. And a crystal pool sparkling below me. And the scent of freshly cut hay. And the sun-washed stone walls of the terrazza dripping with the thick green leaves and fire pink blossoms of bougainvillea, and birds singing in the treetops—

Well, what else could I do but slap on my swimsuit and hit the water?

And it was so very, very . . .

COLD!!!!

OK? The water is REALLY cold. Like ice-cube-tray cold. I'm writing this half-shivering to death on one of the lounge chairs, completely draped in towels.

But even though it's only like nine in the morning, or something, the sun is already beating down. Steam is coming up from the damp towels on my legs. Soon I should be toasty. . . .

YES. Now THIS is how I've always pictured a European vacation. Just me, the water, clear blue sky, bright hot sun, and a bottle of <u>acqua con gas</u> (sparkling water, which I found in the fridge). It's SO quiet here. No car alarms. No sirens. No neighbors squabbling over possession of the remote control next door. Just birds tweeting, and horses neighing, and the wind rustling through palm fronds and the leaves of the olive tree beside me, its branches heavy with little round balls deepening from a pretty pale green to a deep brown color . . . totally bitter and indigestible (yes, I tasted one. Who knew they had to be marinated or whatever? The pomegranates from the tree at the other end of the pool are MUCH better).

In the air is the crisp, clean smell of chlorine from the pool, the scent of freshly cut hay from the field beyond the hedge, and . . . OK, well, the smell of horse manure drifting over from the Centro Ippico, but it's very faint.

And off in the distance, atop a deep green rise that seems to come from the middle of the hay field, sits another fortified city, topped by a castle . . . Castelfidardo, where we're going to go today to apply for Mark and Holly's marriage license. If they can pry me from this spot. Which I sincerely doubt. Because the only way I'm moving is if—

AAAAAAAAAHHHHHHHHHHHHHHHHHHHH!!!!!!!!!!

Greetings! I have served breakfast to JANE HARRIS! I surprise her very much with the brotchen and hot coffee! She had just had her morning swimming when I come into yard with tray prepared by my grandmother! She scream very big!

But then she sees it is only me, and I put down tray beside her pool couch, and we have the coffee and brotchen. I bring also the Nutella, and JANE HARRIS likes this very much! We have nice chat, and I find out IMPORTANT NEWS FLASH:

JANE HARRIS HAS DEVELOPMENT DEAL WITH CARTOON NETWORK FOR WUNDERCAT ANIMATED SERIES!!!!!!!!!!!

Yes!!! Perhaps we will be seeing Wundercat on television soon!

I am very interested as JANE HARRIS is telling this to me, but then one of the mans she is traveling with (don't worry, boys, he is NOT her boyfriend. In the words of JANE HARRIS: "HIM? MY BOYFRIEND? NO WAY!") Cal Longdon comes out of the house and says he wants to speak alone with JANE HARRIS.

So I start to go, but JANE HARRIS says "No, Peter, you stay." And so I give Cal Longdon some brotchen and coffee too and we three sit and talk about politics for very long time before daughter of the sister of the man who owns the villa where JANE HARRIS is staying comes out and says they must go to Castelfidardo.

I am thinking I will ride on my motorino to Castelfidardo also today to see if JANE HARRIS needs anything more.

That is the report from WUNDERCAT CENTRAL! More news as it is received!

Over and out,

Peter, #1 Wundercat Fan Of All Time

....

✉

To: Peter Schumacher <webmaster@wundercatlives.com>
Fr: Martin Schneck < m.schneck@comixunderground.com>
Re: JANE HARRIS

How is JANE HARRIS looking in a bathing suit? You did not tell!

Martin Schneck

✉

To: Jane Harris <jane@wondercat.com>
Fr: Cal Langdon <cal.langdon@thenyjournal.com>
Re: Time to talk

Since you seem so reticent to discuss this face-to-face, I see no alternative other than to continue our e-versation. I believe you were saying something to the effect that I ought to mind my own business where matters of Mark's heart were concerned, and I was busy maintaining that I felt it my duty as a loyal friend to warn him of the emotional and financial jeopardy in which he is placing himself. Have you given the matter more thought, or are you still blinded by the romance of the thing?

Cal

✉

To: Cal Langdon <cal.langdon@thenyjournal.com>
Fr: Jane Harris <jane@wondercat.com>
Re: Time to talk

Oh my God, I can't believe you're e-ing me from the front seat AGAIN. CUT IT OUT!

J

✉

To: Jane Harris <jane@wondercat.com>
Fr: Cal Langdon <cal.langdon@thenyjournal.com>
Re: Time to talk

What other choice do you leave me when you won't speak to me in person? I haven't budged from my position that these two are making an enormous mistake. Have you, perhaps, come around to my way of thinking? I notice you seemed reluctant to leave the pool today when your friend Holly was urging us to get ready for the trip to Castelfidardo. . . .

Cal

....

✉

To: Cal Langdon <cal.langdon@thenyjournal.com>
Fr: Jane Harris <jane@wondercat.com>
Re: Time to talk

Because I was having a nice time at the pool! At least until YOU showed up there.

And no, I haven't changed my mind. Holly and Mark belong together, and I don't understand why anyone would think otherwise.

And I'm not "blinded by the romance of the thing," as you put it. It's sweet, that's all. And if you do anything to try to ruin it, you're a creep!

J

....

✉

To: Jane Harris <jane@wondercat.com>
Fr: Cal Langdon <cal.langdon@thenyjournal.com>
Re: Time to talk

A creep?

Cal

✉

To: Cal Langdon <cal.langdon@thenyjournal.com>
Fr: Jane Harris <jane@wondercat.com>
Re: Time to talk

You heard me. Or read me. A CREEP. Only a creep would try to talk his best friend out of marrying the girl of his dreams. Don't even tell me that isn't what you were up all night doing down there on the terrazza.

J

✉

To: Jane Harris <jane@wondercat.com>
Fr: Cal Langdon <cal.langdon@thenyjournal.com>
Re: Time to talk

How do you know what I was up all night doing? You went to bed at ten.

Cal

✉

To: Cal Langdon <cal.langdon@thenyjournal.com>
Fr: Jane Harris <jane@wondercat.com>
Re: Time to talk

I just happened to get up to get a drink of water, and I saw you out there. You and Mark.

But it didn't work, obviously. Or we wouldn't be making this trip to Castelfidardo, now, would we?

J

✉

To: Cal Langdon <cal.langdon@thenyjournal.com>
Fr: Jane Harris <jane@wondercat.com>
Re: Time to talk

I didn't get a chance to speak to Mark, due to the fact that the excessive amount of alcohol he put away at dinner rendered him comatose. Not, I would like to add, a good sign that he is looking forward to his impending nuptials with joy.

Cal

✉

To: Cal Langdon <cal.langdon@thenyjournal.com>
Fr: Jane Harris <jane@wondercat.com>
Re: Time to talk

Oh, please. *I* could drink Mark under the table. He's always been a lightweight. He was probably just trying to keep up with you. That doesn't mean ANYTHING.

Besides, every guy has the right to let off a little steam before he gets married.

J

✉

To: Jane Harris <jane@wondercat.com>
Fr: Cal Langdon <cal.langdon@thenyjournal.com>
Re: Time to talk

> every guy has the right to let off a little steam before he gets married.<

Proving my point that marriage is an unnatural and antiquated institution that ought to be abolished. The fact that it is traditional for men to get blind stinking drunk the night before their wedding just shows that it is a state into which they are entering against their better judgment.

WOMEN want marriage. Men do not. Mark's behavior last evening proves deep down, he doesn't want this. And you know it.

Cal

....

✉

To: Cal Langdon <cal.langdon@thenyjournal.com>
Fr: Jane Harris <jane@wondercat.com>
Re: Time to talk

You're so weird. Seriously. Are you this way about EVERYTHING? I mean, do you have to overthink every little thing? Don't you ever just DO stuff, without thinking about it first?

Or is it BECAUSE you did something once, without weighing the consequences, and got burned, that you are so anti-marriage?

J

....

✉

To: Jane Harris <jane@wondercat.com>
Fr: Cal Langdon <cal.langdon@thenyjournal.com>
Re: Time to talk

And I suppose you're going to claim you haven't been dreaming about your wedding day since you were seven? Dressing your Barbies up in bridal veils and walking them down the aisle with poor hapless Ken since you were nine? Sketching designs of your dream wedding gown since your teens, and viewing every male you met after the age of twenty as potential husband/father-of-your-children material, weighing his earning potential against his looks and assessing the chances of his remaining faithful to you?

Cal

....

⊠

To: Cal Langdon <cal.langdon@thenyjournal.com>
Fr: Jane Harris <jane@wondercat.com>
Re: Time to talk

You didn't answer my question.

J

....

⊠

To: Jane Harris <jane@wondercat.com>
Fr: Cal Langdon <cal.langdon@thenyjournal.com>
Re: Time to talk

You didn't answer mine.

Cal

....

⊠

To: Cal Langdon <cal.langdon@thenyjournal.com>
Fr: Jane Harris <jane@wondercat.com>
Re: Time to talk

Fine. Yes, I had Barbie weddings. Yes, I've sketched bridal gowns.

And, yes, I've sized up potential boyfriends, wondering whether or not they were going to be faithful to me.

But I've never cared about their EARNING potential. Truly. You can ask Holly.

And as for being good father material, how can I worry about who's going to be the father of my children when I'm not even sure I WANT children? My career is just starting out. I want to see how that goes before I attempt to bring another life form into this world.

Besides which, I already have a cat. That is quite enough responsibility right now.

J

....

✉

To: Jane Harris <jane@wondercat.com>
Fr: Cal Langdon <cal.langdon@thenyjournal.com>
Re: Time to talk

Are you seriously comparing owning a cat to raising a child?

Cal

....

✉

To: Cal Langdon <cal.langdon@thenyjournal.com>
Fr: Jane Harris <jane@wondercat.com>
Re: Time to talk

Um, you haven't met The Dude.

J

✉

To: Jane Harris <jane@wondercat.com>
Fr: Cal Langdon <cal.langdon@thenyjournal.com>
Re: Time to talk

Who is The Dude?

Cal

✉

To: Cal Langdon <cal.langdon@thenyjournal.com>
Fr: Jane Harris <jane@wondercat.com>
Re: Time to talk

My cat. And you still haven't answered MY question.

J

✉

To: Jane Harris <jane@wondercat.com>
Fr: Cal Langdon <cal.langdon@thenyjournal.com>
Re: Time to talk

I can't remember what it was.

Cal

✉

To: Cal Langdon <cal.langdon@thenyjournal.com>
Fr: Jane Harris <jane@wondercat.com>
Re: Time to talk

Isn't it true that the only reason you're so anti-love-and-marriage is because your own didn't work out?

J

✉

To: Jane Harris <jane@wondercat.com>
Fr: Cal Langdon <cal.langdon@thenyjournal.com>
Re: Time to talk

Absolutely not. The failure of my own marriage plays absolutely no part in my conviction that human beings are genetically incapable of monogamy. I believe we were meant to have seven or eight partners in a lifetime, not one. The idea that as a community we applaud those couples who manage to stay together forty or fifty years or longer is simply ridiculous. There's something inherently wrong with celebrating couples like that. It simply isn't natural to want to spend that much time with another human being.

Cal

✉

To: Cal Langdon <cal.langdon@thenyjournal.com>
Fr: Jane Harris <jane@wondercat.com>
Re: Time to talk

My parents will be celebrating their fortieth wedding anniversary next year. Are you saying there's something inherently wrong with them?

J

✉

To: Jane Harris <jane@wondercat.com>
Fr: Cal Langdon <cal.langdon@thenyjournal.com>
Re: Time to talk

No offense to your parents, but basically, yes. Are you going to tell me that in all of those forty years, they've never fought or cheated on each other?

Cal

✉

To: Cal Langdon <cal.langdon@thenyjournal.com>
Fr: Jane Harris <jane@wondercat.com>
Re: Time to talk

Sure they've fought. They're HUMAN. But cheated on each other? No way.

J

PS You're an ass.

✉

To: Jane Harris <jane@wondercat.com>
Fr: Cal Langdon <cal.langdon@thenyjournal.com>
Re: Time to talk

I never said my theory was a very popular one. But it happens to be true.

Cal

PS Has anyone ever told you that you're kind of cute when you're mad?

✉

To: Cal Langdon <cal.langdon@thenyjournal.com>
Fr: Jane Harris <jane@wondercat.com>
Re: Time to talk

Are you FLIRTING with me?

It won't work. I'm a little brighter than the women you're so obviously used to.

Stop e-ing me, we're here.

J

PS You're still an ass.

Marriage of an American Citizen in Italy

An American citizen planning to marry in Italy must obtain a declaration (called STATO LIBERO) sworn by four (4) witnesses before the Italian consulate, stating that according to the laws in which the citizen is subject in the United States there is no obstacle to his/her marriage. Therefore he/she must appear at this Consulate General with four unrelated friends not related to him/her nor to each other. Each of them has to bring a valid identification (Passport or Drivers License).

The citizen's passport must also be presented and, if applicable, evidence of the termination of any previous marriage (final divorce decree or death certificate) translated into Italian and legalized by the competent Department of State with an "Apostille" (see page 2). The sworn statement has three months' validity.

Travel Diary of

~~Holly Caputo and Mark Levine~~

Jane Harris

Cal Langdon is a stupid jerk.

He's the KING of all jerks. He's the undisputed CHAMPION of all-time jerks. How can Mark even be friends with him? Really? How?

I mean, I GUESS he can be interesting, and even witty, when he's talking about some arcane topic such as the accordion-making industry. Which, considering that Castelfidardo is apparently the accordion-making capital of the known universe, is at least kind of useful. Who knew Zio Matteo is a world-renowned accordionist, and that's why he bought a villa so close to the town that makes his chosen instrument?

There is even an accordion MUSEUM here, featuring—what else?—the world's largest playable accordion. It's as tall as Cal Langdon.

There's also a statue on the village green of a large man playing the accordion. He is, oddly, in the buff. I'm not sure this would fly in America. I mean, a statue of a naked accordionist in the town square.

Still, topics unrelated to human relationships, such as Saudi Arabia's declining oil reserves and the history of accordion-making? Those are the only subjects about which Cal Langdon ought to be allowed by law to converse. Because when it comes to people, he's totally and completely in the dark.

No wonder his wife left him.

I honestly don't even see how he lasted as long as he did on the foreign correspondence trail. I mean, Cal Langdon has been flying around the world—when he wasn't apparently bouncing around it in the back of a jeep—interviewing dignitaries and world leaders and guerrillas alike.

And yet he seems to know less about people than ME, and I've barely left my apartment these past five years, I've been so busy drawing. How can someone who knows so many people know so little about them? That's what I'd like to know.

Whatever. I'm not going to let him spoil this beautiful moment for me. We're sitting outside the Office of the Secretary of Castelfidardo, which is where they give out the marriage license applications and schedule the town weddings. Mark and Holly are up at the desk, trying to make the clerk understand what they want. They already have all these forms they filled out back at the Italian consulate in New York. It turns out that if an American citizen wants to elope in a foreign country, they can't just do it all willy-nilly. You have to fill out a bunch of paperwork first, back in the States. For one of the forms, Mark and Holly even had to drag four separate witnesses—unrelated to them, or to each other—to the Italian embassy to swear that they weren't already married to anyone else (Holly and Mark, I mean).

I don't know why this is taking so long. Or why Cal Langdon felt compelled to go up there too, and listen in. I'm keeping an eye on him to make sure he isn't trying to sabotage the proceedings. Now the <u>secretario</u> himself has come out to join in the conversation.

Still, the <u>secretario</u> keeps going, "<u>Non</u>."

This doesn't sound good. Shouldn't he be saying, "<u>Si</u>"?

Holly keeps gesturing to the paperwork from the Italian consulate and going, "But in New York they said—"

And the <u>secretario</u> keeps going, in his broken English, "Yessa, but, in New Yorka, thees is not how we do theengs here in Italia."

Hmmm. Holly looks stressed. I sense trouble brewing.

Now the <u>secretario</u> is starting to look annoyed.

"I donna understand," he's saying. "Why you have to get married here in Castelfidardo? Why not Las Vegas, like normal Americans?"

Uh-oh. Holly's mad now.

"Because we're NOT normal Americans," she says. "We want to get married here in Castelfidardo. We have the right forms. What's the problem? Just open your calendar and tell us when the mayor has a time available to perform the ceremony, and we'll be on our—"

Oh, my. Peter Schumacher just walked in. He must have followed us on his little motorino.

Poor boy. He must really not have anything else to do. . . .

Oh, the <u>secretario</u> is handing something to Holly—

HAGUE CONVENTION ABOLISHING THE REQUIRE-MENT OF CONSULAR LEGALISATION FOR FOREIGN PUBLIC DOCUMENTS

The United States of America and Italy and some other countries have signed a convention abolishing the requirements of diplomatic and consular acknowledgements or legalizations of public documents originating in one convention country and intended for use in another convention country signatory of the convention.

This consulate general, therefore, will not henceforth acknowledge or legalize public documents: notarial documents, deeds, certificates of vital statistics, wills, court decrees, etc.

To be valid in any other of the countries signatories of the convention, all documents must carry an APOSTILLE.

To obtain the "APOSTILLE" in any of the United States, a document is first notarized by a Notary Public in that state and then authenticated by the Country Clerk in the country in which the notary is qualified.

✉

To: Listserv <Wundercat@wundercatlives.com>
Fr: Peter Schumacher <webmaster@wundercatlives.com>
Re: JANE HARRIS

NEWS FLASH! JANE HARRIS is here in Italy to be the witness for the wedding of her friends. Today they go to the Ufficio di Secretario of Castelfidardo for the license to marry, and the secretario said NON! He would not allow it, as the friends of Jane Harris did not get APOSTILLE from the US consulate in Roma!

I have driven my motorino straight from the Ufficio di Secretario myself to let you in on the news, and also to tell my grandmother, who says she will speak to the secretario herself after lunch, because she knows his mother! And she says his mother will be very angry when she learns her son would not let the American lovers marry! Grandmother says she will take this to Mayor Torelli himself, if she must!

At the Ufficio di Secretario, JANE HARRIS was wearing pink short-sleeved shirt, trousers in black cotton, and pink sandals! Her toenails are painted pink to match! JANE HARRIS is still looking very cute!

More later from #1 fan of Wundercat!

Wundercat Lives—4eva!
Peter

To: Claire Harris <charris2004@freemail.com>
Fr: Jane Harris <jane@wondercat.com>
Re: You

Disaster! The city of Castelfidardo won't allow Holly and Mark to get married here! Not without some stamp from the US consulate in Rome!

Which means we have to drive all the way there and back to get it. That's another eight hours there and back in the car! And we only have the house until Friday, when Holly's uncle comes back from his latest accordion tour. And the Secretario says the mayor's calendar is totally booked, and only the mayor can perform wedding ceremonies!

Everybody is pretty bummed. Well, except for Cal, of course. He is totally against marriage on principle. He thinks there must be something inherently wrong with you and Dad for having been together for so long. He has absolutely no idea how normal human beings function. It's possible he's a robot.

Anyway, we're going to grab lunch in town and reconnoiter back at the secretario's office later. Holly's uncle's housekeeper might be able to do something, according to her great-grandson. Apparently, she knows everybody's mother, and can shame them into doing whatever she wants.

Hope Dad's back is feeling better! Good thing, those gloves.

Love,
Janie

PDA of Cal Langdon

Insisted on buying lunch, as everyone in our party was completely dejected (excepting myself, of course).

It seems that Italian bureaucracy is doing my job for me, insofar as keeping Mark and Holly from wedded bliss (or bust). It appears the young couple cannot be wed unless they get a specific stamp on a form that can only be secured at the American embassy back in Rome. Their choices are to skip the whole thing or pile back into the car and drive back to Rome tomorrow.

At this point, Mark seems to be leaning toward making the trip. Surprisingly, it's his lady love whose resolve seems to be flagging. I wonder if Holly is quite as enthusiastic about the idea of marrying Mark as I—and her friend Jane—once presumed.

This, at least, explains why Ms. Harris insists upon carrying on our conversations via text. She must have known that her friend's enthusiasm was not all it should be.

And I must say, if a small detail like a stamp on a form and an eight-hour drive are enough to drive Ms. Caputo into such dudgeon, perhaps Mark really is better off single.

The girls are in the ladies' room, doing whatever it is women do when they enter such facilities together. Mark is on his cell with the car rental agency in Ancona. Apparently, the replacement vehicle *New York Journal* promised him earlier this morning is no longer available. Good thing he called before we made the trip.

Lunch was delicious, by the way. We found a small family-run establishment popular with the many accordion-factory workers in town. For twenty euros total we enjoyed an exquisitely prepared lemon pasta, grilled scallops, insalata caprese, and a carafe of bianco frizzante. We received a number of odd looks, to be sure, from the natives. This is clearly a restaurant that doesn't see many Americans.

And clearly has never heard of a non-smoking section.

Still, a pleasant meal, in all.

Now, I presume, we shall be trekking back to town hall to argue some more with the presiding officials. With any luck, we'll be joined by Inga Schumacher—taking this tragi-comedy to a whole new level of hilarity—and her great-grandson, who seems to have glued himself to our sides . . . not that his near-constant presence seems to bother Ms. Harris. In fact, I'm starting to believe she actually likes having the kid around. Peter's presence makes it very difficult for me to say all the things I'd like to say to the object of his devotion. . . .

Perhaps this is just as well. I always seem to be thinking—and saying—the oddest things around that woman. Telling her I think she's cute when she's angry? What was I doing? I NEVER say that kind of thing, much less write it.

That's right. She has it in *writing*, permanent proof of my idiocy.

I ought to be shot.

Especially since it's more than clear that she thinks I'm—what was it? Oh, yes. An ass. That's very nice. Being called an ass by a woman who makes her living drawing a cartoon of a cat. Excuse me, did *I* create something that people have forever since been forcing me to look at, dangling from suction cups on the back windshield of their car? No, I did not.

It's all this damned fizzy wine. That's what it is. I just need a beer. Maybe this afternoon, since it doesn't look as if we'll be changing cars in Ancona, I'll talk Mark into going to a bar with me—there's that Crazy Bar and Sexy Tattoo Shop in Porto Recanati—and we'll talk this whole marriage thing out over a couple of cold ones. . . .

Though I think I'll keep my thoughts about Ms. Harris to myself. And the fact that today she's got on a pair of shoes I haven't seen before. Open-toe, of course, with these pink straps that criss-cross over the cat tattoo—

I need some air.

Travel Diary of

~~Holly Caputo and Mark Levine~~

Jane Harris

Poor Holly. She's crushed.

Stupid <u>secretario</u>. And stupid Italy. I hate it here again!
How can they be so mean? Can't they see they're destroying
one of the sweetest, gentlest girls in the world with their
ridiculous bureaucratic red tape?

At least Frau Schumacher understands. She's really letting that <u>secretario</u> have it. He looks kind of scared. He keeps
saying something about the mayor. Apparently, he doesn't
have the authority to do . . . something.

But the mayor does.

I think Frau Schumacher told him to let us in to see the
mayor, then.

Wow! For an old lady, Frau Schumacher sure can be intimidating!

Thank God for Peter running home to get her. Well, really,
thank God for Wondercat. Because without Wondercat, Peter
wouldn't have even known about our problem and gone to get
his great-grandmother.

And of course, there'd be no Wondercat if it weren't for
The Dude. So really, none of this would be happening if it
weren't for my cat.

As usual. Just further proof that The Dude, as I've always
suspected, really is God.

Now the <u>secretario</u>'s left his own office. Frau Schumacher
looks very pleased with herself. I asked Peter what's going on,
and he said, "The <u>secretario</u> is going to see if ze mayor vill
change his schedule to let your friends get married on Vednes-
day. There is maybe an opening in ze calendar on zis day."

When I commented that this seemed like a positive devel-

opment, Peter nodded and said, "Yes. Zey are all very fright-
ened of my grandmuzzer. She will go to the mayor's muzzer,
and zat zey do not want."

Yes! Joy!

You would think Holly would be happier to hear that. But
she's just sitting next to me, holding her stomach and looking
kind of queasy.

Well, I guess I can't really blame her. She's been looking forward to getting married for so long, and all of these delays
have to be—

The secretario is back. Oh my gosh! We're being summoned
to the mayor's office!

✉

To: Jane Harris <jane@wondercat.com>
Fr: Claire Harris <charris2004@freemail.com>
Re: You

Oh, sweetie, that's horrible news about poor Holly! Sorry it took me so long to get back to you, but Daddy dropped a picture frame on his big toe so we were just at Promptcare getting it X-rayed. Not broken, thank God, but a bad bruise. I sent him to bed with a bowl of Breyers.

I do hope you're able to work something out for Holly. It would be such a shame for she and Mark—well, all of you, really—to have gone all that way and then not be able to have your little elopement. I feel just terrible.

But, even if they can't get married, you can still have a nice vacation, can't you? What is Holly's uncle's house like? Is it pretty? Do the windows lock? Because you know I just saw on the news that in a lot of those oceanside communities, people leave the windows open at night to let in the sea breezes, and it's like an invitation to thieves and rapists! They just slip in on through the windows and take whatever they want! I hope you're making sure all the windows are locked at night.

And I hope you're not being too mean to that handsome Cal Langdon. You're a very vibrant and pretty girl, Janie, and you know men can't help falling in love with you. Remember how many of them asked you to the senior prom? Well, it's true a lot of them were freshman boys who couldn't have taken you anyway. . . .

But the way they mooned around the house, asking Daddy if they could mow the lawn, when we knew perfectly well they just wanted a glimpse of you. Keep in mind that some of those boys you wouldn't give the time of day to went on to have very good jobs at Pfizer.

And Helen Shipley told me her son Curt makes six figures in the cruise ship industry!

Why you keep insisting Curt is one of those bisexuals, I can't imagine. Helen says it simply isn't true. Curt's not married yet because he just hasn't met the right girl, according to Helen. Probably YOU were the right girl, and he's just waiting for you to get in touch.

Also, according to Charlie Rose, Mr. Langdon got a VERY nice advance for that little book he wrote. That's not something you ought to turn up your nose at, you know. Wondercat is darling, but it won't always be as popular as it is now. You need to think about your future, you know, Janie.

Love,
Mom

PS Daddy says to tell you it looks as if that cartoon about the flying serving utensils has been canceled. That might open up a slot for the Wondercat animated series, don't you think?

....

✉

To: Listserv <Wundercat@wundercatlives.com>
Fr: Peter Schumacher <webmaster@wundercatlives.com>
Re: JANE HARRIS

SUCCESS!!! My grandmother has arranged it all! The friends of JANE HARRIS will be married Wednesday morning at nine o'clock, before the mayor had to go and coach the American football game at the primary school, where he is also the athletic director when he is not being mayor.

But they must get the stamp from the consulate of the US before they can be married. So tomorrow they will go to Rome to receive it.

All is done, and by my grandmother! Everyone was much excited! Except for the secretario and the mayor.

But best of all—

JANE HARRIS KISSED ME!!!! YES!!!! To say thank you for making it so that her friends can have their marriage!!!

Never will I wash this face again.

That is all for now. I am Peter Schumacher, #1 fan of Wundercat, saying

TSCHUSS!

Wundercat Lives—4eva!
Peter

GE. SP. AL. S.N.C
Viale Europa 44
Porto Recanati (MC)
GROCERY

	EURO
PelliCola Co	0,50
6 Minibiscot	2,50
Olive Bella	2,50
Kinder Sorpr	1,80
Birra Peroni, 24	12,76
Insalata Rom	0,66
Tomato Ketch	2,23
Uva Italia P	1,95
The Twinings	1,90
Insalata Tro	0,41
Puro Succo	1,33
Naionese Cal	1,22
Latte Fr.A.Q.	1,37
Insalata Gen	0,38
Latte Fr. Int	1,30
Oro Duepic'c	2,34
637 Pom.Ross	1,90
Banco Taglio	1,01
Oro Piu'caca	1,53
Olive verdi	0,78
Bisc. Conad G	0,89
Pane Dolci I	0,55
Pomodori Pel	0,55
Doricream	0,65
Mais Pop Cor	0,60
Banco Taglio	27,21
Caffe Classi	2,09
Caffe Classi	2,09
Arance Taroc	2,55
TOTALE	77,55
Contanti	100,00
Resto	22,45

N.Pezzi 50
Oper: 10
Cassa 1 1
Regalo Bollini: 15
Codice: Bollini

Arrivederci e Grazie!

```
        La Cantinetta
          Enoteca
   Ricrea di Morresi G. & C.
     SNC Viale Europa 36
        Porto Recanati


                        EURO
   Vino   1             8,66
   Vino   1             7,80
   Vino   1             7,40
   Vino   1             5,40
   Vino   1             7,00
   Vino   1             9,00
   Vino   1             9,00
   Vino   1             6,50
   Vino   1             6,50
   Vino   1             5,00
   Vino   1             5,00
   Vino   1            10,20
   Vino   1             9,00
   Vino   1            14,00
   TOTALE             110,46


            Grazie!
```

Travel Diary of

~~Holly Caputo and Mark Levine~~

Jane Harris

The mayor said yes!!!!

It seemed touch and go there to me for a while, but Frau Schumacher totally came through for us! I couldn't tell what she was saying to the big man behind the desk—a very intimidating desk, too, with lots of important looking documents all over it, for a very intimidating man, wearing a big green shiny sash over his track suit—but Cal later translated that basically, she said, "Marry these two delightful young people or I will make you sorry."

Cal says he doesn't know HOW Frau Schumacher was going to make him sorry, but the mayor apparently believed her enough to make a time in his schedule for Holly and Mark.

And OK, it's super-early in the morning for a wedding— 9 A.M.—but it's better than nothing! Frau Schumacher was right about wedding breakfasts, I guess. That's what they do here, instead of receptions.

Now all we have to do is drive to Rome tomorrow, get the form Holly and Mark need, and drive back.

At last, we can relax a little. We went grocery shopping for food for the rest of the week (and Cal and Mark hit the liquor store, this cute little shop called La Cantinetta in Porto Recanati. Frankly, I think 14 bottles of wine, champagne, J & B, and something called limoncello might be a bit much, but it IS a wedding, after all, even if it's just four of us attending) and then came home and hit the pool right away. At least, Holly and Mark and Peter and I did. Cal got a call from his editor or somebody, so he's sitting in the terrazza, yakking into his cell, saying things like, "But I said you'd have it next month. No, I never said that."

Sounds like somebody's a little late on a project. Ha ha.

I got the skinny on Peter while we were in the mayor's office, too. When we walked in, I was surprised to see a girl about Peter's age sitting on the mayor's desk, going "Papa" in the unmistakable wheedle of a teenaged daughter. She was a pretty little thing named Annika—all big blue eyes and blonde ringlets and knobby knees—and when she saw Peter, she completely forgot about whatever favor she was begging her father for. Her eyes narrowed in that mean way only teenaged girls' eyes can, and she went, "What are you doing here?"

And Peter was all, "I am here on official business with the mayor."

And the girl started laughing and said, "What business can you have with my fazzer?"

And everything was suddenly SO clear to me, just from those—let me see—OK, eight little words. You know, that Peter adores Annika with a passion that cannot be denied, and that she wants him, too, but Peter isn't considered cool enough to date in their social set, and so she has to act scornful towards him.

It was all so obvious and sad.

Then the mayor hung up the phone and went, "Annika. Shush."

Then he and Frau Schumacher started going at it in Italian, so I used the opportunity to ask Peter who the girl was, sotto voce (Italian for "in a soft voice." I am really getting this language down, if I do say so myself).

And he was like, his voice dripping with (obviously feigned) scorn, "Zat's Annika. She is the mayor's daughter. She zinks she is queen of all of Castelfidardo even zo she is not."

And I asked Peter if he and Annika went to school together, and he told me he goes to "Internet school" because the schools in Castelfidardo aren't "adwanced" enough for him, and that he can't go to school back in Germany because there's no one there for him to live with, his "fazzer" currently being "in the jail."

In the jail! Peter's dad—Frau Schumacher's grandson—is in the jail!

For what, I don't know. But now I understand why it is that Peter is able to hang around us all day. Annika, presumably, was on her (three-hour) lunch break from school. Can you imagine all the trouble American teens could get up to if we gave them a three-hour lunch break? And all of the malls were CLOSED during it? My God, civilization as we know it would break down completely.

Anyway, after the mayor and Frau S. negotiated their little compromise, there was a lot of cheering and relieved sighs (and, from Cal Langdon, a frown), so I took the opportunity to lean down and give Peter a peck on the cheek—to thank him, you know, since if he hadn't gone and got his great-grandmother, none of this would have happened.

And, while Peter turned bright red, I had the pleasure of seeing Annika, who'd witnessed the kiss, scowl prettily.

Score one for Peter.

Poor Annika. One of these days she's going to wake up and realize Peter was the one for her. Only by the time that happens, Peter will have his own software company and be making millions and be dating a starlet from some Fox sitcom . . . or whatever the Italian equivalent of Fox might be.

Cal Langdon just barked, "You'll get it when you get it, Art," into his phone.

God. He is so Type A. He really needs to learn to chill, like me, or he's going to have a coronary before he's forty.

And how dare he suggest that there's something wrong with MY parents for staying together so long? I asked him while we were in the hallway outside the mayor's office, out of earshot of Holly, how long HIS parents stayed together, and he said, "They were married twenty years, and are much happier people now that they've gone their separate ways."

Which is all very well and good for them, but if Cal Langdon were MY kid, I'd want to get away from him, too. No wonder they split up. The North Pole and Antarctica aren't far enough to get away from that voice: "I told you, Arthur, I will have the proposal for you when I get back. No, not the DAY I get back. But a few weeks later—yes, well, I still haven't figured out exactly what I'm going to write about. No, not dirty diamonds. No, I'm not going to Angola—"

Some women, I suppose, might find Cal Langdon's voice sexy. And IT is kind of deep and gravelly, in a Robert Redford kind of way.

But the stuff he SAYS with it! EW!

And OK, he's hot. I mean, I'm not going to lie and say he's not. All I have to do to KNOW that isn't true is flip back to the beginning of this journal and read the part where I first saw him—God, was that really only four days ago? It seems like months—to know that initially, I thought Cal Langdon was hot.

And it's true that even now, knowing what I do about him, he still has his moments. Like when he pried my foot out of that crevasse between the cobblestones, and his whole hand fit around my ankle.

And sometimes when he looks at me with those too-blue eyes, it seems like there's a light shining from out of his head, like a jack-o'-lantern—a light only I can see, and which makes it very hard to maintain eye contact.

But still. In the car on the way back from Castelfidardo, I made a comment about how ludicrous it is that everything in this country closes from noon until four, sometimes five, every single day, and that really, it isn't any wonder that America is a superpower and Italy isn't, given that we only take half-hour lunches, for the most part.

And Mr. I Know Everything There Is To Know in the Entire Universe has the nerve to go, "Believe me, if the average temperature in America during the summer months was forty degrees Celsius, we'd be shutting down everything between noon and four as well."

Whoa! I am sorry, but that is nothing but showing off. CELSIUS? What American knows how to tell the temperature in Celsius?

OK, enough ranting against Cal Langdon. Not while I've got all this delicious sun to bask in. It's actually kind of hard to get worked up about anything, you know, with this sun beating down and the palm fronds overhead swaying gently in the breeze from the sea—carrying with it, as always, that slight hint of horse manure—and the only sounds those of bees buzzing and the crystal blue water in the pool gently rippling and Cal pecking at his Blackberry.

The sun is so hot, in fact, it seems to seep into your skin like thick heavy lotion. Really, it's hard to tell whether it's the bianco frizzante (SOOOOO good mixed with a little Orangina) or the sun, but I really feel, I don't know, like nothing matters right now . . . not even what happens to Dr. Kovac on ER. I feel like I could just lie here forever. . . .

✉

To: Cal Langdon <cal.langdon@thenyjournal.com>
Fr: Arthur Pendergast <a.pendergast@rawlingspress.com>
Re: The Book

Would you cool it? I'm not trying to bust your chops. I know
you've got a lot going on right now. Hell, if I'd moved back to
the States after a ten-year absence, and had to find a place to
live, furniture to put in it, buy a car, etc., I'd be going stark raving mad.

Well, not really, since I'd just leave all that to my wife. But you
don't have a wife. So don't worry about it.

Just, you know. If you could give me a rough idea of what you're
thinking about doing for your second book. That would be nice.

Arthur Pendergast
Senior Editor
Rawlings Press
1418 Avenue of the Americas
New York, NY 10019
212-555-8764

✉

To: Jane Harris <jane@wondercat.com>
Fr: Holly Caputo <holly.caputo@thenyjournal.com>
Re: Did you see that?

???????????????

Holly

✉

To: Holly Caputo <holly.caputo@thenyjournal.com>
Fr: Jane Harris <jane@wondercat.com>
Re: Did you see that?

Hello. Aren't you getting married the day after tomorrow? What are you doing ogling other men's naked chests?

J

✉

To: Jane Harris <jane@wondercat.com>
Fr: Holly Caputo <holly.caputo@thenyjournal.com>
Re: Did you see that?

I'm getting married, but I'm not DEAD. My God, who knew that under that mild-mannered Oxford lurked a chest of such exquisite proportions? Did you notice the abs?

Holly

✉

To: Holly Caputo <holly.caputo@thenyjournal.com>
Fr: Jane Harris <jane@wondercat.com>
Re: Did you see that?

They were slightly hard to miss. Don't you think he was showing them off just SLIGHTLY by ripping off his shirt and diving in like that? I mean, DIVING?

J

✉

To: Jane Harris <jane@wondercat.com>
Fr: Holly Caputo <holly.caputo@thenyjournal.com>
Re: Did you see that?

Well, he's been working, while the rest of us were just out here lounging around. I think he just got frustrated and gave up, turned off the Blackberry, and went for it. I didn't catch anything "stagey" about it.

Wow, look at him go. That's a lot of laps. He must really be annoyed about something—or somebody—to be swimming that fast.

Holly

✉

To: Holly Caputo <holly.caputo@thenyjournal.com>
Fr: Jane Harris <jane@wondercat.com>
Re: Did you see that?

He's ruining my afternoon of total relaxation. How can I relax when someone is exercising that hard in front of me? He's making me feel guilty about all that pasta I had at lunch.

J

✉

To: Jane Harris <jane@wondercat.com>
Fr: Holly Caputo <holly.caputo@thenyjournal.com>
Re: Did you see that?

He'll stop soon. Oh, see. There you go. Oh, look, how sweet.
He's coming to sit by YOU, Janie! I *told* you he likes you. Maybe
even as much as PETER does.

Holly

....

✉

To: Holly Caputo <holly.caputo@thenyjournal.com>
Fr: Jane Harris <jane@wondercat.com>
Re: Did you see that?

I hate you.

J

Travel Diary of

~~Holly Caputo and Mark Levine~~

Jane Harris

Why are men—and boys—so weird?

I mean, they certainly LOOK nice enough, for the most part. Cal Langdon, in particular, though it GALLS me to admit it. I mean, look at him, sitting there in that lounge chair, with the sunlight winking off the drops of water still clinging to his golden body hair.

Oh my God, I can't believe I wrote the words <u>golden body hair</u>.

Still, not like he's got so much of it. Just enough, really.

Just enough to make me wonder how much more he's got, you know, below the waistband of his shorts.

I can't believe I wrote <u>that</u> EITHER!!!

Still. It doesn't matter how good they look—and just how, I'd like to know, does a guy whose job entails sitting behind a desk, typing stuff, get such defined biceps?—men are still weird.

Seriously. Just look at what they're doing now. The Modelizer, Mark, and Peter are having this totally in-depth—and boring—conversation about the Hubble space telescope and dark energy—whatever that is—and they are WAY into it. I mean, as much into it as Holly and I get when we're talking about <u>ER.</u>

They're going on about how dark energy—whatever it is—fills up most of the universe, along with dark matter, and how no one knows what either of those things is (which is a bit of a relief, since, um, I was thinking I'd missed something), but they seem to think it's responsible for the anti-gravitational force that is causing the universe to expand, rather than contract, the way everything else does, when gravity pulls on it.

Hello. Don't they realize they're in ITALY? Can't they shut up for FIVE MINUTES and enjoy the way the light is trickling through the green leaves as the sun sinks down, dappling the pool and veranda in golden half-light? Or the way the setting sun seems almost to create a mist across the patchworked hills, making them seem blurry to the eye—except for where the outbuildings on them are silhouetted against those great big purple clouds built up behind them, the aftereffects of a fleeing storm?

THAT's what they should be talking about. The miracles of nature right in front of them. Not some stupid dark energy, billions of miles away.

Oh, great. Those clouds, that I thought were fleeing? They're headed this way. It's going to rain in a second.

Aw, screw it. It's time for dinner anyway.

To: Cal Langdon <cal.langdon@thenyjournal.com>
Fr: Joan Langdon < joan.langdon@artintucson.com>
Re: Mary

Hi, Calvin! It's me, Mom. I don't know where you are right now—are you still in Riyadh? I know you were on *Charlie Rose*—one of my neighbors told me. But of course I missed it, because you know I don't own a television—so you must have been back in the US for that.

I did buy your new book. It was very long.

But they have it in the window at Books-A-Million, so I'm sure you'll sell lots of copies.

Anyway, I hope you're well, and not working too hard . . . but knowing you, I'm sure that's the case. You were always such a workaholic. Remember in high school, when you were so deter-mined to get into Yale? Your dad and I couldn't understand it. What's so wrong with a state school? We went to one, and didn't turn out so badly.

But you got your way, in the end. As always. Well, I mean, you got in. Too bad they wouldn't give us enough financial aid to let you go. But hey, you turned out all right! Looks like Ohio State didn't hurt you too much!

I myself am doing extremely nicely—I have a show at the Tucson Senior Center next month, featuring my latest series of "lint peo-ple." I really think these latest pieces are going to put me on the map in the art world. I see myself as a sort of middle-aged, fe-male Matthew Barnye. You know, the artist who made a name for himself with Vaseline sculptures?

I can't tell you how good it feels, Cal, to finally be expressing my creative side. I felt so STIFLED all those years I ignored the artistic part of me. I really hope you're finding a way to let your own creativity flow, Cal. I know some people call writing art, but what you write . . . well, I don't think nonfiction counts. You've always looked down on your sister and me, I know, calling us "flakes."

But there's nothing "flakey" about creative expression, Cal. Nothing at all.

Speaking of your sister, I was wondering if you'd heard from her. I only ask because I had the oddest dream last night, in which you, your dad, and Mary and I were trapped on a frozen pond, and the ice had begun to crack. Oddly, you were the only one who managed to pull yourself to safety.

So I was just wondering if you knew if Mary was all right.

That's all.

Mom

....

✉

To: Cal Langdon <cal.langdon@thenyjournal.com>
Fr: Hank Langdon < hank.langdon@expat.net>
Re: Hey

Hey! Whaddaya think? I got myself online! Yeah! I know! It's a miracle!

So when are you coming for a visit? I got an extra set of clubs. The courses here ain't bad at all. Well, you know, except for the spics. But you can't escape the spics in Mexico City, let me tell you!

Hey, I heard you landed some big book deal, or something. Think you can loan your old man ten grand or so? I got myself in a little deep with this guy over a horse—

Well, let me know. And if you talk to your mother or sister, tell 'em to lay off me. They've bled me dry. I don't have two pesos left to rub together.

Mañana.
Dad

....

✉

To: Cal Langdon <cal.langdon@thenyjournal.com>
Fr: Mary Langdon <m.langdon@internetcafenetwork.com>
Re: You

So I take it from your not emailing me back that you have no interest in me or my life. I guess the word FAMILY doesn't mean anything to you.

Whatever. I can get along fine without you—which is why the judge granted me Emancipated Minor status in the first place.

I'm in Canada, now, in case you're interested. Not that MY travels could be of any interest to such a jet-setter like yourself. Where are YOU now, anyway? Gstaad? Ougoudagou? Some place more fabulous than where I am, I'm sure.

Don't worry (like you *would*), I'm sure I'll be fine. It's not that cold here yet. Well, except at night. But I've been sleeping in the van. Too bad Jeff can't leave the heat on overnight, but it wears out the battery.

See you in the next life.

Mare

✉

To: Mary Langdon <m.langdon@internetcafenetwork.com>
Fr: Cal Langdon <cal.langdon@thenyjournal.com>
Re: You

What is wrong with you? Why are you sleeping in some guy's van? I thought you'd have learned a lesson about that, given what happened last time.

And I DID reply to your last email. If you'd quit changing your email address every two days, you might actually hear from some of the people you've written to once in a while.

I can give you another thousand bucks if you let me know where I can wire it. But what happened to the grand I sent you last month? What are you doing with all of my money, anyway? If I find out you're blowing all of my money on drugs, Mary, I'm cutting you off. Do you understand me? Because I don't think you're quite getting the Emancipated part of being an emancipated minor. Which, by the way, at 25, you're not anymore.

Cal

✉

To: Cal Langdon <cal.langdon@thenyjournal.com>
Fr: Mary Langdon <m.langdon@internetcafenetwork.com>
Re: You

Oh my God, you are the best big brother any girl's ever had EVER! Send the money to the Western Union here in Whistler, BC.

And we have to live in the van because all the cheap apartments and hotel rooms are taken by Winter X boarders right now, gearing up for the games. But it's cool, because we're selling TONS of tie-dyed shit. We can't dye it fast enough, it seems.

And I need the cash for necessities, tampons, and food and stuff, until we start showing a profit. Jesus, Cal. I would never do drugs. I need my brain cells for my ART.

Thanks—U R the BEST!!

Much love,
Your little sis

....

✉

To: Mark Levine <mark.levine@thenyjournal.com>
Fr: Ruth Levine <r.levine@levinedentalgroup.com >
Re: Hello!

Sweetie, I'm sorry to bother you, I know you're having fun on your little European jaunt, but I need to know ASAP: What size sweater are you wearing lately? I know usually you like a Large, but you joined that gym, didn't you? So maybe you've bulked up a little, and need an Extra Large?

I only ask because it turns out Susie Schramm—you remember, I told you about her in my last email—she knits! Yes! On top of being a high-powered legal eagle AND a size four, she knits in her spare time (I mean, the time she spares from her work and volunteering for B'Nai Brith, of course).

And I've commissioned a sweater for you from her. Apparently, she isn't afraid to use bold colors, either. I know how much you love yellow, so that's what you're getting. . . .

Ooops, it was supposed to be a Hannukah surprise! Oh, well!

Write soon and let me know.

Love,
Mom

To: Holly Caputo <holly.caputo@thenyjournal.com >
Fr: Darrin Caputo <darrin.caputo@caputographics.com >
Re: Hello, it is your mother

Holly, it is your mother again. Darrin says I'm not to use his email anymore to write to you, but you do not pick up your cell phone when I call. Either your cell phone doesn't work in Europe, or you are using that Caller ID, and not picking up when you see it is me.

Which is fine. I understand that you do not want to speak to your mother. Even though I am the one who gave birth to you, and wept with joy when I heard the doctor say you were a girl, the little daughter I had almost given up hope of having after four boys in a row.

I am writing now because I saw Jane Harris's mother at the Kroger Sav-On yesterday, and what she said to me there disturbs me very much. Your father says it is nothing, but I do not agree. I was telling Mrs. Harris how lucky she is to have a daughter like Jane, who sees only nice Christian boys, like that very pleasant British boy, Dave, and the investment banker, Malcolm.

And Mrs. Harris says to me, "But Mark Levine is very nice, too. Listen, Maria, you must stop thinking of it as losing a daughter, but instead, of gaining a son."

What does Claire Harris mean by this? Why would she think I am gaining a son? I do not need any more sons, I already have four . . . five if you count Darrin's Roberto. Holly, you are not thinking of doing something foolish when you are in Italy, are you?

I hope you know that if you marry this boy Mark, he will NOT be a son to me. Just as you will no longer be my daughter. Think on this, I beg you.

I will pray for you.

Your mother

Travel Diary of

~~Holly Caputo and Mark Levine~~

Jane Harris

Somebody needs to take Cal Langdon aside and tell him that
that shirt he is wearing, which I am sure he thinks is very cutting edge and SoHo, actually makes him look gay. How can a
straight man not know this?

And I know Cal is straight. Not just because he was married before, or the skank I saw slinking from his hotel room, because you know, those don't really prove anything anymore, in
today's day and age (just look at Curt). I know because of
what happened just now at the restaurant we're having dinner
at since it was raining again (what is WRONG with this country?) and nobody felt like cooking outside, much less risking all
the electricity going off again by turning the oven on inside.

Plus everybody seems to be in a really bad mood, although
no one will tell me why.

It must be the rain.

Anyway, they only let us into this restaurant after we
stood at the door for like ten minutes tapping at the glass,
then begging the proprietors in broken Italian to please please
serve us, as they, like every restaurant owner we have encountered in Porto Recanati (except of course the Crazy Bar and
Sexy Tattoo Shop), are actually very reluctant to prepare food
and sell it to people, though they haven't bothered to put a
closed sign in their window. Apparently in the off-season what
Le Marche restauranteurs do is invite all of their aged friends
to sit in their restaurant at night and watch <u>Magnum PI</u>—in
Italian of course—and ignore any actual paying customer who
might wander in.

Thank God Mark is incapable of taking no for an answer,
or we would never get fed. He carries this <u>Guide to Le Marche</u>

handbook around with him and insists we have to eat at all the places Holly's uncle marked for us. He even showed the restaurant proprietors their ranking, and insisted they feed us. Maybe it's something to do with him being around sick patients all day, but Mark just exudes this "Be nice to me" vibe, which people totally seem to respond to.

I mean, except for Holly's mom.

And it's not really as sickening as it sounds. On him, it works, and doesn't leave you feeling like you want to hit him over the head with a pool cue or anything.

Anyway, the way I know Cal is not gay, in spite of the shirt and the model ex-wife—and Holly's assurances to the contrary, of course, but hey, the future wife of the best friend is not always the first to know—is that after <u>Magnum</u>, the movie <u>Babe</u> came on, the one about the little pig who can herd sheep, and all of the Marquesians or whatever they are sat there, enrapt, in their traditional Le Marche-wear of jeans and Bon Jovi T-shirts, but Cal never blinked an eye. He just went right on drinking his grappa like it was actually good and not something that should only be sold as a facial astringent.

No gay guy can resist the lure of <u>Babe</u>. Not that I think the restauranteur and all of his aged friends are gay. They're just foreigners. They probably cried at the end of <u>Magnum</u>, only I missed it because I was in the men's room, trying to smuggle out a roll of toilet paper, because of course there wasn't one in the ladies' room. Ditto a toilet seat.

Which, by the way, I have to say <u>What's up with that?</u> about. Clearly, Italian women never go to the bathroom outside of their own homes. That is the only thing I can think of to explain the state of some of the ladies' washrooms in Le Marche. What do all the Italian ladies do, anyway, when they have to go? Just squat? I can barely make it into a squat during Pilates, and that's in drawstring pants. What are the chances of me squatting in control-top panties and a pair of tight capris around my knees? Seriously? Think about it. The restaurant owners obviously haven't.

And yes, I know, it's a summer community and we're here on the off-season, but I highly doubt the owner of this place has all the toilet seats stored somewhere in the back until the beach starts getting crowded again. I mean, clearly this is a culture where toilet seats just aren't that important.

To which I say, Um, again, this is why America is a super-power and you, Italy, are not. Because we care about our comfort in the john.

Anyway, now everyone is arguing about tomorrow. You know, who's going back to Rome to visit the US consulate. At first I just figured Holly and Mark would go by themselves, and I could lounge by the pool drinking bianco frizzante and reading the latest Nora Roberts. Um, hello, this is my vacation, right?

But no. Cal had to be all, "I'll come with you," to Holly and Mark.

Hello? Go <u>with</u> them? Why? Don't you have a book you're supposed to be writing, or something? They don't need you, Cal Langdon. A translator, maybe. But not a modelizer.

I know what he's up to. He might think I don't, because I am just a lowly cartoonist and he is the big Saudi Arabian oil crisis guru journalist. But I am ONTO his devious plan. He thinks he's going to go with Holly and Mark and make subtle anti-marriage remarks that will feed into Holly's insecurities and make her so freaked out about marrying against her parents' wishes that she's going to call the whole thing off!

Well, I am not going to let it happen. I just declared that if Cal's going, I'm going, too!

Now he's staring at me all squinty-eyed-Robert-Redfordy across the table, like I'm going to be so intimidated, I'm going to back down.

But it won't work. I am staring squinty-eyed right back at him, while Holly and Mark argue over whether they should let either of us come with them. Mark says it will give us a chance to try one of the Roman restaurants Holly's uncle recommended in the <u>Guide to Roma</u> book Mark found back at the villa.

But Holly says it's our vacation too, and we shouldn't have to spend it shuttling back and forth between Rome and Le Marche in a Toyota. Even though this time there won't be a suitcase in the backseat, since it's just a day trip.

I could see Cal wasn't going to back down, so I said, "I happen to be extremely fond of Toyotas," causing Holly to look at me and go, "Oh, God, what's WRONG with you? And what are you writing in that book?"

I've been outed. More later.

Travel Diary of

~~Holly Caputo and Mark Levine~~
Jane Harris

The horror continues.

As soon as Cal got up to go use the facilities himself just now, I told Mark if he was any kind of friend he'd tell Cal to stay home at the villa with me (even though I don't want him there, as it will mean spending the day alone with him while Holly and Mark are off US consulating tomorrow, but whatever). Also, that he should tell Cal his shirt looks gay. Mark pointed out that he had already encouraged Cal to stay home to no avail, and that the shirt is from Bangladesh and it's the only clean thing left in Cal's backpack. Apparently, he's sweet-talked Frau Schumacher into doing his laundry while we eat.

I can't believe he'd take advantage of that sweet old lady's crush on him in such an obvious manner, even if he DID give her ten euros for her trouble, according to Mark.

Still.

At least the food is good. REALLY good. Even when it's prepared by someone who won't take their eyes off <u>Babe</u>. Although Cal and I both eschewed the raw oysters, Cal because he doesn't like them, and me because I may be a travel neophyte, but I am not eating raw fish in a foreign country. Holly and Mark were both like, "Oh, well, more for us," and slurped down like twenty each.

Whatever. It's their funeral.

After this, since it's stopped raining, we're going to get gelati from the Gelateria and take a moonlit walk along the beach. Romantic! Well, for Holly and Mark.

Uh-oh, back to the Who's Going To Rome Tomorrow argument. . . .

Who buys their shirts in BANGLADESH??? What is wrong with the Gap, for God's sake?

To: Jane Harris <jane@wondercat.com>
Fr: Claire Harris <charris2004@freemail.com>
Re: Holly

Hi, honey! Don't worry, everything's fine. Well, I mean, your dad burst a blood vessel in his eye just now trying to move the stereo, but he says it doesn't even hurt.

Anyway, I hope I didn't mess anything up, but I saw Marie Caputo in the grocery store just now, and she was down in the mouth as usual about Holly (and telling me how lucky I was that you only date boys like Dave—whatever happened to him, anyway? He was so sweet) and I might have mentioned something about how she shouldn't think of Holly's marrying Mark as losing a daughter, but as gaining a son.

Then I remembered she's not supposed to know anything about Holly marrying Mark this week.

I hope I didn't let the cat out of the bag, or anything!

And as for that Cal, well, I agree, Saudi Arabia is a very boring subject for a book.

But still, he looked quite nice in that turtleneck he was wearing on *Charlie Rose*. I think it might have been cashmere. I'm just saying it wouldn't hurt to give the boy a chance.

And what do you mean, I shouldn't worry about him falling in love with you? I don't want to hear that kind of negative talk from you, young lady. You know you're irresistible. At least when you don't have PMS and you wear your hair out of your eyes.

Love,
Mom

To: Claire Harris <charris2004@freemail.com>
Fr: Jane Harris <jane@wondercat.com>
Re: Holly

MOM! THIS IS REALLY REALLY BAD!!!! I TOLD YOU NOT TO SAY
ANYTHING!!!

DO NOT SAY ANYTHING ELSE TO ANYONE UNTIL I TELL YOU
IT'S OK!

AND DON'T GO TO THE KROGER SAV-ON OR ANYWHERE
ELSE WHERE YOU MIGHT MEET HOLLY'S MOM!!!!!!!!!!!!!!!!!!!

J

To: Darrin Caputo <darrin.caputo@caputographics.com>
Fr: Jane Harris <jane@wondercat.com>
Re: Your mother

Oh my God, Darrin, does your mother know? About Holly and
Mark, I mean? Because I think my mother might have spilled
something. YOU know, right? I mean about them—

Oh my God, what if you're not supposed to know either? Holly
will KILL me if she finds out I told. She really wanted to surprise
you, on account of all those times you kidded her that she would
settle on one guy.

But whatever, this is an emergency. Holly's been acting all weird
since this afternoon, kind of down, and I think it might be because she heard from your mother. Darrin, Holly and Mark are
eloping this week! But everything is going wrong! The marriage
license people here in Le Marche aren't cooperating and your

uncle's oven doesn't work and there's this friend of Mark's who keeps saying the meanest things and—

Well, never mind all that. Anyway, you have GOT to keep your mom from figuring out what's going on, because I don't think Holly can take much more. Can you do something to throw her off the scent? Pretend you and Bobby are adopting or something?

Oh, I know! Tell her you're going to have a sex change operation!!! YES!!! Transgenderism will TOTALLY distract her!

Thanks, Darrin, you're the best! I'll write when I know more. . . .

AND DON'T TELL HOLLY I TOLD!!!! WHEN YOU HEAR SHE'S MARRIED, ACT SURPRISED!!!!!!!!!!!

J

Travel Diary of

~~Holly Caputo and Mark Levine~~

Jane Harris

AAAARRRGH. MOTHERS. I mean, I love her and everything—
how great is it to have someone in your life who, every time
you complain about a guy, is all, "He must be secretly in love
with you, that's why he's acting that way"?—but she has the
BIGGEST MOUTH.

I mean, this is a CRISIS, her spilling the beans—well, sort
of, anyway—to Mrs. Caputo.

And really, it's my own fault, because I never should have
said anything to her in the first place . . . to Mom, I mean. She
hasn't been able to hold a secret since . . . well, ever.

I just don't know how to fix it. This new crisis, I mean. This
is something Frau Schumacher's not going to be able to shout
at anybody about until it's, you know, done.

As soon as I got that email I went to Holly and Mark's
room—Holly went to bed as soon as we got home from the
restaurant, saying she had a headache . . . and no wonder, if
she'd heard from her mother the way I suspected she had—
and tapped on the door, since I knew Mark was down on the
terrazza having a nightcap with Cal.

Anyway, Holly called "Come in" all weakly—she looked
awful! Just AWFUL! I asked her if she'd heard from her mom
and she said she had, and I said I was sorry and that it was
all my fault.

Holly was just sweet as could be, and told me not to
worry, that she didn't blame me a bit. . . .

But it's all my fault. I just know it.

"I'm starting to think this wedding's just not to be, anyway," Holly said.

!!!!!!!!!!!!!!!!!

I told her that she HAS to marry Mark. That if she doesn't, it will shake my faith in romantic love to its very core. That the two of them were made for each other. I mean, look at the way he has those really big feet, and hers are so little and dainty! And look how she hates tomatoes and he loves them, and he hates sauerkraut and she loves it. . . . They routinely finish each other's plates.

And they BOTH love <u>Seventh Heaven</u>, not just Holly. Mark won't admit it, but HE doesn't answer the phone when I call on Monday nights, either. And Holly says HE always cries at the end, too.

I told all this to Holly and she just nodded weakly and said she guessed she was just tired. So I told her to go to sleep and that she'd feel better in the morning.

But of course this was not the most reassuring of conversations. So I went downstairs to find Mark—and ran smack into him coming up the stairs, since he said he wasn't feeling so hot either, and had decided to go to bed early as well.

So I grabbed him by the arm and dragged him into one of the empty bedrooms—I guess Cal didn't end up taking the pink one after all—and told him what happened with my mom and Holly's mom.

All he said was, "Aw, Jane. I wouldn't worry about that."

"But Holly's devastated!" I cried. I can't believe he couldn't see that! I mean, it's true I've known Holly since the first grade when her family moved onto my street and I went over and rang the bell and asked if they had any little girls for me to play with.

But Mark's been living with her for the past two years! You would think he'd know her at least as well as I do! I mean, they sleep in the same bed!

"Holly's just tired," Mark said. "She's beat, same as me. It's been kind of a long day."

"Then . . ." I have to admit, I had tears in my own eyes, as if I had just watched the end of <u>Babe</u> or an episode of <u>Seventh Heaven</u>, "you're not thinking of calling it off?"

"The wedding?" Mark looked down at me like I was crazy. "No way. Why would I do that?"

"Well, because—"

And then, before I could stop myself, it all came tumbling out. The truth. About his friend Cal.

I know it wasn't very nice of me. To tattle, I mean. Especially to a groom about his best man. Especially just thirty-six hours before the wedding.

But still. Cal totally deserves it. Who does he think he is, anyway, with his phenylethylamine and his thinking he can sabotage my best friend's wedding by planting doubts in her—or worse, her husband-to-be's—head?

Mark listened to everything I had to say (I talked really <u>sotto voce</u>, so Cal, still down on the terrazza, wouldn't overhear) and, when I was done, he did the weirdest thing.

He threw back his head, and <u>laughed</u>.

Yes! Actually laughed! Like it was the most hilarious thing he'd ever heard!

Frankly, I don't see what was so funny. I mean, if <u>I</u> had been about to get married, and I found out one of my friends was planning on using whatever influence she had over me to talk me out of it—

Well, that's just ridiculous, because if I were set on marrying someone, no one would be able to talk me out of it.

Which is exactly what Mark said to me.

Mark: "Janie, Cal's one of the best friends I've ever had. But no one is going to talk me out of marrying Holly. Particularly not someone whose own marriage was such a spectacular disaster."

This information dried my tears right up.

And I know it was really wrong of me, but I totally couldn't help going, "You knew Valerie, Cal's ex?"

Mark: "Knew her? Yeah, I knew her. About as well as he did, anyway. And for about as long. I was there the night they met."

Me: (extremely interested in this) "Really? And was she really beautiful? She was a model, right?"

Mark just shrugged. I have to admit, he didn't look so hot. But maybe it was the light from the harsh Italian bulb inside a pinky shade.

Mark: "She was all right. Not my type. Tall and blonde and skinny. You know. Typical model."

Me: (nodding sympathetically) "And very, very dumb, right?"

Mark: "Well, not so dumb that she didn't know she'd latched onto a guy flush with his first-ever paycheck. And the whole modeling thing wasn't going as well as she'd have liked. Contrary to what she was apparently led to believe by the Barbizon School or wherever she trained, modeling is quite hard. You have to get up early. And she didn't like that."

Wow! Mark really hated Cal's wife! He hardly EVER says anything bad about anyone, seeing as how he's, you know, nice and all.

"So . . ." I still wasn't sure it was safe to leave Mark alone with his friend. "If Cal DOES try to talk you out of marrying Holly . . ."

"He's not going to try any such thing," Mark said. But at my skeptically raised eyebrows, he added, "Fine, well, he can try, but it won't work. I can't believe you, of all people, would even think such a thing is possible, Janie. I love Holly, and no one's going to talk me out of marrying her. Not Cal. Not my mother. Not even Holly's mother. Nothing is going to stand in the way of our doing it. NOTHING."

Sadly, the conclusion of this very inspiring speech was somewhat anti-climactic, since about the time he uttered the words 'Holly's mother,' Mark got kind of green around the gills, and went, "Um. Excuse me. I don't feel so hot all of a sudden" and ducked into the bathroom, from which some explosive sounds soon emanated.

So I wished him well and left him for my own room, happy in the knowledge that, should Cal try anything, Mark, at least, would stay strong.

As for Holly . . . well, we'll have to see. I THINK she knows she's doing the right thing.

I'll work on her some more in the car tomorrow.

Now to let Cal Langdon know he won't be able to talk Mark out of it. . . .

Travel Diary of

~~Holly Caputo and Mark Levine~~

Jane Harris

Oh my God, you'll never guess what I just caught Cal Langdon doing!!!! Mr. Hardened News Journalist was down on the ter-razza, holding out a plate of Zio Matteo's tuna to all of these scrawny stray cats that had come slinking over to the villa from the stables.

He jumped like I'd shot him when I said his name, and the cats all ran, but I saw them.

Oh, I saw them, all right.

Between the being-afraid-of-snakes thing, and now a soft spot for cats, I guess Mr. No Heart might just have one after all.

Still, I didn't let on that I knew. About his heart, I mean. Instead, I told him—because I couldn't help myself—that I'd spoken to Mark, and that he (Cal) was living in a fantasy world if he thought he could talk him (Mark) out of marrying Holly on Wednesday.

To my surprise, Cal just totally ignored that. Instead— while staring at my Christian Louboutins, as usual—he asked me instead if I knew Indian women sometimes decorate their feet with henna.

?????????????

There is something seriously wrong with this guy.

Me: "Um, no. But I do know if they show their ankles in public, they can be punished by having their feet cut off. Why don't you write a book about how unfair that is, instead of what's going to happen to the Saudis when the oil runs out?"

Cal: (finally looking away from my feet) "Do you think women's lives there are going to get easier when their country is essentially shut off from contact with the outside world, due to their no longer having a product we want to ex- ploit? Or do you think they'll get harder?"

Me: "Harder, obviously. But what can I do about it? Use fewer water bottles?"

Cal: "Yes, overconsumption of petroleum-based products is a leading cause of global warming."

Seriously, I can't believe he ever got any woman to marry him. I mean, with a line like that. Even a model.

Hey, maybe that's why he only dates foreigners now. Be-cause they can't tell what's coming out of his mouth.

Me: "Well, then maybe we'd better just use it all up and get it over with so we run out already and can go back to how things were before."

Cal: "You mean before they started bottling spring water and selling it for a buck fifty a pop and pretending it's better for you than tap?"

!!!!!!!!!!!!!!

Me: "I don't know. You're the one who wrote a book about it. Why do you keep looking at my feet, anyway?"

Cal: "Why do you keep looking at my crotch?"

I SWEAR TO GOD!!! THAT IS WHAT HE ASKED ME!!!!

Then THANK GOD Peter showed up from out of nowhere and went, "Jane Harris, I am hearing your woice and knew you vere avake. Now will you be drawing me the sketches of Vunder-cat you promised for my Veb site?" and handed me a sketch pad and some markers.

So I said, "Of course, Peter," in my most gracious voice—even though I was FREAKING OUT about the crotch thing—and drew him about fifty Wondercat sketches, while Cal sat there scowling in the candlelight and going, "Peter, shouldn't you be in bed by now? Don't you have school in the morning?"

But of course Peter explained that he goes to Internet school and doesn't have to log on by any particular time.

And all I could think was, what if Peter hadn't shown up right then? I mean, Cal and I had basically been in each other's face over that whole petroleum thing. Close enough that, you know, it occurred to me—just kind of randomly—that if we didn't hate each other so much, we might have started, I don't know.

Kissing or something.

I KNOW! I don't even LIKE him. He's a totally pompous know-it-all—a modelizer!

But still, he does kind of . . . <u>exude</u> something. I don't know what it is. I mean, I was having a pretty good time hating his guts right up until I saw him with those cats. CATS!!!! HE LIKES CATS!!!!

And he so clearly didn't WANT to be caught feeding them. He looked so GUILTY when he saw me.

And then, when we got close there, during our little argument . . .

BAM. There it was. I couldn't stop noticing how handsome he looked in the candlelight, with those too-blue eyes and his messy Brad Pitt-y hair and his shirt open a little at the neck so I saw a tiny bit of that chest he'd had out on display earlier by the pool and—

WHAT'S WRONG WITH ME??? I ALREADY HAVE A BOYFRIEND!!!!!!!!!

Well, okay, not really.

But I have one if I want one. All I have to do is go to British Columbia, and WHAM, there he is, the boyfriend. A boyfriend who BELIEVES in love. A boyfriend who would NEVER say love is a mere chemical reaction in the brain caused by surges of phenylethylamine (um, especially since Malcolm doesn't know any words that big).

SO WHY AM I EVEN THINKING ABOUT CAL LANGDON IN THAT WAY????

It can't just be the cat thing. It must be all this fresh air. It DOES things to a girl. As soon as I get back to the city and breathe in good old New York exhaust fumes, I'll be all right again.

I hope.

In the meantime, I've just got to STAY AWAY from him and his pheromones or whatever it is that makes me keep thinking about what it would be like to sleep with Cal Langdon.

Tomorrow I'll make sure to wear my Adidas, too. No guy looks at your feet when you're in your Adidas.

God, how am I supposed to get to sleep NOW?

PDA of Cal Langdon

I have GOT to stay away from prosecco. It makes me do the most damnable things, things I'd never do were I in my right mind . . . feed perfectly fine tuna to a lot of stray cats, for example. Or admire the way the moonlight brings out the highlights in a certain cartoonist's hair . . .

Who drank all the scotch?

✉

To: Jane Harris <jane@wondercat.com>
Fr: Darrin Caputo <darrin.caputo@caputographics.com>
Re: Your mother

ARE YOU SERIOUS???? HOLLY AND MARK ARE ELOPING????
In Castelfidardo?

Well, that's kind of a weird place to do it (have you seen the
whang on that naked accordionist statue in the town square?
That dude is HUNG), but I couldn't be happier for them. OF
COURSE we'll do something to throw Mom off the scent. I don't
know what, exactly. . . . Bobby's going to think something up,
he's better at this kind of thing than I am.

Oh my God, that is just the BEST NEWS. NO ONE deserves a
romantic wedding in Italy more than my sister Holly. Give her a
big kiss from me, and don't worry, I won't tell a SOUL!!!!

Love,
D

✉

To: Jane Harris <jane@wondercat.com>
Fr: Claire Harris <charris2004@freemail.com>
Re: Holly's mother

Really, Jane, you don't have to SHOUT at me. That's what they
call it when you write an email in capital letters, you know.
SHOUTING. And it's very rude.

I didn't mean to say anything to Marie. Obviously. It just slipped
out. You should be a little more understanding, you know. I'm
under a lot of stress these days over at the Salvation Army, where
I've been volunteering. The past three Saturdays in the row I've

signed up to work in the thrift shop, and each and every time they've put me in the back, ironing the donated baby clothes! I know I'm very good with an iron, but can't they at least once let me work the cash register? Or help the poor people find the right clothes for their body type?

But no. "Oh, look, here comes Claire. Get out the ironing board."

I am seriously considering quitting and going over to Good Will. Marcy Clark told me they don't make anybody iron ANYTHING over there.

Plus your dad touched a mango yesterday, and you know how allergic he is. I WARNED him there was a mango in the fruit bowl. I was going to use it in the fruit salad I'm bringing to the gourmet potluck at Helen Fogarty's this weekend.

But Dad had to go and cut it up, thinking it was a papaya, and now he's got hives all over his hands and arms. I've been putting calamine lotion on them, but I think we're going to have to take another trip over to the Promptcare for some prednisone. . . .

So don't be so snappy with me, young lady. I have a lot going on.

I don't know what Marie's problem is, anyway. At least *her* daughter's got a man who wants to marry her. All MY daughter has is a development deal with the Cartoon Network. And while Daddy and I are very proud of you, sweetie, you can't exactly honeymoon with a development deal, now, can you? Or gaze into a development deal's sweet angelic eyes while you're changing its diaper.

So cut your mother some slack.

Love,
Mom

Travel Diary of

~~Holly Caputo and Mark Levine~~

Jane Harris

Okay. Okay. Everything is going to be all right. I can figure this out. I can totally figure this out—

No, I can't. This is a disaster. A total and complete disaster. What am I going to do????

✉

To: Listserv <Wundercat@wundercatlives.com>
Fr: Peter Schumacher <webmaster@wundercatlives.com>
Re: JANE HARRIS

Good morning fellow lovers of Wundercat! There is BIG NEWS today about JANE HARRIS! Her friends who will be getting the marriage both eat the bad oysters last night, and this morning are sick as dogs! YES! They cannot get up out of the beds!

And this is bad because they are supposed to get the form from the Consulate of the US today, so they can have the marriage tomorrow!

But when I drove by the villa this morning on my motorino, to bring JANE HARRIS fresh brotchen, she is very upset, and says, "Ask your grandmother what can be done." So I get my grandmother, and she comes to the villa and says that nothing can be done from eating the bad oyster, they will have to wait until it has passed through.

Which, if it does not do soon, there will be no marriage tomorrow!

So this is BAD NEWS for JANE HARRIS.

I will keep you informed as news continues! This is Peter Schumacher, #1 Fan Of Wundercat!

Wundercat Lives—4eva!
Peter

Travel Diary of
~~Holly Caputo and Mark Levine~~
Jane Harris

Oysters. They just HAD to have the oysters.

I warned them. They can't say I didn't warn them. Who eats raw shellfish in a foreign country, I ask you? Who? This isn't Japan. Italy is not known for its raw seafood. What were they THINKING?

Poor Mark. I guess that's what I heard him throwing up last night. And he's STILL throwing it up. He can barely move from the bed.

And Holly . . . my God, when I knocked on their bedroom door to see why they weren't up yet for our drive to Rome, and Holly answered, she looked like . . . well, the undead. She hasn't looked this bad since that Fourth of July we invented the drink with the watermelon balls and vodka (Rockets' Red Glare).

"I don't think there's going to be any wedding," she said. And then had to run to the bathroom.

What could I do but follow her? It's not like I haven't held her hair for her while she barfed plenty of times before—Rockets' Red Glare in particular.

"Holly," I said, as gently as I could, when she'd sunk back down onto the bathroom tiles in exhaustion. "You guys HAVE to make it to Rome today. You know tomorrow's the only day the mayor said he could fit your wedding into the schedule."

Which turned out not to be the right thing to say, since Holly promptly started to cry.

"I know!" she wailed. "But what can we do? We wouldn't last five minutes in the car. We'd have to pull over every thirty seconds to throw up. Oh, God, Janie. It's over. We're not getting married. Not now, anyway. Not in Italy. And the way everything seems to be going against us . . . maybe not ever. Maybe my mother is right. Maybe HIS mother is right. Maybe we should just forget it. Maybe it's just not meant to be."

I know! I couldn't believe what I was hearing.

"Not meant to be? Holly, I know you don't feel well, but are you NUTS? You can't just forget it. You guys HAVE to get married. And you have to get married here, in Italy."

She just looked at me through miserable, swollen eyes. "Why?"

"Because I already told Darrin!" was what I ALMOST said. I remembered that I wasn't supposed to have told anyone, though, and at the last possible second changed it to, "Because it's what you've always wanted to do. You've been planning this forever. And Mark wants it, too, I know it. More than anything. You can't just give up because of a little food poisoning!"

To which she responded by barfing some more.

I got her back to bed, somehow. Then I found Peter outside with more of those breakfast rolls, and asked him to get his grandmother. Frau Schumacher came over, looking very concerned, and went in to see the stricken couple. Her expression, when she came out of the room again, was grave.

"No good," she said to me. "Zey vill not make the drive to Roma and back today. Tomorrow, yes. But not today."

"But it HAS to be today," I cried. "There's no other time! The mayor said Wednesday was the only day . . .and we leave Friday anyway."

But I know Frau Schumacher is right. She's downstairs making some hot broth for Mark and Holly to choke down—it doesn't matter if the lights go out right now, since it's daytime. A beautiful day, as a matter of fact. The sun is beaming down, and the pool is sparkling, and the breeze is causing the palm fronds to sway gently. . . .

Damn it! Why did they eat those oysters?

And why does this country have to be so BACKWARD??? If a person wants to get married here, and has all the right forms from back in the US, why CAN'T she??? Why do they have to send her all over creation for MORE forms??? Is it some kind of test to see how dedicated they are to the idea of being married? I mean, it's just a FORM, <u>anybody</u> can get a form—

Holy crap.

<u>Anybody</u> can get a form.

PDA of Cal Langdon

Honest to God, I don't know how this happened. Last thing I knew, I was sleeping blissfully.

Then, not five minutes ago, a small but very determined missile hit my bed, tearing off my very comfortably arranged sheets and shouting in my ear that it was time to get up and get in the car.

I vaguely recall that this missile seemed feminine in form—not an unpleasant way to be roused. Until I realized just which, precisely, female the form belonged to.

Then a cup of coffee was shoved in my hand, and I was urged to dress. Which I did. And then, when I wandered downstairs, wondering what was happening and why Frau Schumacher was at the stove, making what appeared to be soup of some kind, I was very rudely snatched, shoved outside, pushed into the passenger seat of the car, and driven off at considerable speed down the driveway by someone who is apparently not exactly familiar with a stick shift.

A someone who looks remarkably like Jane Harris.

On crystal meth.

Oh, that's right. It's all coming back to me now. We're supposed to be escorting Mark and Holly to Rome so that they can apply for some sort of form at the US embassy.

Except that for some reason, Mark and Holly do not appear to be in the car with us.

"Um, Jane," I ask, in what I hope is a soothing tone that won't startle the young woman beside me, looking so wild-eyed behind the wheel. "Aren't we forgetting something? Or should I say, someone? A *pair* of someones?"

She seems barely to register my presence in the car, she's checking so frantically in the rearview mirror for a hole in the oncoming traffic so she can make the turn onto the strada principale.

"Mark and Holly have food poisoning," is her surprising response. "They won't be able to make it. We have to go without them."

"I see." I'm trying to sound as reasonable as I can, seeing as how she is clearly unaccustomed to driving and conversing at the same time. "And am I to understand that we'll be applying for whatever form it is they're lacking?"

"Yeah." She tosses something into my lap. Looking down, I see that it's a pair of passports. "Don't worry, I got their passports. Their birth certificates, too."

This strikes me as highly amusing.

"And do you really think that the US embassy is going to issue this form to us just because we're holding our friends' passports and birth certificates," I ask, playing along, "simply because we ask them to, as a favor?"

"No," comes Jane Harris's somewhat startling reply. "They're going to issue the form because we're going to tell them we're Mark Levine and Holly Caputo."

This is definitely the funniest thing I've heard all morning.

"Isn't that going to be a little difficult?" I ask. "Seeing as how Mark is dark-haired and wears glasses, and I'm fair-haired, and have twenty/twenty vision?"

Next thing I knew, Mark's glasses were hurled into my lap.

"I filched them off his bedside table," my kidnapper explained. "And you can't tell his hair is that dark in the picture. It's black and white. You could say it got bleached in the sun, or whatever, if anybody asks. Which they won't."

Sadly, I'm starting to wake up now. Even more sadly, this is all starting to seem less and less like a dream, and more and more like a real-life nightmare.

"Wait a minute. Are you serious?" Because she LOOKS totally serious. And we are hurtling down the strada principale—past signs that say ROMA—at a very serious speed. "We're going to POSE as Mark and Holly?"

"Why not?" She is passing a large truck carrying—predictably—numerous live chickens, stacked high. They squawk at us hysterically. "All we have to do is show our IDs and sign some forms. What's the big?"

"The BIG," I say (since when did people start leaving off the word 'deal' when asking what the big deal is, anyway? Is this an artist thing? Mary does this, as well), "is that that is what I believe is called forgery. And probably perjury. And maybe a whole bunch of other things, as well."

Jane Harris has not once turned her head in my direction. She is wearing sunglasses, which makes it extremely difficult to see her eyes, and thus whether or not she has gone absolutely and completely bonkers.

"Oh, please," she's saying. "Like we'll get caught. Mark's a doctor, remember? No one can read his signature anyway. And I'm an artist. I've been forging Holly's mom's name on report cards and tardy slips for ages. I think I can easily manage to do Holly's. You can just scribble something for Mark's."

This has progressed from a pleasant game to an entirely unpleasant situation.

"Jane," I try again. "Are you kidnapping me and forcing me to go to Rome with you to commit fraud against the US government?"

She refuses to see the gravity of the situation, replying merely, "Oh, shut up and drink your coffee and keep writing in your little machine there, if it makes you feel better. There's some of Peter's brotchen in the back if you want it. And I'm not kidnapping you. I'm not demanding a ransom from anybody for you. As if anybody'd pay it if I did."

There must be some sort of Italian law that forbids this sort of thing . . . taking advantage of a man in a less than wakeful state, and forcing him to drive hundreds of kilometers to a city he only just came from a day or two before, where he will be forced to impersonate another man. . . .

She's wearing Adidas, but I can see still see the cat tattoo. Is it because it's so early, or can it really be . . . well . . . winking at me?

Travel Diary of

~~Holly Caputo and Mark Levine~~
Jane Harris

This is going to work. This HAS to work.

I know Cal doesn't think it's going to (big surprise).

But what does HE know? He's been against those two getting together since before any of this even started. Look at him now, asking for the key to the men's room. He STILL looks as if he doesn't know quite what hit him. His hair is sticking up in the back in the most peculiar—but strangely erotic—fashion.

EROTIC???? What am I THINKING???? I am on a MISSION here. I can't be thinking about sex at a time like this!!!

This HAS to work. We're halfway to Rome now, and it's only a little after ten. We should get there before lunch . . . well, probably just as they're closing for lunch.

But that's okay. It's the US embassy. They can't POSSIBLY take a four-hour lunch at the US embassy. They're AMERICAN, for God's sake. They probably take an hour lunch, like all normal people. So we can fill out the form, get the APOSTILLE, and get back on the road by two or three o'clock, and be home before dark.

PLEASE let them only take an hour for lunch. . . .

✉

To: Jane Harris <jane@wondercat.com>
Fr: Holly Caputo <holly.caputo@thenyjournal.com>
Re: Where are you?

Sorry if there's typos in this, I can't really see very well, my head is pounding so much. But where are you guys? Frau Schumacher—who is being so sweet to us—says she doesn't know, that you just took off without a word to anyone. . . .

Well, I'm glad, anyway. I mean, that you're not here to see this. I hope you're off having fun somewhere. I'm so sorry for spoiling your vacation. And the wedding. I know how much you were looking forward to it. Almost as much as me—02q9375)(*&@

Sorry, I couldn't stop crying there for a minute, and lost sight of the keyboard.

Anyway, I'm glad you and Cal seem to be getting along now, and hope you've gone to Loredo or somewhere. There really is some lovely sightseeing in the area. The Madonna's house, for instance. Apparently angels lifted it and brought it from the Holy Land and dropped it here in Le Marche. . . .

I was just wondering, though, have you seen Mark's glasses? He swears he left them on the nightstand, but now they're gone.

Not that it matters, since the only place he's going is the bathroom. Still, it's strange.

Well, write when you get a chance. Oh, God, not again—I have to go—

Holly

Travel Diary of

~~Holly Caputo and Mark Levine~~

Jane Harris

We're here!!!! The US embassy!!! We made it with minutes to
spare!!!! Cal took over the driving after the Mobil station, and
we practically FLEW the next few hundred kilometers.

.Plus, he insisted on taking this different route, which didn't
go through the mountains. Which was good, since I forgot my
Dramamine. We reached Rome at five minutes to twelve.

And now we're here!!!!

I must say, this place isn't at all like what I would have
thought. I mean, inside, it's kind of like my dentist's office.
There are all these chairs and people waiting and a glassed-in
reception desk and you have to take a number (well, that's
more like at my butcher's than at my dentist's, but whatever).
Our number is 92.

I have to say, the Modelizer is being much better about
this than I'd thought he'd be, judging by his initial reaction in
the car, when he finally woke up. I admit I kind of shanghaied
him. I knew he wasn't really awake when I made him get in the
car.

Still, he's taking it like a total sport. He hasn't uttered a
peep of anti-marriage propaganda all morning. Maybe the
guy's finally coming around after all.

<u>Fat-bottomed girls/They make the rockin' world go
round</u>—

Oh my God, I can't BELIEVE that's all we had to listen to
the whole drive! We are heading STRAIGHT to a music store
the minute we get out of here and buying another CD. I don't
care what. ANYTHING but Queen.

Although I have to admit, Freddy Mercury is totally grow-
ing on me. <u>We are the champions, my friends</u>—

Ooooooh, they're calling a number. 92, 92, let it be 92!!!!!!
28?

28?????

Cal just looked at me and went, "Looks like we're going to be here awhile."

Understatement of the year.

And all they've got to read is <u>International Time</u> magazine! <u>International Time</u> is like watered down real <u>Time</u>, which is already so watered down it's like watching the local news, without the grisly power mower accidental decapitations.

I'm going to DIE.

But it's worth it. It's worth it for Holly. This is for her. And Mark. This is—

OH MY GOD, THIS IS MY WEDDING PRESENT TO THEM!!!!

YES!!! Why didn't I think of it before??? Since I can't give them this journal—um, especially not now that I've mentioned Cal's pheromones—I'll give them this . . . the form that will allow them to be married tomorrow.

Genius. Total genius. This is MUCH better than candlesticks or something dopey like that.

Ooooooh, they're calling another number . . . 92. COME ON!!! Maybe 29 through 91 left already.

Wait. That's not a number. The guy's putting a sign up on the glass. What's it say?

Office Closed
for Lunch
12:30 P.M.—
3:30 P.M.

Chiuso
12.30 a 15.30

PDA of Cal Langdon

I can't believe this is happening. I can't believe this is what I've been reduced to. I'm in Rome, possibly one of the most gastronomically diverse cities in the world, renowned for its cuisine, the long and languid lunch hour . . .

And I'm having warmed over eggplant pizza at Amici Amore, a ubiquitous Italian fast-food joint.

There's a VIDEO ARCADE in the back.

I should have put my foot down. I should have explained that when a Roman hangs a sign that says the office will be closed until a certain hour, he absolutely means it.

But no. She kept insisting. She's convinced if we scarf down a quick meal and get back to the embassy, we will somehow move up further in the line. Even though there is no line, and she is, in fact, holding a number that will doubtlessly not be called until tomorrow, or possibly next week.

Why didn't I insist? This trip didn't have to be an entire waste. We could be having a leisurely, romantic lunch in some restaurant's cozy back garden right now—listening to doves coo rather than the sound of asteroids being blasted by a computer-generated laser gun—enjoying the sunshine instead of the obscene purple neon of this place.

Why did I let her have her way? Especially when her way is so often so very, very wrong?

I don't even *like* eggplant.

I have to take a stand. When she gets back from the ladies' room, I *will* take a stand. I'll tell her this whole scheme is destined for failure. I'm going to tell her that this is a ridiculous waste of time, and that we're heading back to the villa to salvage what's left of our vacation time. I'm going to tell her—

Here she comes.

Oh. She says we're leaving.

~~Holly Caputo and Mark Levine~~
Jane Harris

Stupid restaurant! Stupid Rome! Stupid Italy!

What is the DEAL with the bathrooms here???? Seriously. I had to go at that stupid Amici Amore, so I head on off to the ladies', and first off, the whole place is lit by black light— why? Oh, because (Cal just told me) it's to make it impossible for junkies to find a vein if they take it into their heads to shoot up in there.

But that's not the worst of it. Oh, no!

THERE WAS NO TOILET. No. None. Where a toilet ought to be was a hole. A HOLE IN THE FLOOR. With two cut-out foot-prints on either side of it, and two bars to hold onto.

Okay, maybe ITALIAN WOMEN know what this is. But I've never seen anything like it, and I have NO IDEA what you're supposed to do there. Obviously you put your feet on the cut-outs. And clearly you're supposed to hold onto the bars.

And then do what? Squat?

I DO NOT SQUAT.

Oh my God, what is WRONG with this country?

Cal says he knows of another restaurant we can go that isn't far from here, and that he swears will actually have a toilet in the ladies' room. I'm so traumatized, I'm actually letting him drive me there. A HOLE. A HOLE. What does Amici Amore even MEAN, anyway? BIG HOLE HERE?

Oh. Cal says it means Love Friends (<u>amici</u> = friends, <u>amore</u> = love).

Love Your Friends. Ha! Fuck Your Friends is more like it. By telling them to go there. TO SEE THE HOLE.

Where is he TAKING me, anyway? I told Cal we better not go too far from the consulate, since I'm SURE they won't actually be taking a three-hour lunch. I mean, they're AMERICAN, for crying out loud. That sign was probably just a scam to throw off the people with dumb, petty problems like lost passports or whatever. It won't daunt ME. I'm in this for the long haul. I don't care how long it takes. I'm going to sit there until I get—

Oooooh, what a beautiful building!

Hotel Eden

Sesto piano, la nostra terrazza ristorante da dove si può ammirare uno dei più bei panorami sulla Città Eterna.

Gli altri ce la invidiano, noi ve la offriamo.
Oltre all'incantevole panorama, "La Terrazza dell'Eden" è da segnalare per i prestigiosi riconoscimenti tra cui uno Stella Michelin.

Hotel Eden

The Sixth Floor of Rome:

Our Restaurant which will delight you with the best Mediterranean cuisine accompanied by the unrivalled view over the Seven Hills of Rome.

"La Terrazza dell'Eden" is one of the most prestigious gourmet Restaurant in Rome and is proud to be awarded with one Michelin Star.

Degustazione

Carpaccio scottato di branzino e capesante
con olio extra vergine al basilico

Mezzi rigatoni grezzi all'aragosta con crema di zucca

Ravioli di barbabietola con polenta e taleggio

Coda di rospo al forno con speck e lenticchie

Medaglioni di vitello in crosta di pecorino senese
con zucchine croccanti

Crostata aromatizzata con mele e mandorle,
semifreddo alle nocciole e Ferrari Maximum Demi-sec

Caffe
Delizie friabili

Gourmet Menu

Warm sea-bass and scallops carpaccio,
extra virgin olive oil flavoured with basil

Rigatoni with lobster and pumpkin cream

Beetroot Ravioli filled with polenta and taleggio cheese

Oven-baked monkfish with smoked ham and lentils

Veal medallions in a Pecorino cheese crust,
crispy courgettes and marjoram

Apples and almonds on pastry, hazelnuts semifreddo
and Ferrari Maximum Demi-sec sauce

Coffee
Petits fours

PDA of Cal Langdon

Now *this* is more like it. Sunshine. A nice prosecco. Panoramic views of the entire city. La Terrazza Dell-Eden at the Hotel Eden never fails in a pinch. Since 1889, it's been pampering guests, battle-worn from Roman sightseeing and psychically scarred by the traffic. This is where we ought to have come from the start.

Let that be a lesson to us all: Never let an artist choose the restaurant.

Travel Diary of
~~Holly Caputo and Mark Levine~~
Jane Harris

Oh my God, I totally know this place! This is where Britney Spears and Pink stayed when they were filming that Pepsi commercial in the Colosseum, the one they showed at the Superbowl! And the photographers got all these shots of Britney up on this very sundeck, hanging out with that married dancer.

Cool.

It's just GORGEOUS here, all yellow and green, with this view to DIE for. You can see all the way to the Vatican. You can wave to the Pope. Hi, Pope! Holly's mom sends her love! I'm sure Dan Brown didn't mean it!

And prosecco . . . yum. The food is delicious, too.

But we better hurry up. The office opens again in 45 minutes. Cal wants to go to the Spanish Steps, which are down the street from here. Like we've got time for sightseeing.

Still, I don't want to say no. He's being so NICE, all of a sudden. I mean, taking me here, and showing me this place, and buying lunch, and just being . . . well, like a nice guy, for a change.

And he looks so . . . well, hot too, sitting there in his jeans and chambray shirt. He finally got his hair under control, I see—which is good, if he ever hopes to pass for Mark, who doesn't have as much of it as he does—hair, I mean. The sun is really bringing out his golden highlights.

And he's telling such funny stories, about things he and Mark did in school. You can hardly tell he's the same person who just the other day was insisting that marriage is an outdated institution, and that love is nothing but a chemical reaction in the brain.

You know, between this and the cat thing last night, I'm almost starting to LIKE him.

Maybe that's just the prosecco. God, this is so <u>romantic</u>, sitting up here on top of the city, looking down on all the treetops and ancient ruins, drinking sparkly wine and eating these luscious olives. I can't believe Holly and Mark are missing it—

Holly and Mark! We've got to go!!!!

✉

To: Jane Harris < jane@wondercat.com>
Fr: Claire Harris < charris2004@freemail.com >
Re: You

I don't know if you're just ignoring me now, or if something's happened to you. I hope it's the former, of course. I was flipping through the channels last night and I happened to see that on the Travel Channel they were doing a show on the lesser-traveled regions of Italy, so I watched it, and sure enough, they did a story on Le Marche, and they said there are WOLVES there.

Yes. WOLVES. In the hills.

I hope there are no hills near Holly's uncle's villa, and that if so, there are no wolves in them. And that you're keeping your window closed at night. Because wolves can jump very high. At least according to this documentary.

I suppose you aren't writing back because you're angry about my telling Holly's mother that she is gaining a son, not losing a daughter. I still don't see how Marie is going to extrapolate from this that Mark and Holly are eloping in Italy.

But I just thought I'd let you know that it looks like Marie is going to have a lot more important things to worry about soon: Daddy and I were just at the Promptcare for a splinter he got in his foot (I TOLD him the dining room floor needs sanding) and ran into Holly's sister-in-law Brandy, who was there with little Heather because she'd stuck a Red Hot up her nose.

Heather, not Brandy.

Anyway, according to Brandy, the Caputos are fit to be tied because Darrin just announced that he's getting married. To his boyfriend, Bobby. Apparently, they are having some sort of commitment ceremony on the steps of City Hall to rub the mayor's nose in it.

And I already phoned her—I HAD to, to let her know Angela di Blasi has the flu and book club is going to have to be at my house this week—and she was STILL in hysterics over the fact that Darrin is inviting the paper to cover the event and Father Roberto will know Darrin is gay.

I hope you're happy now.

Nancy Jansen wants to know if you'll autograph a copy of *Wondercat: The Early Years* for her nephew Jeff. I told her you would. She's sending it to you in New York with a self-addressed stamped envelope so you can just pop it in the mail back to her when you're done.

Love,
Mom

~~Holly Caputo and Mark Levine~~
Jane Harris

Those Spanish Steps weren't anything so big. I mean, they were all smooth from being walked on so much, since they're like three hundred years old. They are definitely a safety hazard. I nearly twisted my ankle a couple of times going down them.

And yeah, okay, so Shelley's house was right next door. Shelley. Wasn't he the one whose wife wrote <u>Frankenstein</u>?

I don't know why Cal got so tight-lipped when I asked him this. How am I supposed to know stuff about literature? I was an art major. I bet <u>he</u> doesn't know that Michelangelo got so sick of people complimenting him on his David statue's hands that he cut them off.

So I asked him if he knew this, and he said he didn't. Also that he didn't understand why, if so many people liked the hands, Michelangelo would cut them off.

So I explained about how artists want people to view their work as a whole, not parts. If people were too busy concentrating on the hands, they wouldn't see the rest of the statue. And that's not what Michelangelo wanted . . . to make a great pair of hands. He wanted to make a great <u>statue</u>.

I could tell he was impressed by this. I think it made up for when I told him about the Britney thing back at the Hotel Eden. He'd looked kind of scared then.

Whatever! I can't help it if he's the <u>Wall Street Journal</u> and I'm <u>Us Weekly</u>. I obviously have to know SOMETHING or I wouldn't have had to switch over to quarterly income tax returns this year, would I?

There were all these hippies sitting on the steps, playing guitars and singing about peace and stuff. Seeing them obviously reminded Cal of something, since he was like, "I have to go to Western Union." I was all, "Why?" and he was like, "I've got to wire some money to my sister."

So we went to Western Union—fortunately the Spanish Steps are in this totally high-tourist area, so we found one right away—and Cal wired a thousand dollars to someone named Mary Langdon. I know I shouldn't have looked, but what else was I supposed to do?

Besides, I was curious.

Even though he didn't seem to want to talk about it, I asked him how old his sister was, and he said she was 25. So he's her big brother. It's hard to imagine Cal having a little sister.

It's hard to imagine Cal ever having been a kid. But I know he was one, once, because that's how he and Mark came to be friends.

I wonder if Mary's afraid of snakes too.

Also, what she needs a thousand bucks for. Who hits their brother up for a loan that big? That is just bound to get the two of them on the <u>People's Court</u>, you just know it.

But when I asked, Cal was just like, "Mary's an artist," in this tone that suggested he didn't think much of the profession. Um, MY profession.

But whatever. It's sweet of Cal to help out his little sister. I really wouldn't have pegged him as a soft touch for money, but you can tell that girl's got him wrapped around her gold-digging finger. . . .

Generous with his sister. Nice to cats. Scared of snakes.

Still. Modelizer. And anti-marriage. Hmmm.

We're back at the consulate. Cal wanted to give up, but I wouldn't let him.

And I'm glad I didn't, because things are totally speeding up around here. They're on number 67 now. Don't even ask me how.

One annoying thing . . . there's this woman here, about my age, who I guess is trying to get the same form we are. She's marrying this Italian guy named Paolo. I know because she is telling anyone who will listen about it. Paolo is sitting there beside her, this hulk of a man, who doesn't look very happy. She says he doesn't speak any English. Also, that she can barely speak Italian. She says their relationship is based entirely on physical attraction.

Which, if it's true, is kind of sad. For her. I mean, Paolo's hot, don't get me wrong. But she's nothing to write home about. I wonder if Paolo even knows where they are, and that they're getting married.

I just elbowed Cal, who was busy typing into his Blackberry (as usual) and asked him (<u>sotto voce</u>) if he thinks Paolo knows what he's getting himself into. Before he had a chance to reply, the future Mrs. Paolo was all, "He's a mechanic. My parents don't approve. They think I can do better than marry an Italian mechanic who doesn't even speak English. But the sexual energy between us is so strong, how can I deny it?"

This last question was directed solely at me. Unfortunately, I've made eye contact. Now she won't go away.

"I'm Rhonda," she says. "What are you writing in that book there?"

Me: "Nothing."
Rhonda: "Oh, it's a travel journal. I just love journaling. You know, I can't sleep at night if I don't journal about my day. Sometimes I'll go for twenty, thirty pages."
Me: "Wow."
Rhonda: (batting her mouse brown eyelashes at Cal) "So is this your honey?"
Me: "Um. Yes. Yes, I guess it is. This is Mark. I'm Holly."
Rhonda: "Hi, Holly. Hi, Mark. Aren't you handsome! What are

you two doing here? Lose your passport? I'm here to pick up a form I need to get married."

Me: "So I heard. We're here to pick up a form we need to get married too."

Rhonda: "Oh, you two are getting married? Here in Italy? Why, if you don't mind my asking? I mean, what's wrong with Vegas?"

Cal: "We just can't wait, Rhonda. My love for this woman is so strong, I want to marry her right away, and not wait a minute more. I want to make her Mrs. Mark Levine as soon as is humanly possible."

!!!!!!!!!!!!!!!!!!!!!!!!!!!!!!!

He's funny!!!!!

Who knew?????

Rhonda: "Oh, boy, do I ever understand that! It's just like me and Paolo. Have you met my future husband, Paolo? He doesn't speak any English. And I don't speak any Italian. We met three days ago. My cruise ship stopped here, and I went to rent one of those little scooters, and there he was, and . . . well, I wouldn't get back on the cruise ship. My parents are furious with me—it was a cruise to celebrate their thirty-fifth wedding anniversary—but what can I do? Our physical attraction is overwhelming. Paolo's like an animal in bed."

Me: (patting Cal on the knee) "So's this guy."

Cal: (putting his arm around my shoulders) "Now, honey, don't be modest. You're no slouch in the sack, either."

Me: (looking modest) "Well, we did make love—how many times was it yesterday, sweetie?"

Cal: "Seven, I believe."

Me: (trying hard not to notice that Cal Langdon smells really,

really good) "Well, yes, but that's just because you had that sports-related injury."

Cal: "Of course. Yesterday was kind of a slow day, actually."

Rhonda: (looking excited) "Paolo went nine once! In one day!"

We all looked at Paolo with respect. He blinked back at us, without the slightest glimmer of recognition of what we were talking about—or of intelligence.

Me: (Cal's arm is still around me. It's warm. And distracting.) "That is very impressive. No wonder you're marrying him."

Rhonda: "I know. If only my parents would try to understand! They called from Greece last night, and were furious with me when I told them what Paolo and I were doing today. I thought they'd be happy for me—happy that I've finally found the happiness they've been enjoying for thirty-five years! But no. They think I'm crazy, and that in a week we'll be divorced. But of course Paolo's Catholic, and doesn't believe in divorce. I think. It's hard to tell what he's saying, exactly, but I think that's the deal. Anyway, too many people get divorced these days. They don't understand that a marriage takes work and that you can't just move out because your husband's cheating on you or whatever. You've got to stay and try to MAKE it work. You would think Mom and Dad would understand that."

Cal: "Families can be so difficult sometimes."

Rhonda: "Tell me about it. I was journaling about mine just the other night, when it occurred to me that—-"

Consulate guy: "Ninety-two! Number 92!"

THAT'S US!!!!!!!!!!

MARRIAGE OF U.S. CITIZENS IN ROME'S CONSULAR DISTRICT

U.S. citizens planning to marry in Italy must present certain documents and comply with specific requirements of Italian law in order to obtain a marriage license. Marriages cannot be performed by American Consuls, nor on the premises of the American Consulate. The documents required and the procedure to follow are described below.

1. Valid U.S. passport.

2. Birth certificate (original or certified copy).

3. Evidence of the termination of any previous marriage, if applicable (e.g., final divorce decree, annulment decree or death certificate of former spouse).

4. Affidavit, sworn to by the U.S. citizen before a U.S. Consul commissioned in Italy, stating that there is no legal impediment to the marriage, according to the laws of the State of which the citizen is a resident.

NOTE: Once issued, this affidavit must be stamped by the Legalization Office of any *Prefettura* in our Consular District (there is one in every province capital).

5. Atto Notorio: This is a declaration, in addition to the sworn statement described under point 4, stating that according to the laws to which the citizen is subject in the United States there is no obstacle to his/her marriage. This declaration is to be sworn to by two witnesses (a witness may be of any nationality, but must be over 18, with current photo ID), before an Italian Consul outside Italy or, in Italy, before an official at the *Pretura* (Lower Court) in the city where the marriage is to take place. U.S. citizens coming to Italy to be married must obtain this declaration from a Consul of Italy, before leaving the United States.

6. Declaration of Intention: Bride and groom should present all the above documents to the *Ufficio Matrimoni* (Marriage Office) of the *Municipio* (Town Hall) in the city where the marriage will

be performed, and make a "Declaration of Intention to Marry" before an *Ufficiale di Stato Civile* (Civil Registrar).

NOTE: All documents originating out of Italy (birth certificate, divorce decree, etc.) MUST be translated into Italian. Both the original documents and the translations MUST be legalized for use in Italy, with the so-called "APOSTILLE" stamp, in accordance with The Hague Convention on the legalization of foreign public documents. In the U.S., the "APOSTILLE" stamp is placed by the Secretary of State in the state where the document was issued.

I swear the information contained in the documents submitted herewith is both true and valid.

Signature: *Holly Ann Caputo*   Holly Ann Caputo

Signature: _____   Mark Levine

Stato Civile

✉

To: Cal Langdon <cal.langdon@thenyjournal.com>
Fr: Mark Levine <mark.levine@thenyjournal.com>
Re: Wheere adre you?

Hgey. Il cvan;t find mt glasdes. Whiohe are yyi????

MKal

PDA of Cal Langdon

I am an international fugitive from justice. At any moment I expect our car to be overtaken by Interpol, and for Jane and me to be yanked out, slammed to the asphalt, and slapped into cuffs. I suspect Black Hawk helicopters are hovering over us at this very moment. Undoubtedly, we'll be thrown into an Italian prison, and no one will ever hear from us again.

And Rhonda, ultimately, will have the last laugh.

We did it. We perjured ourselves. Committed fraud. Forged our friends' names on government documents.

And they never suspected a thing.

Jane was right. It was a cinch. The guy behind the bulletproof glass barely even glanced at us or our passports. He just asked us where we were staying, made a laconic comment when he found out it was Le Marche, slid the form through the slot for us to sign, then gave us back our documents with the form stamped appropriately. All that waiting—we didn't get back on the road until almost five-thirty—and we were done in five minutes.

I thought Jane was going to have an embolism, she was so delirious with joy. She kept clutching my shirt—not an unpleasant sensation, by the way—and hissing, "It worked! We did it! It worked!" as we rode down the elevator.

Then she seemed to sober up and asked, "What did that man say about Le Marche?"

So I told her he'd said, with a grunt, when he heard where we—I mean, Mark and Holly—were planning on being wed: "Better a corpse in the house than a man from Le Marche."

This filled Jane with righteous anger—"What did he mean by that? What's wrong with Le Marche? I think it's beautiful. Just because it's not overrun with American tourists like Rhonda, that means there's something wrong with it? That pig," etc.

This struck me as highly amusing, considering her sentiments on Le Marche after coming out of the bathroom at the restaurant where we dined just last evening.

Still, it's true that Le Marche is beginning to have a certain charm. I'm actually eager to get back there.

I haven't been eager to get anywhere since . . . well, ever. I wonder what that's about. It seems as if places have always been just that to me . . . places. I can't imagine what's happened to make Le Marche seem less like a place and more like . . . well. Home.

✉

To: Jane Harris <jane@wondercat.com>
Fr: Malcolm Weatherly <malcolmw@snowstyle.com>
Re: Ciao!

Hey, babe! How's it going? Haven't heard from you in a while.
What happened? You run off with some Italian stallion or what?

Drop me a line, will ya? I miss your face.

And I really need to know if you've seen my lucky hat.

M.

~~Holly Caputo and Mark Levine~~
Jane Harris

Talk about weird.

I mean, that I'm stuck in a car with Cal Langdon, and I'm actually having a not-bad time.

What's HAPPENING to me?

Why did he have to put his arm around me back at the consulate? Not that I didn't like it—far from it, of course—but ever since then, I've been wishing it would happen again. Why do I even want to touch him, anyway? He's a modelizer!

But he did come through for Mark and Holly. And against his will, even. I mean, he never wanted them to get married in the first place.

But I haven't heard a peep of protest out of him all day. In fact, thanks to him, those two are going to have their dream wedding after all.

That's gotta come as a blow to someone who is violently opposed to the institution of marriage. I wonder if he even realizes this.

Me: "Hey, so what happened to being all anti-marriage?"
Cal: "What?"
Me: (turning down Queen) "I thought you were totally against Holly and Mark getting married. So why'd you go along with this whole thing?"
Cal: "Are you recording this conversation in that book?"
Me: "Um. Sort of."
Cal: "Great. What else did you say about me?"
Me: "That you drool in your sleep."
Cal: "I do not."

Me: "You do too. I saw it for myself this morning when I woke you up."

Cal: (making a grab for this book) "Let me see that."

Me: "Hey! Eyes on the road, mister. Seriously, what changed your mind?"

Cal: "About what?"

Me: "MARRIAGE!!! Why are you pro now, when you were anti before?"

Cal: "I'm still anti. Just not in the case of Mark and Holly. I changed my mind."

Me: "Obviously. But why?"

Cal: "They just seem very . . . together. Like a couple should be. I guess."

Me: "I told you."

Cal: "That doesn't make me pro-marriage, you know. It just makes me pro-Mark and Holly."

Me: "That's all I wanted. You remember. Back on the plane?"

Cal: "Well, I barely knew Holly then. I still think Mark would be better off seeing the world before he settles down. Don't snort. It's a big place, there's a lot to see. A man shouldn't let himself get tied down too young."

Me: "Excuse me. Mark is thirty-five. That is middle-aged in many countries. And he TRIED exploring the world, remember? He got food poisoning for his efforts."

Cal: "I realize all of that. That's why I amended my opinion. About Mark and Holly."

Me: "But not love and marriage in general."

Cal: "I still believe marriage is an outdated institution. I also believe it robs people of their individual sense of self. I mean, just look at how women take their husbands' names—"

Me: "Not ALL women."

Cal: "The majority of them. Would you?"

Me: "Um. I'm the creator of Wondercat. YOU may never have heard of me, but lots of people have. If I changed my name, it would confuse my fans. And besides. I like my name the way it is. Even though, of course, it was handed down to me by a patriarchal society that subjugates women by robbing them of their birth identity upon marriage."

Cal: "See? That's what I'm talking about!"

Me: (snorting again) "Hello. I was kidding."

Cal: "Oh. Well, that's still what I'm talking about."

Me: "No, it isn't. That isn't what you said before. You said you don't believe in marriage because mammals are genetically incapable of monogamy, and I cited wolves and hawks as examples. Also that chemicals in the brain cause us to believe ourselves in love, when actually, we're merely in lust. It's right here in this book if you don't believe me, I can look it up."

Cal: "You put that conversation in there, too? Holly and Mark are going to read that!"

Me: "Er. Yeah. Maybe. Stop trying to change the subject. Do you really believe that? That human beings are incapable of monogamy? Because I can cite a lot of examples of marriages in which neither partner strayed—"

Cal: "How do you know?"

Me: "I think I'd know if my own parents were cheating on each other."

Cal: "How? Unless they told you. You wouldn't know. You'd have no idea."

Me: "Well, what about Rhonda's parents?"

Cal: "Who the hell is Rhonda?"

Me: "Rhonda. Of Rhonda and Paolo. Her parents were celebrating their thirty-fifth wedding anniversary."

Cal: "You have no possible way of knowing whether or not

Rhonda's parents have been monogamous for those thirty-five years."

Me: "True. Still. I'll bet you twenty bucks they have been. Nobody goes on a cruise with a cheating spouse."

Cal: "You are unbelievable."

Me: "No, you are. Just because your ex-wife cheated on you, you think all women are incapable of being faithful. Admit it."

Cal: "I never said any such thing."

Me: "You didn't have to. It's totally obvious. When you say you think humans are incapable of monogamy, you mean women."

Cal: "No, I don't."

Me: "Did you cheat on her?"

Cal: "Who?"

Me: "Valerie."

Cal: "HOW DO YOU EVEN KNOW HER NAME?"

Me: "Holly told me. _Did_ you?"

Cal: "Of course not."

Me: "See? I rest my case."

Cal: "HOW? I DON'T EVEN KNOW WHAT YOU'RE TALKING ABOUT!"

Me: "You distrust all women because of what one of them did to you. And that's made you take this anti-marriage stance. But it's not marriage that's the problem. It's ditzes like your ex who don't take it seriously or get hitched for the wrong reasons or whatever. Don't blame the institution of marriage for Valerie cheating on you. It wasn't <u>marriage</u> that made her cheat. She was just a ho."

Cal: "Oh my God. You are <u>unbelievable</u>."

Me: "Yes. But I'm right, too. There's the exit. Don't miss it."

He's acting like he's all shocked now that I would bring up this very private thing from his past.

And I guess it IS kind of rude to call someone's ex a ho. But really, that's what she is. Just like Dave is a male ho. But I haven't let Dave's predilection for humping soul-sucking Human Resource reps behind my back sour me on the idea of matrimonial bliss, or of someday finding that perfect someone, now, have I?

And really, I know that, technically, there's no such thing as matrimonial bliss . . . marriage is work, and there are no soul mates. You just have to find the person who annoys you the least (at least according to Dr. Phil), or rather, annoys you in ways you can stand.

Really, I bet there'd be a lot less divorce if people realized this. A lot less marriages, too. But that might not be such a bad thing.

Ooooh, I smell horse! The Centro Ippico! We're almost home!

To: Listserv <Wundercat@wundercatlives.com>
Fr: Peter Schumacher <webmaster@wundercatlives.com>
Re: JANE HARRIS

FANTASTIC NEWS, KIDS!!!! There is going to be a wedding after all!

This just in:

JANE HARRIS has driven all the way to Roma to get the APOS-TILLE that her friends need to have the marriage! YES! She walked in at approximately 21:00 hours, while my grandmother and I were sitting at the banquet table in the villa, trying to get JANE HARRIS's friends, who ate of the bad oysters but were finally starting to feel better, to drink some soup.

In walks JANE HARRIS holding up the APOSTILLE! The wedding will go on tomorrow morning as planned! The friends of JANE HARRIS, even though they are both still sickly, jump up and shout for joy! And JANE HARRIS says, "This is my wedding present to you!"

It is the best wedding present anyone has ever given to anyone, declares JANE HARRIS's friend Holly.

My grandmother opens the bottle of champagne to celebrate.

So come one, come all, to the Ufficio of the Secretario of Castelfidardo tomorrow morning at 9:00!

This is Peter, #1 Fan of Wundercat, saying GOOD NIGHT!

Wundercat lives—4eva!
Peter

✉

To: Holly Caputo <holly.caputo@thenyjournal.com >
Fr: Darrin Caputo <darrin.caputo@caputographics.com >
Re: Hello, it is your mother

Holly, this is your mother. Something horrible has happened. Your brother Darrin is going to get married. To a man. On the steps of City Hall. Where everyone will see.

You must come home at once. You know your brother has never listened to me or anyone else in this family. You must stop him from doing this. I cannot allow a child of mine to disgrace himself in this way.

I am begging you to talk your brother out of this crazy scheme. Perhaps Mark can help, as well. He's a doctor, surely he must know how wrong it is to flagrantly defy the law in this way.

Counting on you to come home and do the right thing by your poor, confused brother,

Your mother

PDA of Cal Langdon

I was right from the beginning. From the moment I first laid eyes on her—holding all those water bottles in the duty free shop back at JFK—I thought to myself, "There's a nut case."

I called it.

And yet . . . she made some very miserable people very happy tonight. I never saw a bigger pair of sadsacks than Holly and Mark, slumped at that giant dining table, when we walked through the door tonight. Mark, of course, looked particularly lost, since he's blind as a bat without his glasses. I walked in and handed them to him—I actually had to put them on his head, since he couldn't even see me holding them out to him—and then Jane slapped that form onto the table with a big, "Here's your wedding present."

I actually thought Frau Schumacher might have a heart attack, she was so excited.

And to tell you the truth, it was a little upsetting, because I could picture myself, having to give her mouth-to-mouth to revive her, while Mark pounded on her chest. And I have the disturbing idea—maybe from the way the woman hangs on my every word (though surely this is because I'm the only one here who speaks German?)—that if she came to and found my lips on hers, even giving her the breath of life, she might actually . . . well, sort of enjoy it. Maybe even slip me the tongue.

Could it be that Jane is right? Could there possibly be something to her theory that marriage is all right for some people—that it didn't work out for Valerie and me because Valerie was . . . well, a "ho"?

This seems an oversimplification of the problems Valerie and I had.

And yet . . .

Well, marriage certainly seems like it might be all right for Mark and Holly. They're happy enough about it, jumping around as much as they can, considering their still queasy stomachs. I have to say, I can't understand how anybody could be as delighted as they are at the prospect of being married by the socialist mayor of a town devoted to accordion construction, thousands of miles from their families.

But maybe there's something romantic about it that I'm missing. Valerie always accused me of not being romantic enough. The sewing machine I got her for Valentine's Day was always a bone of contention. She said she'd have preferred a diamond tennis bracelet.

But I thought a sewing machine was a much more practical gift, considering how much she was spending on clothes . . .

Now Holly's grabbed Jane and the two of them—followed closely by Frau Schumacher, who seems fairly spry for her age and apparently doesn't like to be left out of anything—have disappeared, apparently in a panicked quest to ease the wrinkles out of the wedding gown none of the rest of us is allowed to see.

With the girls otherwise occupied, Peter and I attempted to throw perhaps the lamest, most pathetic bachelor party in the history of time for Mark. Lame because of course the groom is so weak from food poisoning he can barely lift his glass to his lips. Pathetic because the only entertainment are the stray cats from last night, back for another helping of fish.

That's right. No lap dances or kamikazes for Mark.

But perhaps this is fitting for a man who has chosen such a perverse—and yet strangely right—place to wed.

Now Mark's staggered back upstairs to bed—interrupting the girls while Holly was trying on the wedding gown, judging from the indignant screams I just heard floating down from the window—leaving me alone with young Peter, who just asked me if I thought Jane Harris would be back down, or if I thought she'd go straight to bed.

How touching that this young man believes I am in any way privy to Ms. Harris's private thoughts or intentions. As this is an entirely erroneous assumption, however, I was forced to inform him that I did not, in fact, know.

Then the little malcontent had the nerve to look in my eye and ask me just what, precisely, were my intentions toward the lady in question.

Not in so many words, of course. His exact phrasing, uttered in a highly disapproving tone, was, "Are you and Jane Harris lowers?" by which I am assuming he meant lovers. I can't say I cared for the smug look that crept over the kid's face when I told him that we most certainly were not.

Perhaps I shouldn't have been so adamant?

At least he didn't say anything. Instead, he calmly produced a deck of cards from the back pocket of his jeans and asked if I cared to play a game of War.

Reduced to spending a beautiful, starlit night along the Adriatic coast playing War with a German teenager.

I can't help wondering if the man at the consulate's office wasn't right this afternoon when he expressed his belief that it's better to have a corpse in the house than a man from Le Marche. Not that there happen to be any of those in the vicinity. Just that . . . well, this place seems to *do* things to otherwise normal people. . . .

✉

To: Cal Langdon <cal.langdon@thenyjournal.com>
Fr: Mary Langdon < m.langdon@internetcafenetwork.com>
Re: Thank You

Oh my God, Cal, thanks for the money. I really needed it. Jeff
(the guy who owned the van) turned out to be a total psycho. He
kicked me out just because he happened to catch me talking to
another guy. I don't know who he thinks he is, anyway—the
freaking Taliban? God, I hate it when guys think they own me.

But it's cool because I hooked up with this awesome group of
ski-boarders. They've even got a spare room I can crash in. One
of them, Malcolm, showed me how to ride the halfpipe. He let
me use one of his boards and everything. He says he thinks I
might have a lot of natural talent. Who knows? Maybe boarding's been my calling all along, and I just never knew it, because
Mom and Dad always made us go on those stupid beach vaca-
tions, instead of taking us skiing, like normal parents.

Anyway, thanks again for the cash.

More later,

Mare

✉

To: Cal Langdon <cal.langdon@thenyjournal.com >
Fr: Ruth Levine <r.levine@levinedentalgroup.com >
Re: Hello!

Hi, Cal! I don't mean to be a pest, but I was just wondering if
you got my earlier email, and if you'd had a chance to consider
what I said in it. About Mark and Holly. I know you're with Mark
right now, and I was hoping you'd had a chance to speak to him

about it. For reasons I'd rather not go into just now, he and I aren't really speaking at the moment. Or rather, I'm speaking to him, but he appears to be put out with me. I know it will blow over soon—you know Mark and his moods. But I just hope that, in the meantime, you'll keep an eye on him, and keep him from doing anything . . . well, rash.

I certainly don't mean I think he's going to KILL himself because he got into an argument with his mother, of course. By rash I just mean . . . well, I don't know—PROPOSE to her, or something. Holly, I mean. Not that I don't like her or wouldn't want her as a daughter-in-law. She's a perfectly affable girl. It's just that she's not one of *us*.

Anyway, I don't mean to spoil your nice vacation with my constant emails. I hope you're having a good time. I just also hope that if, you know, you find yourself in a position to maybe give Mark a little dose of reality about how difficult it can be to make a marriage work—especially when two people come from such different cultures as he and Holly do—I'd really appreciate it.

Affectionately,
Ruth Levine

Travel Diary of

~~Holly Caputo and Mark Levine~~

Jane Harris

Holly looked happier tonight than I've ever seen her. Happier even than the day Brad Toller asked her to the senior prom after she'd spent the entire year just trying to get him to notice her. Seriously. She's GLOWING. I mean, she's still pale from having spent the entire day and most of last night throwing up—and her wedding dress is hanging off her, she's lost so much weight—but tomorrow she's going to make the most beautiful bride in the universe.

We so did the right thing, Cal and I, perjuring ourselves, etc., today at the consulate's office.

Now Holly's drifted off to bed in a dreamy haze, and I just heard Mark come in to join her, and Frau Schumacher seems to have left, and I realize I'm STARVING. I mean, we haven't eaten since the Hotel Eden this afternoon, so I'm going to forage for food down in the kitchen, then go straight to bed myself, since we have to get up so early tomorrow for the ceremony.

I noticed Cal was pretty quiet tonight, while everybody else was celebrating. I can't even begin to imagine what was going through his head. That ex-wife of his totally messed him up. I wouldn't mind running into her in a dark alley someday. I bet I could show her a few things I've picked up since living in the East Village, stuff she probably doesn't run into too much in her suburban kick-boxing class. Really, where do girls like that get off? They take perfectly adequate guys (well, OK, Cal needs work, but I imagine back then he probably wasn't as much of a pompous ass) and ruin them for the rest of us. That's just wrong.

Not, of course, that I would want Cal Langdon if he wasn't

damaged goods. Please! The last thing I need is a journalist for a boyfriend.

Although he does look awfully good in a bathing suit—

No! Stop it! I do NOT need to date a modelizer! That is just setting yourself up for heartbreak and many, many pints of macadamia brittle.

PDA of Cal Langdon

This is intolerable. I am in Italy, on a warm, moonlit night by a sparkling pool, with palm fronds blowing gently in the evening breeze, a platter of olives and crumbled chunks of Parmesan and a bottle of extremely excellent wine before me, and a woman radiating a very healthy sexuality across from me . . .

And I'm playing War with her.

What's wrong with this picture?

What's wrong with ME? I shouldn't want this woman. She's everything I can't stand . . . artistic, obsessed with popular culture, set in her ways, *American* . . .

And yet . . .

I want to kiss her.

Maybe it's the moonlight. Maybe it's this damned place.

Or maybe it's because she made me laugh so many times today.

Damn. What's *happening* to me? So she made me laugh. Mark makes me laugh, and I don't want to kiss *him*. I don't even like funny women. And I especially don't like funny *artistic* women.

So why is it that I'm going to kill this kid if he doesn't get the hell out of here in the next five minutes?

One.

Two.

Three.

He's still not leaving. He's telling some story about a comic he loves. Jane is apparently familiar with it, though it's not her own. It appears to have elves and gnomes in it. Peter is gushing over the fact that the final installment is coming out in only two weeks. Jane, who knows the author, says she's heard what's going to happen, but flirtatiously refuses to tell the kid. He is delighted by this, and is begging her. She refuses to divulge what she knows, and lays down an eight. Peter's just lain down an eight.

War.

She won.

The candlelight brings out the highlights in her dark hair, and makes her eyes shine. Her skin looks like butter . . .

What is *wrong* with me? I do NOT want to get involved with this woman. Or any woman, for that matter. I have a book to write. I have to find a place to live. I don't even have a dry cleaner. I can't get into a relationship. . . .

OK, I'm giving the kid another five minutes to leave. It's nearly midnight. Doesn't he have some computer system he has to go hack into somewhere back home?

Now she's asking him about Annika. Who the hell is Annika? Oh, the girl at the mayor's office. The mayor's daughter, apparently. Peter speaks scathingly of Annika, whom he's clearly in love with, and who, judging by his insistence that he loathes her, obviously doesn't return his feelings for her.

I slap down a two. So does Peter.

War.

Oh, it's war, my boy. In more ways than you know.

Wait. What's that?

Meowing. The cats are back.

She leaps up and heads into the kitchen to find something to feed them. Peter and I are alone at last.

By the time she returns with a bowl of what looks to be the contents of several cans of tuna, Peter is gone.

"Where'd Peter go?" she wants to know.

And I can't help but believe that she genuinely doesn't know.

This is a mystery I'm only too happy to clear up for her.

Travel Diary of

~~Holly Caputo and Mark Levine~~

Jane Harris

IS HE INSANE? I mean, I know he thinks I'm silly, what with my
"little cartoon" and my too-high heels that I'm always tripping
over and the whole "carabinieri" thing.

But it never occurred to me that he might think I'm the
STUPIDEST HUMAN BEING ON THE FACE OF THE PLANET.

Because that's exactly who I'd have to be to fall for his
whole "It's just a kiss, it doesn't have to mean anything" rou-
tine.

But you know what? I'm not going to let him. Ruin the wedding, I mean. He can sulk all he wants tonight, but if he comes
downstairs tomorrow morning with anything but a great big
happy smile on his face, I will personally give his arm hairs a
twist he won't forget.

Who does he think he is, anyway, Enrique Iglesias? "I just
want to kiss you. You're an an artist. I thought you people
were used to living in the moment?"

Whatever!

Apparently he thinks just because I am an unmarried
woman of a certain age who lives with a cat, I must be desperate. Or retarded.

Well, I'd HAVE to be pretty desperate—or retarded—to
fall into bed with HIM. What, just because he did me (well,
Holly and Mark, really) a favor today, I'm going to sleep with
him? Because we had a nice lunch and some laughs, I'm easy?
Please.

And okay, the guy is truly, almost unbelievably hot. I'll
admit I was checking out his hands as we played cards.
They're all big and sinewy, exactly the kind of hands a girl
wouldn't mind roaming all over her body.

And he can be charming when he puts his mind to it. Even kind of funny.

And he's definitely intelligent. At least, about stuff other than women. And he can be funny, like today at the consulate, with Rhonda.

And he's nice to cats—when he thinks no one is looking.

But I'm sorry, my days of sleeping with guys just because they happen to have nice hands and can tell a funny joke are OVER. Because you know what that gets you? Another night with a hot, funny guy who's not going to be the least interested in going with you to your office Christmas party or splitting the Con Ed bill—much less actually have the money to pay half the rent, even though he's totally moved in.

I'm over that. WAY over that.

You think that'd have been clear to him from the beginning of our relationship. I mean, I know I'm an artist, a word that to him is obviously synonymous with "wacky madcap." But could I really have struck him as the one-night-stand type? Isn't it obvious, from the way I keep bringing up *Ladyhawke* and the fact that hawks and wolves mate for life, that I am interested in monogamy and commitment?

Apparently he didn't get the message. I mean, I come out with food for the cats and Peter is gone—kind of suddenly, since we'd been in the middle of a card game when I got up.

So I'm all, "Where's Peter?" and Cal's like, "I gave him twenty euros and told him to make himself scarce."

Me: "You WHAT?"
Cal: "You heard me. About time, too. He's been keeping me from being able to do this all night."

And then he took me by the shoulders, and before I had any idea what was happening (no, really, I NEVER suspected he was attracted to me, since he's done nothing but grouse at me since the moment we first met. Well, except for putting his arm around me, back at the consulate. But that was just for show!), he pulled me to him and started kissing me.

Kissing me! Like we were in a romance novel, or something!

And OK, he's no slouch in the kissing department. Clearly, he's had some practice.

And OK, I didn't exactly hate it. Far from it, actually. All the different parts of me that usually go all melty when someone hot kisses me in a purposeful way went all melty, right on schedule, when he did it.

And I will admit that for a split second, I was all, "Oh my gosh! He likes me! He REALLY likes me!" and I entertained a quick tiny fantasy of us strolling down Second Avenue hand-in-hand and going to Veselka's for blintzes and me introducing him to The Dude. And I started to kiss him back. . . .

But then I realized . . . that fantasy? It will never, ever come true. Because he doesn't believe in love, much less marriage, and he will NEVER go to Veselka's for blintzes with me, much less stick around to meet The Dude—at least not long enough to form a meaningful relationship with him. And how long can I keep introducing The Dude to men he isn't ever going to see again? He's very sensitive, and when he does bond, it's forever. He wouldn't finish his Friskies for days after Malcolm left.

And then Holly's voice chimed into my head with *You've got to start thinking about the future, and date people who will actually stick around for a change,* and I remembered that bride we saw outside the church in Rome, and how happy she looked, and how her dad was beaming down at her—

And right then and there, I realized something that I don't think I've been willing to admit to myself since college, or whenever it was that the idea of getting married no longer seemed as cool as it had back during those Barbie games in fifth grade:

And that's that I WANT to get married someday. I do. I really do. I want the bouquet and the red carpet and the gown and the veil and the weepy dad and the flower girls and till death do us part.

So what was I doing kissing some guy who thinks marriage as an institution ought to be abolished?

So instead of wrapping my arms around his neck and kissing him back, as I'm sure he was expecting me to do, and as I have to admit I really did WANT to do—at least, my BODY wanted me to—I put my hands on his chest and shoved.

He staggered back into the metal lawn chair he'd been sitting in, and just sat there blinking up at me, like, "What gives?"

But before he had a chance to say anything, I went off.

Me: "What do you think I am? An idiot? I am NOT sleeping with you."

Cal: "Um . . . it was just a kiss."

Me: "You don't believe in love. You think it's all a result of phenyl . . . phenyl . . . whatever it is."

Cal: "Phenylethylamine. And, not to be pendantic . . . but it was just a kiss."

Me: "But unlike you, I do happen to believe in love. And marriage. So what's the point? One night, and then what? I become another name in your Blackberry. No, thank you."

Cal: "Pardon me if my memory is the one at fault here, and, keeping in mind that it was, again, just a kiss, didn't you e me not long ago that you were in no rush to get married or have children because you wanted to concentrate on your career?"

Me: "I might have. But I want to get married EVENTUALLY. So why in God's name would I fall into bed with some guy who's totally against the very idea of marriage? What's going to happen tomorrow morning, when you can't even make eye contact, and are avoiding me? And how about on the plane going back to New York, when we have to sit by each other again? And when we get back to Manhattan? Are you going to call? Am I ever even going to hear from you again?"

Cal: "Apparently, you've already decided that you aren't. Even though it was, I'd like to point out for a third and hopefully final time, just a kiss."

Me: "You know what? Holly's right. I've got to grow up. I'm not sleeping with any more inappropriate men. No more ski boarders. No more musicians. And certainly no men who hate the very idea of marriage, and who have no intention of pursuing a long-term relationship with me."

Cal: "You got all of that out of one kiss? I mean, about my not having any intention of pursuing a long-term relationship with you?"

Me: "Make fun of me all you want. But you know what? I'd rather go to bed with Paolo than with you."

Cal: "Who's Paolo?"

Me: "You remember. Of Paolo and Rhonda. Back at the consulate."

Cal: "PAOLO? The half-wit mechanic?"

Me: "Yeah, but at least he wasn't going around bleating that there's no such thing as romantic love. At least he believed in marriage."

Cal: "The guy didn't speak any English! I doubt he had any idea he was GETTING married."

Me: "Go on feeling all superior to us poor suckers who believe in love and monogamy and want to find someone with whom we can spend the rest of our lives. Because you know what's going to happen twenty years from now? I'm

going to be with someone—someone I can have breakfast with and read the paper with and watch stupid
movies with and sleep with and go on vacation with,
someone who WON'T cheat on me, the way your wife
cheated on you, because I'm going to marry someone who
loves me for me and not my money or whatever—and
you're going to be all alone. I hope you like it."

Cal: "Well, thank you very much. I'm sure I will. And I hope you
and Paolo will have a happy and prosperous life together.
For your thirty-fifth anniversary, might I recommend a
cruise?"

Me: "Thanks, I'll keep it in mind."

Cal: "Well. I guess we have nothing more to say to each other,
then."

Me: "I guess we don't. Good night."

Then I swept off the terrazza and came up here and wrote
all this.

I think I made quite an impression on him.

I just wish I hadn't tripped over the threshold when I was
going inside.

But I really don't think he noticed.

Now it's quiet—I guess he must still be down there, since
I didn't hear him come up. All I can hear are the crickets outside.

Still . . .

I can't help wondering if I did the right thing. I mean, I
think we WOULD have had a good time. He really is a good
kisser.

And you know, he can be fun—like in the consulate's office—
when he lets himself.

And he's obviously smart. It's not like we'd ever run out of
things to talk about.

Okay, argue about. But whatever.

Maybe I shouldn't have been so hasty to shove him away. . . .

No. No, I did the right thing. Because what would have been the point? A night of bliss and then what? He'd just go back to his skanks.

Only this time, I'd be one of them! Oh my God, I wouldn't be able to BEAR the idea of him thinking of me that way. As another woman he'd scored. I couldn't. I just think I'm *worth* more than that.

You know, I'm starting to think that The Dude might actually be my soul mate. He's everything you'd want in a man . . . loyal, trustworthy, attentive, handsome, smart, not afraid of commitment . . . he even has a good sense of humor.

Too bad about the fish breath, though.

Oh, damn. I left my bottle of water downstairs. I wonder if I can sneak down and get it without running into him again. . . . Maybe if I don't put on any shoes.

PDA of Cal Langdon

Well.

That was . . . unusual. I mean, it was just a *kiss*. . . .

A really good one. An exceptional one, I'd have to say. I've kissed quite a few women in my day, but that one certainly stands out.

Obviously, however, I made an error in judgement. A grave one.

Still, it wasn't like she didn't kiss back. At first.

But she's right, of course. It would have been a mistake. I don't know what I was thinking. I *never* do things like that. Act on impulse in that way, I mean. I can't imagine why I thought. . . . It isn't as if it could go anywhere, she's completely right. We live in two entirely different worlds.

Still, she's an artist. You'd think she'd be a little more receptive to taking a risk.

Well, it's lucky she resisted. She's clearly one of those clingy, needy ones, if she can jump straight from a kiss—which was all it really was, no matter what she thinks—into a full-blown relationship. She'd probably have asked me to move in after our first time making love, then spend every weekend in the foreseeable future whining about wanting to take me to meet her parents.

Or worse, be her date to some friend's wedding.

Shudder.

No, I made a lucky escape with this one. She's clearly no Grazi. There'd be no more pleasure for pleasure's sake, here. Obviously, I overestimated her intelligence.

It was those damn shoes.

Why does she even wear the stupid things, when she clearly can't even walk in them?

Anyway, this is all for the best. The last thing in the world I need right now is to be saddled with some marriage-crazed cat cartoonist. I need to get to work on my next book, and it'll be much easier to do that if I'm unfettered, relationship-wise.

And despite what she might think, I happen to *like* eating breakfast alone. And I've never had to sleep alone if I didn't want to.

Well, except for tonight.

PDA of Cal Langdon

Ski boarders? Musicians? Just who has this girl been sleeping with? Must remember to ask Mark tomorrow.

PDA of Cal Langdon

I can't ask Mark tomorrow—or today, I should say. It's his wedding day. He's hardly going to be likely to want to discuss his wife's best friends's love life.

Still. It was just a *kiss*. I don't know why I did it. I couldn't help myself, honest to God. It's not like I'm in love with her. God forbid!

It was just a kiss.

So why can't I stop thinking about it?

PDA of Cal Langdon

Upon ambling through the kitchen just now on my way up to bed, I made a rather startling discovery. Ms. Harris appears to have come back downstairs to retrieve something she forgot to bring up the first time she stormed off to her room, and in doing so, has left by the refrigerator something I'm sure she didn't mean to leave behind: that little book she's constantly scribbling in, the one that says Travel Diary of Holly Caputo and Mark Levine on it.

Oddly, I've noticed she's scratched out Mark and Holly's names and inserted her own. And yet, when I—quite by accident—opened it to the first page, I couldn't help noticing the words:

Dear Holly and Mark,

Surprise!

I know neither one of you would bother to keep a record of your elopement, so I've decided to do it for you!

Surely if she really is keeping this diary for Mark and Holly, it wouldn't be wrong of me to read it. Obviously she intends to give it to them.

And I think I have every right in the world to see what's being said about me, as I imagine she's had some rather choice things to say on the subject. Perhaps there's even a libel suit in my future. Who knows?

And yet I can't help feeling that I'm overstepping some boundary here.

Hmmmm. Quite a moral dilemma.

....

PDA of Cal Langdon

Anal retentive?

....

PDA of Cal Langdon

Modelizer??

....

PDA of Cal Langdon

I'm going to kill Mark for the appendage thing.

....

PDA of Cal Langdon

Apparently I'm a sardonic bastard, as well.

....

PDA of Cal Langdon

I . . .

I don't know what to say. Except . . .

Except I'm starting to think it wasn't just a kiss after all. In fact, seeing it all laid out there like that in her book, in black-and-white—all of my interactions with this woman, I mean, in more or less graphic detail—I'm starting to realize that it might be . . . it could ONLY be.

But that's IMPOSSIBLE. I'm overtired, that's all. It's nearly three in the morning, for Christ's sake.

And yet there's no denying that sometimes when I look at her, I think—

No. It's the tattoo. That damned tattoo and those stupid shoes. They're DESIGNED to make a man think things like that.

Except that . . . well, that drive to Rome today, and that wait in the consulate's office . . . that drive and that wait could have been so tedious, but I actually had more fun than I've had in a really, really—

I've got to snap out of it. This CAN'T be happening. Not now. I'VE GOT A BOOK TO WRITE. I've got an apartment to find. I've got a sister to support.

My God. I think . . . I really do think . . .

So. It wasn't just a kiss.

But she thinks—because of my big mouth, she's convinced—

Only how can I show her that with her, it's different? I can't just tell her, she'll never believe me, she's obviously convinced I'm a "modelizer."

Holy crap. Grazi.

✉

To: Graziella Fratiani <grazielle@galleriefratiani.co.it>
Fr: Cal Langdon <cal.langdon@thenyjournal.com>
Re: You

Grazi, I've left two messages on your cell. I realize it's late—or early, as the case may be. Still, I wanted to let you know—about your coming out to the villa this week: I really don't think it would be a very good idea after all. I know we'd talked about it and I said I thought it would be fine, but actually, I think it might be really awkward at this point. Mark and Holly really want to make it more of a family thing. I know you understand. Thanks so much, and I'll call next time I'm in town, I swear.

Cal

PDA of Cal Langdon

How could I have been so stupid? How could I have missed all the signs? They were all there . . . I mean, I even fed those stupid *cats.* How could I for one second not have wondered what was happening to me?

I just kept blaming the prosecco.

I ought to be shot.

✉

To: Listserv <Wundercat@wundercatlives.com>
Fr: Peter Schumacher <webmaster@wundercatlives.com>
Re: JANE HARRIS

GOOD MORNING! It is the day of the marriage of the friends of JANE HARRIS! YES!!! Come one, come all, to see the marriage of the friends of JANE HARRIS! I will be riding my motorino to get the marriage brotchen, and many other surprises! My grandmother and I have been working on many plans for the wedding couple!

Come to the Commune di Castelfidardo to see the marriage of the Americans today! It will be a marriage never to forget!

From the #1 Fan of Wundercat!

Wundercat lives—4eva!
Peter

Dear Holli and Marc,

For your marriage we wish you unlimited thirst
for a double good life that you both
grow and thrive and your luck may
increase and not burst!

Love,

Inge and Peter Schumacher

Travel Diary of
~~Holly Caputo and Mark Levine~~
Jane Harris

Oh my God, Peter and his grand-mother have OUTDONE themselves. They are the sweetest people EVER. We woke up this morning to the smell of fresh coffee, and we went downstairs to find the dining table practically sinking under the weight of all the pastries, fresh fruit, breakfast meats, and fluffy scrambled eggs piled onto it.

Plus someone (Peter swears it wasn't him) decorated the front gate with wildflowers from the horse pasture and two pairs of blue socks (still not sure about the significance of this). Apparently, wearing blue socks on your wedding day is important for good luck in this community. However, since Holly's wedding dress is above the knee, I'm afraid this won't do at all.

Speaking of whom, the bride is still glowing. You can't even tell she spent all day yesterday with her head in a toilet. She just looks pretty and happy and . . . well, like a bride!

Even Mark is glowing . . . I mean, if you can say that about a man. There is a bounce in his step that I haven't ever seen before, and he can't seem to stop smiling. He was too nervous to eat—it was so sweet! He keeps looking at his watch and going, "Shouldn't we start getting ready? We don't want to be late. The mayor has that football game to coach."

Cal's the only one who wasn't downstairs on the stroke of seven, bright-eyed and bushy-tailed. He finally showed up a little before eight—from OUTSIDE. Apparently, he'd taken the car and gone somewhere.

But when Mark asked him where he'd been, he went, "To get the paper," and slapped a <u>Herald Tribune</u> down on the table.

Yeah. Nice job, Cal. Way to help out your friend on his wedding day. Get him the paper.

Who cares about him, anyway? Um, not me.

Now Holly and Mark are getting ready. I am on call in case Holly has a hair emergency, but I can already tell that she won't. Her hair is doing exactly what she wants it to. It's behaving perfectly, exactly the way hair SHOULD be on a girl's wedding day.

I am in charge of the paperwork (already in my bag), camera (ready), and lucky socks (ditto). Peter is in charge of the rings. Cal is in charge of driving. He appears to be taking this with the same kind of stoicism you might expect from a man preparing to step in front of a firing squad. How flattering to Holly that her husband-to-be's best friend apparently equates his marrying her to being shot.

Whatever. I'm not going to let that freak spoil the day. This is what we came here for, and everything is going so well: There isn't a cloud in the sky; Holly looks prettier than I've ever seen her; Mark is being the perfect nervous bridegroom; and someone else even made breakfast.

I bet there are a lot of brides who'd gladly sacrifice having their families attend their wedding in exchange for just ONE of the above.

Ooooh, we're leaving—

PDA of Cal Langdon

My God. The entire town has turned out for this wedding. Or at least, that's how it appears. There's nearly a hundred people gathered outside the Commune. And they're all wearing . . .

They're all wearing Wondercat T-shirts.

Seriously. Every last one of them.

Some of them are holding Wondercat banners. And have on Wondercat baseball hats. There's even a baby in a Wondercat COSTUME.

Jane looks completely mortified.

Especially when she stepped from the car, they surged forward, clamoring for her autograph.

She tried to explain to them that she's here for a wedding, and not a comic-book signing. But to no avail. It took us ten minutes just to get into the building. And most of the Wondercat fans have followed us, with the apparent intention of witnessing Holly and Mark's marriage for themselves.

I blame Peter. He's looking particularly pleased with himself. Yes, this has Teenaged Stalker written all over it.

Ah, here comes the secretario. He looks oddly surprised to see us. He keeps stammering something about how he'd heard the bride and groom were too ill to make it to Roma for the APOSTILLE. Jane's shoved our paperwork beneath his nose, but he's looking very skeptical—

Travel Diary of

~~Holly Caputo and Mark Levine~~

Jane Harris

Oh my God, this is HORRIBLE!!! THE MAYOR WON'T MARRY HOLLY AND MARK!!!! HE DOESN'T BELIEVE THE SIGNATURES ON THE APOSTILLE ARE THEIRS!!!! He says he heard that Mark and Holly were sick in bed all day yesterday, and so how could they have gotten the Apostille? He says the signatures on the Apostille have to be forgeries!!!

I'M GOING TO KILL PETER!!! THIS IS ALL HIS FAULT!!!! I know he must have posted something on his Web site or something about it. Because why else would there be all these Wondercat fans here? How else could they have known? And how else could the MAYOR have known about Holly and Mark????

Oh, God, I am DYING for them. Holly looks SO pretty, and Mark is so handsome. HOW can the mayor be so heartless? Should I confess? Should I go up there and be all, "OK, it was me, it's my signature, not Holly's, but I did it for a good cause, and you should still marry them because look how cute they are together"? Would he even go for that?

I don't think so. He was completely unmoved by Frau Schumacher's tirade, which lasted five minutes, at least.

And now he's taking his sash off! His mayoral sash! Like he's done for the day! He's heading off for soccer practice like he hasn't left a roomful of broken-hearted people behind! How can anyone be so—

Oh, no. What's Cal doing? Oh, God, he's not going to confess that it's his signature, is he? I KNEW he'd do something to ruin Holly and Mark's chance at—

Wait. Wait a minute, he's not—

To: Claire Harris <charris2004@freemail.com>;
    Darrin Caputo <darrin.caputo@caputographics.com>
Fr: Jane Harris <jane@wondercat.com>
Re: Holly and Mark

We're here! At the Commune di Castelfidardo, in the Municipale building, for Holly and Mark's wedding!

For a minute it looked as if it weren't actually going to happen. The mayor seemed to suspect all was not right with Holly and Mark's paperwork.

But then Cal Langdon—CAL LANGDON, Mr. I Don't Believe In Marriage Himself—stepped up and, whipping out a notepad, asked the mayor for his full name.

And when the mayor asked him just what he was doing, Cal went (according to Peter, who translated for me), "Oh, I'm a foreign affairs correspondent for *The New York Journal*, and I think my readers would be very interested in learning about how Le Marche officials treat American visitors to their region."

The mayor couldn't put his sash on fast enough! He started the wedding ceremony then and there!

CAL LANGDON SAVED THE DAY!

I wasn't the only one who started cheering, either. Half the town seems to have turned out for the ceremony, as well!

Holly looks so pretty in her dress, which is—even though I helped her pick it out, so I am sort of complimenting myself by saying this, but it's true—stunning. Her waist looks TINY, and she's got a tiny bouquet of white flowers that this kid Peter made her . . .actually they're garlic flowers from the garden, so you don't want to sniff them. But she doesn't know that, so DON'T TELL HER.

And then, solemnly, with all this dignified grace, they began the ceremony, with Holly and Mark holding hands and looking so sweet and nervous in front of them, and all of the rest of us—including, I am astonished to note, a good number of school-children, including the mayor's own daughter, who surely should be in school—crowded all around the sides of the room. Every-one seems to be on his or her best behavior.

Well, except for Cal Langdon, who despite his earlier heroics for some reason won't stop looking at my feet. I do have on my new Christian Louboutins, though—the ones with the rhinestone flow-ers over the toe straps—so that might be why. Possibly he thinks they aren't suitable wedding attire?

The mayor opened this big book and began to read, while the secretario translated in not very good English. It's a very moving ceremony so far, all about how they promise to live in the same house and educate their children. Marriage is obviously taken very seriously here in Italy, but they don't seem much concerned about the for richer or poorer, in sickness and in health stuff. They just seem to want everyone to live under the same roof and go to school.

This seems very reasonable to me.

Ooooh, it's the ring part, I have to start taking pictures, more later—

J

Art. 147· Doveri Verso I Figli

Il matrimonia impone ad ambedue I conuigi l'obligo di mantenere, istruire ed educare la prole tenendo conto delle capacita, dell'inclinazione naturale e delle aspirazioni dei figli

(domando allo sposo)
Sig. *LEVINE MARK* dichiara di voler prendere in moglie la qui presente Sig. *CAPUTO HOLLY ANN?* *(si)*

(ed alla sposa)
Sig. *CAPUTO HOLLY ANN* dichiara di voler prendere in marito il que presente Sig. *LEVINE MARK?* *(si)*

I testimoni hanno sentito *(si) (si)*

Io *Antonio Torelli*
Ufficiale di Stato Civile del Commune di Castelfidardo
Diacharo che il Sig. *LEVINE MARK* e la Sig. *CAPUTO HOLLY ANN* sono uniti in matrimonio

Commune di Castelfidardo
Provincia di Le Marche

Ufficio Dello Stato Civile
Certificato di Matrimonio
L'Ufficiale dello Stato Civile

Certifica

Che dal REGISTRO degli ATTI DE MATRIMONIO
atto N. 1 Parte II Serie C, risulta che nel giorno
23 del mese di settembre contrassero
matrimonio in Castelfidardo

Mark David Levine　　　　Holly Ann Caputo
Celibe　　　　　　　　　Nubile
Nato a Ohio USA　　　　　Nata a Illinois USA
Cittadino Statunitense　　　Cittadina Statunitense

✉

To: Listserv <Wundercat@wundercatlives.com>
Fr: Peter Schumacher <webmaster@wundercatlives.com>
Re: JANE HARRIS

IT IS DONE!!! The friends of JANE HARRIS have had the marriage! It was very beautiful. I hold onto the rings, and when the secretario say to me, "The rings, please," I give them to the friends of JANE HARRIS. JANE HARRIS took many photographs. One photograph was of me giving the rings.

Then the mayor said, *"Io diacharo che sono uniti in matrimonio,"* and everyone in the room gives big cheer!

And then the marriage couple kiss, and everyone gives bigger cheer!

And then the friend of JANE HARRIS named Cal Longdon says to everyone, "To thank you all for making this day so special for my friends, I'd like to invite everyone back to La Beccacia, where a champagne brunch is currently being set up."

Then everyone looks at Cal Longdon strange because we do not know this word, *brunch.*

Then JANE HARRIS says, "Are you serious?"

And Cal Longdon says, "Yes, I am serious. I ordered it this morning."

So now we have the lunch with JANE HARRIS and her friends! I bring my boom box so there is the music for dancing! I will dance with JANE HARRIS! YES!!!

This is Peter, #1 Fan of Wundercat!

Wundercat lives—4-eva!
Peter

```
W E S T E R N   U N I O N
T E L E G R A M

To:   Ruth and Ira Levine
From: Mark Levine

Dear Mom and Dad,

Well, Holly and I did it. We're married.
Wish you could have been there. Mom, stop
crying. Susie Schramm has nothing on my
Holly.

                              Love, Mark
```

```
W E S T E R N   U N I O N
T E L E G R A M

To:   Salvatore and Marie Caputo
From: Holly Caputo

Dear Mom and Dad,

Mark and I got married this morning in
Castelfidardo. Please don't be mad. We'll
come for a visit when we get back to the
States. I know you'll love him as much as
I do someday.

                              Love, Holly


P.S. Darrin made up the thing about
getting married to cover for me, lay off
him.
```

Travel Diary of
~~Holly Caputo and Mark Levine~~
Jane Harris

I'm in total shock.

I can't believe he did this. <u>When</u> did he do this? He must have snuck out at the crack of dawn to get all this done. He couldn't have arranged any of this before this morning. I KNOW he didn't arrange it yesterday. I was with him all day yesterday. He was still vehemently opposed to marriage all the way up until last night. I KNOW that.

So the only way he could have done all this—the only TIME he could have done all this—was this morning, before eight. Before EIGHT IN THE MORNING.

<u>How</u> did he do it? I mean, there is enough food here for a small army. He must have had to wake people up to get them to start cooking this much food—much less get it delivered on time. What did he do, stand outside a restaurant and bang on the door until someone let him in?

You know what? He must have. He totally MUST have.

But WHY? Why would someone as ethically opposed to love and marriage as he is DO something like this?

Maybe for the same reason he stepped up and made sure Holly and Mark got their wedding after all—because he has a heart after all?

I'm serious. He MUST have one. This—and what happened back in town—PROVES it.

Cal Langdon is actually . . . well . . . <u>nice.</u>

Seriously! The terrazza looks so beautiful—someone's put vases of fresh flowers everywhere. There are tables set up across the lawn covered in white table cloths, and there are plastic lilies—actually, quite tasteful ones—floating in the pool. The champagne corks are still popping—it's a real party!

A party of people we never met before this week—some we never met before today—but a party nonetheless. Thrown together at the last minute by a man who, as of midnight last night, was still insisting love is nothing but the result of a chemical imbalance in the brain.

Holly looks so happy over there, dancing with the mayor! It's almost as if she were dancing with her dad after all.

And Mark, dancing with—well, whoever that is. Oh, wait, Annika called her Mutti, so she must be the mayor's wife. He looks blissfully happy too. The two of them seem to be over the moon. This is SO MUCH better than eloping down at City Hall back home. This is like . . . well, what the reception would have been like if Holly's mother had planned it.

It wouldn't have happened—any of it—without the man who's been insisting from the beginning that Mark and Holly were making a horrible mistake. Cal Langdon did it. Cal did it ALL.

This is just unbelievable. I wish I had thought of something so sweet. Why didn't he ask me? I totally would have chipped in.

But apparently I'm the enemy now, judging by the way he's avoided speaking to me all morning—except once to say that my Christian Louboutin pump had come unbuckled. Only he didn't call them Christian Louboutins. He said, "Your, um, shoe is coming undone."

I guess I can't really blame him. I mean, about the not-speaking-to-me thing. I really was pretty brutal to him last night. It <u>was</u> just a kiss, after all. I don't know why I had to jump to the conclusion that all he wanted was a roll in the hay. I'm so STUPID sometimes. I've blown it with yet another great guy.

But how was I to know he was planning this lovely party all along? I mean, what's someone who claims not to believe in love doing, throwing a wedding reception? Not to mention rushing in and SAVING the wedding in the first place. How could I have misjudged him so BADLY?

But the brain-chemical thing. I mean, there's still THAT—

Peter just wandered over here and asked me to dance again. This is the third time. I was like, "Peter, why don't you ask Annika to dance?"

I said it kind of loudly, since Annika is standing nearby. She doesn't exactly look like she wishes I hadn't mentioned it.

Then again, her English isn't as good as Peter's. In fact, she should probably be in school. Half the wedding guests look like they're skipping calculus to be here. Did Cal get this declared as a local holiday on top of everything else? Or is it Italian tradition for everyone in the village to abandon their schools and workplaces whenever zany Americans take it into their heads to be married in their town?

Anyway, Peter is telling me he CAN'T ask Annika to dance, as she'll just say no.

"Annika," I say. "If Peter asks you to dance, will you say no?"

Ha. Annika just shook her head, blushing. BLUSHING!

So I shoved Peter over there, and the two of them are slow-dancing to "Killer Queen."

Because of course Holly keeps insisting Peter play Cal's Queen CD over and over again. "Fat-Bottomed Girls" really IS her official wedding theme song.

Oooh, Cal is smacking one of Zio Matteo's spoons against the side of a champagne flute. He's going to make a speech!

Oh, dear. Considering how he feels about the occasion—or did until his mysterious change of heart this morning—"Down the hatch, and through the gums, look out stomach, here she comes," is about as eloquent as I imagine this is going to get.

To: Darrin Caputo <darrin.caputo@caputographics.com>
Fr: Holly Caputo <holly.caputo@thenyjournal.com>
Re: I'm MARRIED!!!!

Well, I did it. Mark and I are married. I sent Mom and Dad a telegram, but they won't get it until tomorrow.

Still, I wanted you to be the first to know.

I hope you're happy for me. I'm over the moon, myself. The only thing that could possibly be better than this is if you were here.

Jane's been so great—there was a snag with our paperwork, and they almost weren't going to let us go through with it, but Jane drove all the way to Rome and perjured herself on our behalf, along with Mark's friend Cal, who's also thrown us the sweetest reception right here at Zio Matteo's. He just gave the most elegant toast, and since I know Bobby collects them, I tried to write it down as best I could. It went:

"Thanks everyone for coming here today. I know not all of you speak English, so I'll try to make this brief. I've known Mark Levine since the two of us were in OshKosh overalls. And though I haven't always approved of every choice he's made—I still think he should have gone out for the MLB instead of medical school, but he always did have a rescue complex, and wanted to save lives instead of hit homers for a living—this one—marrying Holly—is one even I can support. People in Mark's field can't leave anything well enough alone. They've even analyzed the chemical make-up of love. When we fall in love, our brains are flooded with something called phenylethylamine. It's a stimulant that can be found in chocolate, and, like the effects of chocolate on the mood, it doesn't last.

"But for the lucky few—and I believe Mark and Holly fall into this category—even as the human body builds up a tolerance to the "love" drug, other chemicals—endorphins—rush in. Endorphins are what flood the brain when long-term lovers touch. They're what give them that secure, comfortable, old-shoe feeling. But to keep things from getting TOO comfortable—and keep them exciting—a healthy dose of naturally occurring oxytocin gets released too, increasing desire, and stimulating—

"Well, I think I can leave the rest to your imagination. Right now I'd like you all to just raise your glass and say, Congratulations, Mark and Holly. May your lives together be blessed with health, happiness, and many, many endorphins."

Isn't that sweet? Everyone else really seemed to think so. I had no idea Mark's friend could be so eloquent. I think he really knocked poor Janie for a loop, too, because she just stood there staring at him with the funniest look on her face!

Whoops, Mark wants to dance again—more later. I hope you can read this, I have to admit, I'm a little tipsy!

Much love,
Holly

Travel Diary of

~~Holly Caputo and Mark Levine~~

Jane Harris

OK, I'm scared now. Something's happened to Cal Langdon.

Seriously. It's as if he snapped or something in the night. Maybe his Wellbutrin ran out. Or maybe he started actually TAKING Wellbutrin.

What gives???? First that thing this morning in the mayor's office. Then this party he's throwing for two people whom, at the beginning of the week, he didn't even think should get married in the first place. He had to have spent a small fortune on all of this champagne alone.

And Holly just came up to me—three sheets to the wind, but whatever, it's her wedding day, she deserves to enjoy it—and slurred, "Oh my Go', Janie, d'you know what Cal did? D'you know what Cal DID?"

And when I asked what Cal did, she said, "He booked us a shuite—Mark and me—a deluxe shuite at a five shtar hotel right—on the beach—for tonight. For our wedding night. For a little honeymoon. All inclushive, dinner AND breakfasht . . .and there's even a Jacuzzi tub in the room. AN INROOM JACUZZI. Have you ever heard of anything sho shweet in your LIFE?"

I had to admit that I hadn't.

And that toast? WHAT ABOUT THAT TOAST???? THAT was not the toast of a man who doesn't believe in love. Not at ALL. That was, in fact, an in-depth scientific DEFENSE of love. LONG-TERM love.

What was he THINKING?

Maybe he's not. Maybe he's on drugs. That HAS to be it. He got up this morning with some diabolical plan to stop Holly and Mark's wedding, and somewhere between trying to bribe the mayor into calling in sick and phoning a bomb threat into the Commune di Municipale building, someone slipped him a roofie. Or some E.

Except that if this were true, why is he currently dancing with Frau Schumacher in a completely sober (and yet completely engaging and charming) manner? He's navigating her across the terrazza—ahem, and toward me—with perfect ease. In fact, Peter's great-grandmother looks as if she just died and went to heaven, she's so thrilled by the manly embrace she's floating in. She doesn't even seem to be aware of the fact that she's dancing to "Bohemian Rhapsody."

Which is coming to its head-bobbing end shortly. Surely he's not getting any ideas. You know, about asking ME to dance. Not after the dressing down I gave him last night. LIKE THE HUGE IDIOT I AM.

Oh my God. I'm actually considering APOLOGIZING to him for not kissing him last night. That's how much he's psyched me out with this sudden about face of his. I mean, endorphins? ENDORPHINS? He never said a word to me about endorphins. He was all phenylethylamine yesterday. Now suddenly he's Mr. Endorphin?

"Oooooh, such a lowely party!" That's what Frau Schumacher just said, as Cal twirled her into a seat near me, "Bohemian Rhapsody" having come to its rousing (and second in the past hour) finish.

Me: "I'm so glad you're enjoying yourself, Frau Schumacher. I had no idea you were such a good dancer."

F.S.: "Me? I am nozing. Zees man, here" (clutching Cal's hand. He, by the way, looks ready to flee to the other side of the room again)—"he is the party animal!"

Cal: (looking—I _have_ to say it—sweetly embarrassed) "Now, Frau Schumacher. Don't be modest. We know you must have been quite a party girl yourself once."

F.S.: (dismissing this with a wave of her hand) "Vell, yes, of course. But zat vas long ago. Oh, the parties zey used to zrow at the headquarters of the Führer! Zis reminds me of zem, a little. Zere the champagne flowed and flowed, just like here."

Cal and I exchange wide-eyed glances.

Me: "Excuse me, Frau Schumacher. Did you say . . . headquarters of the Führer?"

F.S.: (wide-eyed with innocence) "Yes. But of course. Zat is vhere I go as young girl to dance. Ven I vorked for the S.S.."

Cal: (stunned) "Frau Schumacher . . . you worked for the S.S.?"

F.S.: (waving her hand again) "Of course, of course. Ve all did! Vell, zat is vhat you did back then! Zere is more champagne?"

Cal hastened to refill Frau Schumacher's glass. "Under Pressure" came on over Peter's CD player, and his great-grandmother leaped back to her feet, declaring, "Zis is my favorite!"

Then she threw herself back onto the dance floor/pool deck.

Cal and I are staring at each other.

"We can never," I warn him, "ever tell Mark and Holly that someone who used to work for the S.S. made their wedding breakfast."

Cal shrugs. "Vhat's the big deal, Jane? Ve all did it," he says, in a perfect, deadpan imitation of Peter's great-grandmother.

"Swear," I say to him.

"Sworn," he says. Then: "So. Still writing in that book, I see."

Me: (unable to drag my gaze from his hands, which are looking even sexier holding a champagne glass than they did last night, holding playing cards) "Yes."

Cal: "You're not going to give it to them, then?"

Me: (Is it my imagination, or do his eyes actually match the blue of the sky above our heads?) "Give what to whom?"

Cal: "Mark and Holly. As a wedding present. The travel diary you've been keeping for them."

Me: (He's wearing a jacket and tie in honor of the occasion. Can I just say that he looks almost as good in them as he does without a shirt on?) "Oh, no. Not anymore. I changed my mind. Kind of the way you did."

I know! Bold move on my part!
He looks confused. May I just say that confused, on him, is completely adorable?

Cal: "I beg your pardon?"

Me: "Well, this party, of course. When did you decide marriage is a good thing that ought to be celebrated instead of dreaded?"

Cal: "Oh, that. Well. Listen, would you quit writing in that book for a minute? It's kind of distracting."

Me: "But it's my first trip to Europe, you know, and I don't want to miss a minute."

Cal: "If your head is constantly stuck in a book, you're going to miss a lot."

Me: "I'll quit writing if you tell me what changed your mind."

Cal: "Changed my mind about what?"

Me: "Holly and Mark."

Cal: "Oh. Well. You, actually."

ME???

Me: "ME??? But . . . when? Not last night."

Cal: "Yes, actually. Last night."

Me: "But I was so mean to you!"

Cal: "Maybe I deserved it."

Oh my God, he DID start taking Wellbutrin! He MUST have! There's no other explanation for this!

Me: "Okay, what gives? Why are you being so nice all of a sudden?"

Cal: "I'm always nice."

Me: "No, you're not. What was all that saving the day down at the mayor's office? You blew your perfect opportunity to save your friend from a fate you USED to think was worse than death. So what happened?"

Cal: "I realized I was wrong."

Me: "About Holly and Mark?"

Cal: "About everything."

Me: "EVERYTHING? Even that whole phenylethylamine thing?"

Cal: "Well—that's a scientific fact. But everything else."

Me: "But . . . how? Why? Did you pick up a prescription for anti-depressants while you were in town this morning, in addition to hiring a caterer and all of that? Because you are NOT acting like yourself."

Cal: "Yeah, well, maybe I had a chance to see how I appear through someone else's eyes, and I didn't exactly like what I saw. Now will you put down that book and dance with me? They're playing our song, you know."

"Fat-Bottomed Girls" just came on again.

Nice one. Maybe he hasn't changed that much, after all.

Which wouldn't necessarily be a bad thing. I mean, who wants a guy who can't take—or make—a joke?

Cal: "Come on. Give me a chance to prove to you I've got one."
Me: "Got what?"
Cal: "A heart."

HOW DID HE KNOW????
And how can I say no?

✉

To: Listserv <Wundercat@wundercatlives.com>
Fr: Peter Schumacher <webmaster@wundercatlives.com>
Re: JANE HARRIS

Halloooo! I am writing to you having come home from the party for the marriage of the friends of JANE HARRIS! This was a very good party. If you were not there, I feel sorry for you! There was much feasting and champagne. Some people were getting very drunken. This was very comical!!!

Everyone has very good time when the car from the hotel come to take away the happy couple for their honeymoon. Then we decide to follow the car on our motorinos, because this is very fun. We stand beneath the terrazza of the happy couple at the hotel, and shout many comical things. Then the bride, she comes out and throws her bouquet to us! The bouquet was catched by Annika! Annika will now be the next bride in Castelfidardo (in American tradition)!

But this is not the most comical thing that happened at the party of the marriage of the friends of JANE HARRIS. The most comical thing was when JANE HARRIS was dancing with the very nice Cal Longdon (who gives me 20 euros to spend on MORE WUNDERCAT COMIX) and a very beautiful Italian lady arrive at the villa. She is called Graziella, and she come to see Cal Longdon.

Cal Longdon looked very, very surprised to see this woman. JANE HARRIS looked very surprised to see this woman, also.

Then JANE HARRIS pushed Cal Longdon into the pool.

This was most comical of all! JANE HARRIS is very hilarious—just like Wundercat!

This is Peter, #1 Fan of Wundercat, saying GOOD NIGHT!

Wundercat Lives—4eva!
Peter

To: Holly Caputo <holly.caputo@thenyjournal.com>
Fr: Sal Caputo <salcaputo@freemail.com>
Re: Hello, this is your father speaking

Hello! You didn't know your father had email, did you? Well, I'll admit we don't have much use for it down at the shop, but I do like to have one for bidding on antique Electroluxes on eBay. You never know when you might find one that just needs a little tweaking to get it running again.

Anyway, what is this I hear that you and Mark got married today at Zio Matteo's place in Marche? Is this true?

Well, if it is true, you have made your mother very sad. She is at church right now, making a novena for you. At Mass this evening she plans to petition for a prayer of the faithful to be said for your immortal soul.

I, however, want to be the first to say congratulazioni. Or should I say mazel tov? I know in the past your mother and I have expressed our concern about Mark not sharing our beliefs. But you are a big girl now, and you need to make your own decisions. I have always liked Mark. At least he understands how a motor works, unlike some of your brothers.

And, as I said to your mother, it will be a good thing to have a doctor in the family. Especially since I have a mole I would like for him to look at when the two of you come to visit.

Don't worry about your mother. I will ask Father Bob to have a word with her.

And, of course, now she'll be able to concentrate on making Mark convert. You know how she loves a project.

Much love,
Dad

✉

To: Mark Levine <mark.levine@thenyjournal.com>
Fr: Ruth Levine <r.levine@levinedentalgroup.com >
Re: Hello!

Mark. Tell me it isn't true. Tell me that Marie Caputo, from whom I just received a nearly hysterical phone call, claiming one of her sons told her that you and her daughter have eloped, is suffering from a psychotic delusion.

Mark—what were you thinking? Do you know what you've done? What am I going to tell Gloria Schramm? I promised you'd call Susie just as soon as you got back to New York. Now you're going to call her, not to ask her to meet you at the Cub Room for after-work drinks, but to tell her you're married? The poor girl will have another one of her episodes. Last time they found her wandering around Fifth Avenue in nothing but Uggs and a pair of Spanx.

Tell me it isn't true. Do you know how far in advance you have to reserve the reception room at the country club? A year! If you had just let me know you were planning something like this, I could have put my name on the list months ago, and we might have been able to have a nice party when you two get back. Now what am I supposed to do? Have people over to the house? You know we haven't had the dining room wall replastered yet from when those stupid kitchen people accidentally drilled straight through while they were installing the new cabinets.

We *might* be able to get a room at the Marriott if they've had a cancellation. I'll have to check.

And your father says now you'll be paying taxes this year as if you were a married man for the entire twelve months, when you were only married for three of them. He says you should have waited until January.

What size coat does Holly wear? I'm going to look into having your uncle Isaac make her up a mink. And don't go telling me she's opposed to wearing fur, it gets very cold in New York, and if she's going to be having my grandchildren, I want to make sure she doesn't walk around with a headcold half the year.

You could have told us, you know, Mark. Your father and I would have loved a trip to Italy. You know the last place he took me was the Bahamas and it rained the whole time.

Love to you both,
Mom

....

✉

To: Jane Harris <jane@wondercat.com>
Fr: Claire Harris <charris2004@freemail.com>
Re: Holly and Mark

Honey! I'm so excited for them! I just ran into Marie at the Kroger Sav-On. She was carrying on about how God never gives you more than you can handle and that this just means more time in purgatory for Holly, you know, but I could tell she was over the moon. She was positively glowing.

Although that might have been because it's unseasonably hot here for September.

Still, she was buying Lender's bagels. Bagels! I asked her about them, and she very nearly blushed as she replied, "They're for freezing. For when Mark and Holly come to visit, Then I'll defrost them. He likes to have them for breakfast, you know."

I think that's a good sign, don't you?

Anyway, I hope you're still having a nice time. Daddy and I are fine. He did get a few acid burns while changing the battery in the Volvo, but Neosporin seems to be working just fine on them.

And just in case you got any ideas from Holly and Mark's wedding, I hope you know your father and I don't care WHO you marry, as long as you invite us.

Although I do think that Cal Langdon would probably look very nice in a tuxedo.

Love,
Mom

....

✉

To: Jane Harris <jane@wondercat.com>
Fr: Malcolm Weatherly <malcolmw@snowstyle.com>
Re: Ciao!

Hey, babe. Haven't heard from you in days. Hope things are okay.

Listen, I was just wondering—we're not exclusive or anything anymore, are we? I mean, it's okay to hook up with other people, right? Since I moved out? Because I sort of met someone. Just drop me a line and let me know, will ya? I don't want to do anything to piss you off. But a guy's got needs, you know?

Peace out,
Malcolm

....

✉

To: Jane Harris <jane@wondercat.com>
Fr: Julio Chasez <julio@streetsmart.com>
Re: The Dude

Hi, Ms. Harris. Listen, I was wondering—when are you getting back, exactly? Because The Dude, he's—well, he seems like he misses you, or something. I mean, this morning when I went in to feed him, I caught him gnawing on the screen over the window, trying to get out onto the fire escape, on account of there being a pigeon there. He made a pretty big hole in it, actually. The screen I mean. My dad replaced it, though, don't worry, and I shut the window all the way so he can't do it again.

And just now he kind of bit me again when all I was trying to do was pet him.

So I was just wondering . . . when are you coming home, again?

I hope it's soon.

Julio

PDA of Cal Langdon

It seems fairly obvious to me that I could have handled that better.

Really, Grazi's timing could not have been more unfortunate. I think I had almost gotten *her* to forgive me for my earlier, unfortunate gaffes.

Although I still insist my opinions, especially on marriage, were perfectly valid. You can't tell me there isn't an educated person alive who might, looking at the world as it is today, wonder if bringing a new life into it might not be the wisest course of action. Given the state of the global-economic—not to mention environmental—situation as it exists at this moment, what kind of person could possibly consider having children, when all that child stands to inherit is a planet devoid of adequate energy sources and (as a consequence of this rape of our fossil fuels) an ozone layer; bankrupt Social Security and Medicaid; and a community terrorized by fundamentalists who believe it is their inherent right to exert their values and beliefs on others, through physical force, if necessary?

Only a fool.

And yet, for the first time in my life, I can see how being a fool can have its advantages. Especially if what you're being a fool for is love.

God. I can't believe I just wrote that.

But, incredibly, it's true. I can see now why Mark and Holly felt they *had* to marry, in spite of their parents' opposition, in spite of what they know about this world and the dangers it holds. I can see now why it was so important to them to legalize their union—why having an easily accessible escape route from a romantic relationship isn't always necessarily the best thing, if you want the relationship to last.

I see all these things now.

Too bad I can't convince *her* of that.

Not that I thought it would be easy. But I honestly never anticipated that I might be doing it from the bottom of a pool.

Here is where the Old Cal might start bleating about how She's got some nerve, expecting me to have acted like a damned eunuch in the past, when I didn't even know her. This is when the Old Cal might think to himself, Why am I even bothering to put myself through this? I've got a perfectly beautiful, elegant, sophisticated Italian woman right here who'd be more than happy to make love with me all night long. Why am I worrying about what some American cartoonist is thinking?

Ah, there's the rub. Because I don't want the beautiful, elegant, sophisticated Italian woman. I want the cartoonist with the cat tattoo who can't seem to stop tripping over her own shoes.

God help me.

She, however, has made it perfectly clear she doesn't want me. At least, not anymore. I suppose Grazi strolling in like that, looking as if she owned the place in that hat and those stilettos, was just one strike too many against me.

Grazi was perfectly understanding about it. She apologized for not having checked her email, and said by the time she got my phone messages, she was already on her way. I believe I made quite an ass of myself, trying to explain what was going on, as I drove her back to the train station (after I'd changed into dry clothes, of course).

"I see," was what Grazi had to say about it. "You are in love. With a woman who draws a cartoon. About a cat."

Hearing her put it that way, so baldly—*You are in love*—I actually felt physically ill for a moment.

And yet—here's the strangest thing of all—I felt ill in a *good* way.

"That's not all," I felt compelled to confess. "She thinks I'm a pompous ass, incapable of feeling anything except my own sense of superiority."

Grazi seemed to find this amusing.

"You *can* be pompous," she said. Which I can't say I found particularly reassuring. "You seem to think you know everything there is to know."

"She's categorically uninterested in geopolitical dynamics," I went on, "or world affairs of any kind."

"Yes," Grazi said. "But these things are not important to most people."

"This morning," I added, feeling desperate for someone, anyone to try to talk me out of what I knew perfectly well was already a foregone conclusion, "I saw her put ketchup on her eggs. And she likes Nutella. And that television show, *ER*."

To which Grazi replied, with a calmness I'm sure she was far from feeling, "Yes, but this is a very popular show."

"It's not something I planned on happening," I explained to her.

"Who plans on falling in love?" Grazi asked, with a shrug. "It simply happens. We cannot stop it, however much we might try."

Then, exhaling a plume of blue smoke from her cigarette, she added, "Though I imagine in your case, trying not to just made you fall harder. That is the way, with men like you. When it happens, nothing can stop it. Not even ketchup on the eggs."

"She hates me," I admitted miserably.

"No, she does not," Grazi was kind enough to say. "If she hated you, she would not have pushed you in the water when she saw me."

I hope—but do not actually believe—that Grazi is right.

But even if she is, what can I do about it? By the time I got back to the house after dropping Grazi off at the train station, so she could go back to Rome, the party was over, and the house was shut up tight. *She* was nowhere to be found. I knew she hadn't left . . . her suitcase was still there. Thinking she'd gone into town with the others to terrorize the bridal couple at their hotel, I drove in, but saw only Peter and his little friends on the beach, ripping apart Holly's garlic flower bouquet in some sort of strange pubescent *Lord-of-the-Flies*-like ceremony, and throwing the petals into the sea.

Now I've had too much coffee at the café, and read every English-language paper in town. The sun is starting to set, and I know I should go back to the villa to see if she's there.

But part of me is afraid to leave this chair. Because what happens if I go back there, and she gives me the cold shoulder?

Grazi's reply, when I asked her this very question as she was boarding her train, was hardly reassuring.

"She won't," she said, with a smile, "if you make the grand gesture."

"What grand gesture?" I asked. "I already threw a party that put me five grand in the hole, and all that got me was a view of the bottom of the pool."

"What does she want?" Grazi asked, pointedly. "Besides a wedding for her friend, which you already gave her? That is what you must do, you know. Give her what she wants—what she's never had—and she'll be yours."

I had to think about that one. What Jane Harris wants. I thought about it for a long time after Grazi's train pulled away from the station.

It turned out not to be that hard. I mean, it's not like it wasn't written on practically every page of her diary.

Still, how to show her I really meant it:. that was the hard part.

Of course, if it turns out I'm wrong . . .

Well, here goes nothing.

~~Holly Caputo and Mark Levine~~
Jane Harris

I should have known, of course. That it was all too good to be true.

About him having changed, I mean.

He hasn't changed. They <u>never</u> change.

I don't know what I was thinking. I mean, just because he got Holly and Mark married, then threw them a nice party, and made a sweet toast, the way any normal man SHOULD have, I thought he'd come around.

Ha. HA!

It's so transparently obvious now that the whole thing was some kind of setup to get me into bed.

I have to admit at first I was flattered. I mean, that he went to all that trouble, just to see me naked. No man's ever gone to such elaborate lengths on my behalf. Well, Curt Shipley took me to the prom.

But knowing now that he didn't really care WHO he screwed afterwards, me or Mike Morris, has somewhat spoiled my appreciation of the fact in retrospect.

Same with Cal Langdon. I mean, it was all just a big game to him. I knew it the minute I laid eyes on that art gallery woman. Just a kiss. Ha! Exactly as I suspected, it WASN'T just a kiss. He was just lonely, and wanted to get laid. He didn't care by WHO. Or WHOM. Or whatever. Why else would he have invited her?

And I'll admit, he did look kind of surprised to see her there. He must have forgotten he'd asked her to stop by.

Well, I'm sure that baptism I gave him reminded him plenty fast.

Whatever. It's not like I even care. I mean, it's not like I was

FALLING FOR HIM, or anything. Please. Falling for WHAT? Believe me, I can do better than an egocentric jerk like him.

And okay, he DOES have those nice sinewy, tanned hands. And those blue eyes. And he likes cats. And he's a great kisser. And he's super smart, but can still be funny when he lets himself.

So what? He has a lot of faults, too. He thinks he knows everything, when, very clearly, he does not, particularly when it comes to human relations.

And he writes books I wouldn't pick up to read if I even were dying of boredom.

And, though I can't be sure of it, I think I caught him looked at me a little funny this morning when he saw me putting ketchup on my eggs.

Who needs that? Not me. No, sir. I'm sticking to nice guys. Like Malcolm. Well, not Malcolm, exactly, since he's clearly moved on, which . . . good for him.

But I mean <u>simple</u> guys, like Malcolm. Guys who don't play head games. Guys with a wry appreciation of life's vagaries. Cal doesn't appreciate anything wryly. Well, except for maybe my grammatical errors.

Oh. Wait. War.

Okay. Peter won.

Whatever.

Where was I?

Oh, yeah.

The first thing I'm going to do when I get back home is register for some kind of class at the Learning Annex. I don't know what. But some kind of class a simple guy would take. Like pottery, maybe. Or Italian! Yeah. How to speak Italian. I bet a lot of guys take that class. And then I can meet a nice, simple guy, and next time I come back to Italy, I'll bring him along.

Because even though this country has its faults—the three-hour lunches, where everything, even SHOE stores, is closed . . . not to mention the lack of toilets, like at Amici Amore, or just the seats, like that restaurant in Porto Recanati—it can also be super nice. When I made Peter drop me off in town today after the party, when he and Annika and everyone else went to harass Holly and Mark at their hotel, I walked around a little, got myself a nice gelato, sat down in a little palazzo, and just relaxed.

I haven't been able to do much relaxing since I got to Italy—well, except for like five minutes by the pool that one day—what with the sightseeing and the worrying about Holly and Mark's wedding not working out and the whole Cal thing.

But today I relaxed, and I looked around, and I . . . well, I liked what I saw. Italy, I mean. Well, Le Marche, anyway. They're all so friendly, and say hi to one another as they pass on the street.

And all of the windows have flower boxes instead of fire escapes on them, because none of the buildings is more than two stories high.

And because the buildings are so low, the sky looks HUGE overhead, like in Wyoming, or something. Only it's a blue like it never gets in New York, on account of all the pollution from the traffic. Here, most everyone rides scooters, or at most, they have tiny little Smart Cars.

Even the ice cream tastes better than back in America. That was the best pistachio I ever had.

And the pace of life is kind of catching. I mean, I definitely don't approve of three-hour lunches. But if you NEED to take that long for lunch, it's nice that it's not frowned on. Like it would be in Manhattan. I mean, can you imagine if you worked on Wall Street or whatever and you tried to tell your boss you wouldn't be back for three hours?

There's something kind of nice about the way no one hur-
ries, and how there always seems to be time for a cup of coffee and a friendly <u>Buon giorno.</u>

It's a shame we have to leave Friday, really. I mean, not
that I'll be sad to say good-bye forever to SOME people I've
met here. But I think I'll miss this place. And Peter. And even
his great-grandmother and snotty Annika (whom, when she
asked me what she was supposed to do with Holly's bouquet
after she caught it, I told it was traditional to shred the flowers to pieces and throw them into the sea for good luck) and
the mayor and the smell of horses drifting into my bedroom
window in the morning and those skinny cats and the oven
that you can't turn on without the lights going out and all of
the Virgin Marys and the castles on every hillside and . . .

Well, just everything.

Except HIM.

After I take that class at the Learning Annex—on how to
speak Italian—and I meet that guy—you know, the simple one
who'll be able to appreciate life's vagaries—we'll come back to
Italy, and we'll have a fabulous time, because both of us will
know what carabinieri are, and neither of us will laugh at the
other's mistakes, unlike—

HIM.

Oh, my God. He's back.

He has some nerve.

Oh, and look. His face still has that same hangdog expression that he had on when I left. What happened, Cal? Did
your Italian skank refuse to put out when she saw how stupid
you look sitting at the bottom of the pool?

Huh. He's trying to make conversation. Yeah, nice try,
buddy. But you're not going to get anywhere in front of the
kid. Why do you think I invited him over here? Yeah, not because I have such a burning love for card games. No, it was be-

cause I had a feeling you'd come crawling back. And I know you aren't going to be talking about <u>us</u> if there's a third party—

OH MY GOD! THAT'S BRIBERY!

Wait, two can play at that game—

AARRRGHHH!!! WHY DIDN'T I GET CASH WHEN I WAS IN TOWN?

Fine. Whatever. So Peter's gone. A twenty, and he's off. Traitor.

I don't care. I still don't have to listen to what this guy has to say. I can just go inside and see what Holly's doing—

Um, no, I can't. Because Holly and Mark are at the hotel. The hotel room <u>he</u> bought them. We're all alone. We're all alone in this giant villa because he—

PLANNED IT THAT WAY!!!!

OH MY GOD. I AM SUCH AN IDIOT.

But whatever. Still not listening. No. Not listening to you, Mr. My Only Goal In Life Is to Break the Heart of the Stupid American Girl. NOT LISTENING.

Cal: "Jane. Seriously. Quit writing in that book and look at me. Just for a minute."

Me: "No."

Cal: "Fine. But I'm not going to go away. Not until we have this out."

Me: "There is nothing to have out."

Cal: "Yes, there is. Look, I know I've acted like a jerk almost from the first moment I met you—"

Me: "Almost?"

Cal: "Okay, from the first moment I met you. But I want you to know that I feel terrible about it now. You were right. I <u>am</u> an ass. And a creep. The things I said—the stuff I did—all of it. You were right. You were completely right about Mark and Holly, and I was completely wrong. I see that now."

Hmmm. This is an interesting turn of events. He's apologizing. And conceding wrongdoing. I've never had a guy do THAT before. What can this mean?

Oh, wait. I know. Silly me.

Me: "If this is all just an act to get me to go to the hotel too, so you can have the villa to yourself for the night for you and your skank, it's not going to work. I happen to like it here, and have no intention of leaving, even for a Jacuzzi tub."

Cal: "Jane. If I wanted to spend the night with Grazi, don't you think I'd be at the hotel with her now, and not here, trying to reason with you?"

DAMN HIM AND HIS GENIUS LOGIC!

Me: "Well, whatever you're trying to do, cut it out. It's making me nervous. I liked it better when you hated me."

Cal: "I never hated you—"

Me: "HA! HA! HA! CARABINIERI!"

Cal: "What? I can't even joke with you?"

Me: "That wasn't joking with me. That was a joke ABOUT me."

Cal: "And you haven't made plenty of those about me this past week?"

Me: "Not to your face."

Oooooh. He just swung one of the wrought-iron chairs around, set it directly in front of me, sat down in it, and leaned forward, so that I can see the blond five-o'clock shadow dusting his jaw. Also those blue eyes.

LOOK AWAY. LOOK AWAY FROM THE HYPNOTIC BLUE EYES.

Cal: "Jane. Quit writing in that book and listen to me."

Ha. So not going to happen.

Cal: "Fine. If that's the way you're going to be, then I'm just going to say this. I will admit that when I met you, I might have been laboring under some misconceptions about male-female relations. I'm not going to tell you I've never been in love, because you and I both know that's not true. I was in love once, and it didn't work out, and because of that, I have worked very, very hard to convince myself that love doesn't actually exist. Because I didn't want to admit that I'd screwed it up. And if I couldn't have it, I didn't want anyone else to, either."

Hmmm. Nice little explanation there. Neat. Tidy. Almost believable.

Cal: "But meeting you changed all that. You made me see that two people—like Mark and Holly—_can_ fall deeply, madly in love, without any ulterior motives, and that that love isn't just in their heads, a result of a chemical imbalance, but the result of attraction, mutual trust, and sheer, genuine affection. The love those two have for each other—the kind of love that would make them throw caution to the wind and get married in spite of almost everyone else in the world that they cared about being totally against the idea—that's the kind of love I've always wanted, but never thought actually existed. Until yesterday."

Hmmm. That's pretty good, too.
Wait. What the hell is he talking about?

Me: "What happened yesterday?"
Cal: "Yesterday, I was stuck in a car with you for eight hours."

Bastard. I didn't even sing along with the radio. Much.

Me: "Yeah. And?"
Cal: "Something happened."
Me: "If you're referring to my driving skills, may I just say I
     didn't TOUCH that truck. What you felt was just the
     wind. We were going pretty fast. And there wasn't even a
     scratch. I checked."
Cal: "I'm not talking about that. I'm talking about the fact
     that I fell in love with you. And I'm pretty sure you're in
     love with me, too."

!!!!!!!!!!!!!!!!!!!!!!!!!!!!!!!!!!!!!!!

Cal: "Can you stop writing in that book now?"

How can I stop? I mean, I can barely hold onto my pen, my
fingers are shaking so badly. . . .
This can't be true. This has to be some kind of elaborate
boy scheme to . . . I don't know what.

Me: "Okay, I understand that guys like you will stop at NOTH-
     ING to make a sexual conquest. I mean, telling a girl
     what you think she wants to hear . . . that's par for the
     course. But it's never a good move to presume you know
     what she feels for you. Because I can assure you, I am
     NOT in love with you."
Cal: "I'm not presuming. I know exactly what you think about
     me. You think I'm an anal-retentive Armrest Nazi . . . an
     arrogant Modelizer. You can't stand the way I talk, any
     of the subjects I choose to talk about, the imperious
     manner I order food in restaurants or tell cab drivers
     how much we owe them. You find my taste in women odi-

ous, the fact that I don't own a television an unforgivable sin, and the fact that I would choose to write a book about Saudi Arabia completely unfathomable. And you're also totally and completely in love with me. If you weren't, you wouldn't have pushed me into the pool earlier today when you saw Grazi walk in."

Me: Speechless.

Cal: "Now will you put that book down and kiss me?"

Me: "No, I will NOT. What are you—how did you—did HOLLY tell you all that?"

Cal: "No. I read that book you're writing in."

WHAT?

Cal: "Could you write a little bigger? I'm not sure China saw that. Yes, I read your diary. It does say, on the first page, that you intend to give it to Holly and Mark as a wedding present. I didn't think it would be any big deal for me to read something you obviously meant for them to read. It wasn't until I was much too deeply engrossed in it to put it down that I realized you'd changed your plans."

Me: "Ngh."

Cal: "Well put. Yes, I know all your darkest secrets, Jane Harris. How much you pine for Dr. Kovac, who is, I'd like to point out, a fictional character. Your mistaken impression of the size of a certain part of my anatomy. What, exactly, you think about my book—not that your facial expression whenever I bring it up doesn't say it all. I know you've got a soft spot for humpbacked dwarves, stray cats, and your friend Holly, and I know you want to go to Veselka's with me and eat blintzes. I

don't know what Veselka's is, but I'm a big fan of
blintzes. I've never enjoyed myself more than I have the
past forty-eight hours, during which I've been trapped
in a car with one of the worst drivers I have ever seen,
run up the Spanish Steps and then down again so I
could be on time to wait in line to perjure myself at the
American consulate. And I'd like to continue doing
those sorts of things with you on a regular basis for
the foreseeable future. Although I would also like to in-
clude sex with you, if possible. And if none of that con-
vinces you, perhaps this will: I have every intention of
sticking around long enough to form an intense, un-
breakable, long-term bond with The Dude. And to prove
it, this afternoon, I went and got this."

Oh, my God. He's rolling up his sleeve. Why is he rolling up
his sleeve? What could he possibly—
NO!
IMPOSSIBLE!
It's a tattoo!!! He's got a tattoo. Of Wondercat!
Just like the one on my ankle.

Me: "But—How? Where?"
Cal: "Crazy Bar and Sexy Tattoo Shop in town. They say Won-
dercat's one of their best sellers."
Me: "But—but—but that's PERMANENT!!!!"
Cal: "So is how I feel about you. Now. Could you put the pen
down and kiss me, please?"

And suddenly, I find that I can.
Because my heart has become filled with something.
Something I can't really describe.
Except that it feels like bianco frizzante.

Travel Diary of

~~Holly Caputo and Mark Levine~~

Jane Harris

Oh my God. He lied. It's totally true, what Mark told Holly about Cal's—

Travel Diary of

~~Holly Caputo and Mark Levine~~

Jane Harris

Poor Frau Schumacher. She's going to have a LOT of sheets to wash when we leave. I think we've done it in every bedroom at least once.

Oh well. I suppose she's used to hard work, considering all the time she put in over at the Führer's place.

Travel Diary of

~~Holly Caputo and Mark Levine~~

Jane Harris

Even Cal admits that Nutella on strawberries, washed down with champagne, makes a lovely midnight snack.

Travel Diary of

~~Holly Caputo and Mark Levine~~

Jane Harris

Must write fast, as he's downstairs, getting more strawberries.

He loves me! At least as much as I—I can't believe I'm ad-
mitting this—love him. YES! It's true! I love him! I could shout
it from the rooftop: I LOVE HIM!

And I don't think that's the phenylethylanamine talking,
either.

Endorphins? Definitely.

Oh, my God. I love Cal Langdon. CAL LANGDON.

And you know, really, the only reason he doesn't like <u>ER</u> is
that he's never seen it. It turns out they don't have <u>ER</u> in
Libya or wherever it is he's been all these years. I'm sure he'll
come around as soon as he's caught up with everything that's
happening at County.

I showed him my Wondercat sketch book, too, and he
laughed at my most recent cartoon. Cal Langdon LAUGHED.
At one of my cartoons!!!! And called me a comic genius!

Which I already knew. But it was nice to hear it from him.

Oops, here he comes. I promised I'd stop writing about him
in here.

For now.

✉

To: Arthur Pendergast <a.pendergast@rawlingspress.com>
Fr: Cal Langdon <cal.langdon@thenyjournal.com>
Re: The Book

Hey, Arthur. I was thinking. How would you feel if my second book was on Le Marche? In case you don't know, Le Marche is one of Italy's lesser-known regions, filled with breathtaking vistas of ancient castles atop rolling picturesque hillsides, shady olive groves, curved white beaches, delicious seafood, and earthy but delicate wines like the Verdicchio, considered among the finest of the *vini da meditazione*.

This is a region in which family-run businesses thrive. It's a nearly self-sufficient area that many countries—for instance, those formerly dependent on the exportation of oil—might do well to emulate.

I'm thinking about renting a place here for a few months with my girlfriend to do some research. You might have heard of her—Jane Harris? She's the creator of *Wondercat*, that hilarious comic strip about the cat. I'm sure you've read it.

Anyway, let me know what you think.

Cal

✉

To: Cal Langdon <cal.langdon@thenyjournal.com>
Fr: Arthur Pendergast <a.pendergast@rawlingspress.com>
Re: The Book

Le Marche? What the hell are you talking about? No one's ever heard of Le Marche. Who the hell is going to buy a book about some place they never heard of?

Let me tell you something: if *Sweeping Sands* wasn't Number 2 on the *Times* Bestseller list right now, I'd tell you what you can do with Le Marche.

But as it is . . . .

Go with God.

Arthur Pendergast
Senior Editor
Rawlings Press
1418 Avenue of the Americas
New York, NY 10019
212-555-8764

PS Girlfriend? Since when do you have a girlfriend? I thought you were monogaphobic.

PPS What the hell is a Wondercat?

✉

To: Listserv <Wundercat@wundercatlives.com>
Fr: Peter Schumacher <webmaster@wundercatlives.com>
Re: JANE HARRIS

Listen up, kids! You are not believing what is happening! JANE HARRIS, creator of our beloved Wundercat, is STAYING here in Le Marche! Yes! At least, this is what she tells me today when I come in the morning to bring the brotchen.

Actually, JANE HARRIS does not come to the door this morning when I bring the brotchen. JANE HARRIS does not come downstairs until very late this afternoon to get the brotchen. And then she is looking very tired. But very good, as usual!

And Cal Longdon, who comes to the door with JANE HARRIS, asks if I know any houses to rent in Le Marche, because he wants to write a book about us! US!!!

YES! Because Le Marche RULES!!!!

And JANE HARRIS says she thinks she had better stay in Le Marche, too, to help Cal Longdon write his very important book about US!!!!

And when I ask her what I know you are thinking—"WHAT ABOUT WUNDERCAT?" she says, "Oh, I can draw Wondercat anywhere."

YES!!!! JANE HARRIS IS MOVING TO ITALY! AND YOU HEARD IT HERE FIRST. Courtesy of me, #1 Wundercat Fan Of All Time!

Wundercat Lives—4eva!
Peter

Private to Annika: When you are done with Wundercat Volume 1, tell me, and I will bring you Volume 2 on my motorino.

....

✉

To: Jane Harris <jane@wondercat.com>
Fr: Claire Harris <charris2004@freemail.com>
Re: Your phone call

Honey, I'm just writing because last night when you called, I could have sworn you said you were *staying* in Italy. With Cal Longdon. Permanently.

Daddy says I must have dreamed the whole thing. But I don't think I would have dreamt the part where you said if your Wondercat development deal ends up going through, of course Cal will move back to New York with you, because the two of you are in a committed relationship and fully support one another in your careers.

That's just not the kind of thing I usually dream about.

And another thing: this morning when I was at the Kroger Sav-On to buy some more Band-Aids for Dad (he put a nail through his thumb hanging up another watercolor from his sister—I wish she'd take up a new hobby), I ran into Marie Caputo, who asked me—with, I must admit, a smile I didn't care for—how it felt to be gaining a son. Gaining a son? What is she talking about, sweetheart? She can't have meant you and that Cal Langdon, can she? Are you two getting married? Does Holly know something I don't know, and maybe told her mother?

How can you marry Cal Langdon, honey? Last time I talked to you, you said you hated him. And that he wouldn't stop looking at your shoes.

None of this makes any sense to me. I don't think you ought to be staying in Italy with—much less marrying—someone you've only known for a week.

I hope Marie misunderstood. In fact, I'm SURE she must have. You've always been such a sensible girl.

Besides, what about Malcolm, that nice investment banker you've been seeing?

Daddy's right, and that phone call last night must have been just a dream. Because you would never move to Italy without The Dude.

Oh, wait, I asked you that last night, didn't I? And you said you were going to pay your super's son to bring The Dude to you there. . . .

But that can't be right. You would never do anything so silly.

Well, ignore me. Hope you have a nice time on the rest of your trip.

And try to be nice to that Cal Langdon. I'm sure he can't help being in love with you. And you always did have very pretty feet.

Love,
Mom

✉

To: Julio Chasez <julio@streetsmart.com>
Fr: Jane Harris <jane@wondercat.com>
Re: The Dude

Hi, Julio! Listen, I was wondering. How would you feel about an all-expense paid trip to Italy?

Want More?

Turn the page to enter
Avon's Little Black Book—

the dish, the scoop and the
cherry on top from
MEG CABOT

Why We Didn't Get Married in Las Vegas Like Normal Americans

Maybe it's because I also write books for younger readers, and so most of the 200 or so emails I get a day are from kids. But the vast majority of the emails in my inbox contain this question: "Where do you get your inspiration?"

Inspiration seems to be a big thing for my readers, but I have to say it's not something I ever think about. Whenever anybody asks, I always have to pause and think, "Where DID I get the inspiration for that story?" The truth is, I usually can't remember. To me, the story is generally the important thing, not how I thought it up.

My book *Every Boy's Got One* is different, though. I got the inspiration for the story—a tale of love and elopement in the Italian countryside—from my own marriage, which was . . . well, an elopement in the Italian countryside.

> *a tale of love and elopement in the Italian countryside*

I didn't think writing a story about a bride would be all that interesting, though, either to me or my readers. It seemed to me that the story of how a woman came to BE a bride in the first place would be the more interesting tale.

So when I decided to write a novel based on my own wedding, I chose for my main characters the best man and maid of honor of the couple who are eloping, basically telling the story of my elopement (with, I'll admit, numerous fabrications) from the point of view of my maid of honor.

Fabrication Number One: I didn't actually have a maid of honor for my Italian elopement. The girl who was sup-

posed to be my maid of honor—the best man's girlfriend—
bailed on him the week before our wedding.

Fabrication Number Two: In *Every Boy's Got One*,
the elopement takes place in Le Marche, in the village of
Castelfidardo, the accordion-making capital of the world.
My own wedding was hundreds of kilometers from there,
in a town near Monaco called Diana San Pietro, in
Ligeria. I changed settings because it's been eleven years
since I was last in Ligeria, and I was in Le Marche less
than a year ago, so I felt the details would be more
authentic.

Fabrication Number Three: In *Every Boy's Got One*, the
characters spend a lot of time emailing people on their Blackberries. I did not actually have a Blackberry, or access to the
Internet, while I was getting married. In 1993, when my wedding took place, the Internet was not yet that widely known or
available. At least to me.

These are, however, pretty much the ONLY ways in which
my real-life wedding differed from the one in my book. And
here's the blow-by-blow to prove it!

"You kid me, *si*?" The *secretario* eyed us suspiciously over
his typewriter.

My husband-to-be and I exchanged glances. The fact was,
we were *not* kidding him. We wanted to get married in Diano
San Pietro, a sleepy village on the Italian Riviera, just a few
miles from Monaco. A popular beach resort in summer, the
Ligurian town was relatively deserted in March, except for
the natives, who farmed the olive groves that dotted the steep,
climbing hills, and ran (when you could rouse them from
their afternoon naps) the many restaurants and cafés that lined
the beautiful shore.

Considering how deserted the town was, the *secretario*'s
reluctance to marry us seemed odd. There certainly didn't appear to be much going on in the Comune di Diano San Pietro,
the city hall. With the exception of ourselves, the white-
haired *secretario,* our translator, and would-be best man,
Ingo, the building was empty. It didn't look to me like there

were a lot of people banging down the doors of Diano San Pietro city officials demanding to be married.

And yet the *secretario* looked extremely unwilling even to entertain the idea of two Americans being wed in his village.

"You do not understand," he entreated us in broken English. "We here in Italy take the institution of marriage very seriously. There is much to be done. There are many forms that must be filled out."

That was when we handed him the *Stato Libero* we had filled out in the office of the Consulate General of Italy back in New York before we'd left for Europe. Signed by four witnesses unrelated either to us or to one another, we had been assured by the consulate that this declaration was the only form we would need in order for us to be married on our vacation in Italy.

But for good measure, we also relinquished our birth certificates, which we'd had translated into Italian, and our passports. Italians, we explained, as nicely as we could, were not the only people in the world who took the institution of marriage seriously.

The *secretario* took the forms from us with an expression of bewildered chagrin. This was clearly *not* what he needed an hour before his lunch break—his *three*-hour lunch break.

Non-Fabrication Number One: In Italy, everything really does shut down from twelve to three, just like in *Every Boy's Got One*: banks; shops; grocery stores; you name it, all in an effort to allow employees to enjoy lunch with their families.

Muttering that he was going to have to speak to the mayor, the *secretario* disappeared into an inner office. When he returned moments later, it was in the company of a large man in a jogging suit, who was eating a somewhat messy salami and onion sandwich. This gentleman, it appeared, held the office of mayor of Diano San Pietro. He took one look at our paperwork and inquired, with a sigh, "Why can't you just get married in Las Vegas like normal Americans?"

Non-Fabrication Number Two: He really did say that, just like in the book.

I'll admit it: I'm wedding-phobic. I have nothing against *marriage*. It's the shower-gown-register-bouquet-cake stuff that gives me the heebie-jeebies. I'm often beseeched by readers to write sequels to my contemporary novels that feature the wedding of such-and-such a character. The fact is, I can't do it because I've never actually planned a wedding myself, and have no idea how one goes about doing so.

Eleven years ago—when our trip to the Comune di Diano San Pietro took place—I was twenty-six, and my husband-to-be, Benjamin, was the ripe old age of thirty-two: certainly old enough to know what we wanted—which was not a big wedding. And certainly not one in Vegas, the wedding capital of the world.

Non-Fabrication Number Three: Like the bride and groom in my book *Every Boy's Got One*, Benjamin and I had decided to elope in Italy—only not because our parents disapproved of our relationship (like Holly and Mark), but because:

a) The idea of looking for a wedding gown actually gave me hives (Benjamin was the one who found the dress I eventually wore, a Bill Blass cocktail gown in white lace with black stripes and polka-dots that hit me just above the knee).

b) While both our families got along, the idea of all of them in one room together was daunting. We both come from very large broods, and, both of us being of Irish/Italian or Irish/Hungarian descent, there was always the possibility of a fistfight breaking out, and

c) Benjamin, like Cal, the hero of Every Boy's Got One (Non-fabrication Number Four) had some pretty negative opinions on the subject of marriage, and had often vowed never to marry at all. Since I'm all for marriage—just not weddings—this created an impasse in our relationship...for about a day. We were able to reach détente on the subject when our German friend Ingo suggested that if he were to get married, it would be in Italy, because it's the most beautiful country in the world. Something about that appealed to Benjamin. And next thing I knew, we were filling out paperwork at the Italian consulate in Manhattan.

Eloping in Italy, back then, seemed the ideal solution to all of our problems . . . providing the Italian bureaucracy didn't get in the way.

The mayor's question about Las Vegas caused us to laugh nervously . . . until we realized he wasn't kidding. Marrying Americans was apparently something the Comune di Diana San Pietro did not do often—in fact, they'd NEVER done it before.

And they weren't very enthusiastic about making an exception for us.

I tried not to take it personally. It probably didn't have anything to do with the fact that they were worried this was going to cut into their lunch hour. Right?

While we stood behind the railing that separated us from the *secretario*'s typewriter, our friend Ingo attempted to explain, in his excellent Italian, that the reason Benjamin and I couldn't get married in Las Vegas like normal Americans was that we were *not* normal Americans. That both the groom and the bride were terrible romantics—that I, in fact, was a fan (though at that time, not yet an author) of romance novels, while Benjamin was a published poet—and that we had long ago decided that if we were ever going to get married, it would only be in the most romantic country in the world, Italy.

I stood there holding my breath, waiting to see if Ingo's argument worked. It wouldn't, of course, be the WORST thing if we didn't end up coming home from Europe married. Neither Benjamin nor I had revealed our marriage plans to anyone except our four unrelated witnesses back in New York. Our plan was to return to the U.S. as a married couple, our wedding a fait accompli with which our doting families were going to have to cope . . . and which would relieve us of all responsibility of having to pick out china patterns or choose bridesmaid dresses. We could always, I figured, try again some other time. . . .

But it wouldn't be in Italy. As a poor graduate student (Benjamin) and administrative assistant (me), we'd blown all of our savings on this trip. We wouldn't be able to make it back to Europe for some time.

To my relief, I could see first the *secretario,* and then the mayor, melting under Ingo's eloquent argument (a miracle, considering how hungover he was after all the prosecco we'd consumed in our rented villa the night before—**Non-Fabrication Number Five**). Finally, with a frustrated sigh, the mayor laid down his sandwich and explained that he would marry us if:

a) We supplied a translator, approved by the Comune, who could tell us exactly what we were agreeing to when we said "si."
b) We provided a "donation" to the "Children's Fund."
c) That we obtained additional paperwork, in the form of *certificatos di cittadinanza* from the Consulate General of the United States in Milan.

Since this last condition entailed a drive of approximately four hours each way, Milano being five hundred kilometers from Diano San Pietro—we argued strenuously against it, insisting that the Italian consulate in New York had said nothing of this additional form.

But the mayor remained firm. It was clear he thought we would bail on the whole thing if it meant an entire day's drive. Because who in their right mind would give up a day of their vacation in Italy to drive back and forth to Milan? This would leave the Comune di Diana San Pietro free to do whatever it was they did all day when they were not marrying Americans . . . which appeared, to my eyes, to be very little.

When, defeated, we finally agreed to do all that they required of us, the *secretario,* looking very official, rolled a sheet of paper into his typewriter and began filling out our request for a *certificato di matrimonio.*

"And when," he asked, "do you want to be married?"

We replied promptly, "April first."

The *secretario* began typing, then suddenly stopped, looked at us over the rim of his glasses, and asked, "This is a joke. You are—who you say?—kidding us, *si?*"

I shook my head. It had been Benjamin's idea to get married in Italy. It was *my* idea to do it on April Fool's Day, playing on Benjamin's belief that only fools get married in the first place.

I will admit that there was a delicious irony to the fact that, when we sent telegrams to our families afterward, they wouldn't know until we returned from Europe whether we'd actually been married, or if it was all a prank.

Hey, at twenty-six, that seemed excruciatingly funny to me.

"You are not kidding," the *secretario* said. He looked back down at his typewriter keys, trying not to smile.

The mayor eyed us suspiciously, then gave us another lecture on how in Italy, marriage is taken very seriously, unlike in America.

Then he picked up his sandwich and announced he could only marry us at nine o'clock in the morning on April first, since he was refereeing the Diano San Pietro boy's football (soccer) game at ten (**Non-Fabrication Number Six**).

We assured him we'd be at the city hall promptly at nine. He looked as if he was thinking, *Yeah. Right.* The *secretario,* typing steadily, continued to smile to himself. It was clear neither man believed he would be seeing us on April first.

But the Comune di Diano San Pietro was sadly underestimating how tenacious a pair of young Americans in love can be.

We received only two speeding tickets on our way to Milano at five the next morning.

Non-Fabrication Number Seven: The wait in the Consulate General's office turned out to be almost longer than the drive itself.

Non-Fabrication Number Eight: While we sat waiting for our *certificatos*, we listened to a young American woman as she tried to convince her older brother that marrying Paolo, an Italian auto mechanic whom she had met the week before, and who sat broodingly beside her, clearly not understanding a word of English, was a good idea. She was still arguing persuasively as we left, four hours later.

Non-Fabrication Number Nine: We really did eat at the Amici Amore restaurant, and the toilet really was just a hole with two footprints around it.

Fortunately, we received only one speeding ticket on our way back to Diano San Pietro.

Non-Fabrication Number Ten: The only CD in the car during this eight-hour drive was a collection of songs by Queen. "Fat-Bottomed Girls" really WAS our wedding's theme song.

The translator was much easier to come by than our *certificatos*. Word of the impending marriage of two crazy Americans spread like wildfire throughout the village.

Non-Fabrication Number Eleven: The eighty-year-old woman from whom we were renting our charming, two-storied house in the hills overlooking the sea, insisted upon going down to the Comune and yelling at the mayor for us, to assure him that we were very serious about being married, and that he had better not wear his referee uniform to the ceremony.

Touched by this gesture, I asked her to be my maid of honor.

Meanwhile, a German tourist staying in a *pensione* a few houses away introduced himself and said he would be happy to translate for us—his Italian was flawless, and he was a translator for a living.

The mother of another young neighbor boy—who regularly volunteered to ride his *motorino* into town each morning to fetch us breakfast rolls (**Non-Fabrication Number Twelve**)—insisted upon acting as official wedding photographer, claiming that our parents would be furious if we didn't at least photograph the big event.

And the night before our wedding, some of the village children came to our house and decorated our front gate with flowers and hung two pairs of bedroom slippers from the wrought iron spikes, an old Italian tradition promising connubial bliss (**Non-Fabrication Number Thirteen**). They also presented me with a beautiful wreath of flowers to wear in my hair on the Big Day . . . garlic blossoms, I found out after I put it on (**Non-Fabrication Number Fourteen**). But it was the thought that counted.

These same children were the ones who, at seven in the morning of the Big Day, tapped on our door. Since I was further dressed than Benjamin, I answered. Two little cherubs looked up at me and explained in broken English, their big eyes soulful, that they were very sorry, but the mayor had telephoned and the soccer game had been moved up an hour, and so there could be no wedding that day.

Gasping in horror, I clutched the front of my wedding gown, my eyes filling with tears.

Then both children burst into giggles and shrieked, "April Fool's!"

I brought my hands down from my heart and asked them to pull the same prank on Benjamin, whose reaction was far more satisfactory to them than mine, since he said a lot of American swear words, to the kids' endless delight.

An hour and a half later, our wedding procession, consisting of our landlady, the translator, his wife and daughter, our self-appointed photographer, her husband and their son, Ingo and two of his friends from Bonn, Benjamin, myself, and assorted village children and their dogs arrived at the *Sala Consiliare* of the Comune di Diano San Pietro.

Clearly surprised that we had actually shown up, the mayor quickly stripped off his referee uniform and donned jacket, tie, and mayoral surplice (**Non-Fabrication Number Fifteen**).

Our marriage took place with much more solemnity and pageantry than either of us was expecting. Ingo, the best man, presented me with a bridal bouquet and my maid of honor with a matching corsage before the ceremony. Then Frau

Schumacher and Ingo witnessed our signing of the Diano San Pietro *registro degli atti di matrimoni.*

According to the translator, Benjamin and I promised, among other things, to live always together and see that our children attended decent schools. No wedding ceremony I have attended since has seemed quite as sweet—and to the point—as our Italian one.

After rings and kisses were exchanged, the mayor announced us husband and wife, and cheers and applause rang out. We were then beseeched by the mayor to pose for photos with him, and by the *secretario* to make a one-hundred-thousand lire donation to the Comune di Diano San Pietro Children's Fund. In the *registro* for the Children's Fund, my husband wrote, "Isn't it a good thing we decided not to get married in Las Vegas like normal Americans?"

Then we all went across the street to the postino's office to send off our telegrams, then to enjoy a wedding brunch at a restaurant that had agreed to open its doors early just for us.

It was at this brunch that we discovered **Non-Fabrication Number Sixteen:** Our landlady had worked for the SS, and had a son who was in jail for robbing all of the homes neighboring hers. Yes, the Nazi mother of a felon was the maid of honor at my wedding. And she'd been so nice! How was I supposed to have known?

Every Boy's Got One ends with missives from the bride and groom's families, expressing their eagerness to throw a party for the young couple whose marriage they'd initially been so vehemently against.

Non-Fabrication Number Seventeen: In real life, our parents' reaction was not much different. At first puzzled as to whether or not the whole thing had been an April Fool's joke, they soon came to believe the event had actually taken place, and began planning a wedding celebration on my mother's back deck in Indiana.

Of course, the morning of the party, a tornado ripped through town, pulling the roof off a nearby church and causing the temperature to plummet and the yard to become strewn with leaves and branches, so that the guests, including myself, were forced to wear sweaters and step over bracken in order to get to the cooler holding the beer.

But then, I'd given up expecting anything to do with my wedding to go right, so I wasn't the least surprised.

Still, nearly a dozen years later, there's nothing I'd change about my wedding day—although I think it would have been a blast to be married in Castelfidardo . . . there's something hilarious about having a wedding in the accordion-making capital of the world—which made writing about it for *Every Boy's Got One* a breeze.

I'm glad that, for this book at least, when people ask me where I got the inspiration, I'll have a ready answer.

Still, it's important to note that there's one thing that's in the book that did NOT happen in real life:

Fabrication Number Four: Unlike some of my traveling companions, I actually knew better than to order the oysters.

Benjamin Egnatz

MEG CABOT

MEG CABOT was born in Bloomington, Indiana. She is the author of seven historical romances under the pseudonym Patricia Cabot, as well as the novels *Boy Meets Girl, The Boy Next Door, She Went All the Way* and the bestselling young adult fiction series *The Princess Diaries*. She lives in New York City and Florida with her husband.

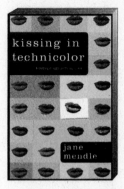